WRIGHT THAT GOT AWAY

WRIGHT THAT GOT AWAY

K.A. LINDE

ISBN-13: 978-1948427548

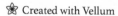 Created with Vellum

PART I

I SEE THE REAL YOU

1

BLAIRE

*T*he number one song in the world was written about me.

And no one knew but me and the asshole who wrote it.

The same asshole who was about to sing it right now.

"Thanks so much for coming out to Wright Vineyard tonight to celebrate the Best in Class Abbey Vintage," Campbell Abbey said into the microphone. He was seated on a stool with an acoustic guitar in his lap. His big blue eyes penetrated the dense crowd packed into the barn at his brother's winery. His dark hair was artfully messy. For once, he'd ditched his signature leather jacket and was in a plain black tee and ripped black jeans. He made rock god look effortless. "Before I go, I have one more song for you."

The crowd went wild.

Including my friends Piper, Jennifer, and Annie. Even my assistant, Honey, was screaming her head off for the lead singer of Cosmere to perform his last song. His most popular song. The one we all knew was coming.

"This song goes out to every person who has ever felt invisible. To the girl in the back of the class, just trying to get by. To the guy on the bench. To you out there. Every one of you. This is 'I See the Real You.' "

Somehow, the audience roared even louder as the opening riff drifted through the speakers. Then Campbell closed his eyes, and his honey-smooth voice filled the room. It was a serenade, an anthem, a fucking spell that he cast on every person who heard this song.

And I'd been ensorcelled first.

If I closed my eyes, I could remember that night so long ago.

The nervous butterflies in my stomach as I waited for the *tap, tap* at my window. Campbell climbing inside my bedroom with his guitar strapped to his back. The quick kisses as we fumbled for one another and the strum of his guitar in the afterglow of his affection. This song brushed across my lips.

I was the girl he had seen.

Until I wasn't.

"I love this one so much!" Honey yelled over the crowd.

"Me too," Annie said. She flipped her red hair, held her hands overhead, and swayed to the music.

"I third this," Jennifer agreed. She had her giant camera up to her face and was taking photos of the crowd.

My best friend, Piper, shot me a look. She didn't know about what Campbell and I had been through. She was three years older than me, and we hadn't known each other in high school. We'd become inseparable in college. Even though she, like everyone else, had no idea we'd been together, Piper suspected. She had been dropping subtle hints ever since Campbell had come back to Lubbock to reunite with his family.

I'd repeated the same thing that I'd been saying since high school—*nothing happened.*

It was a lie. A huge fucking lie. But I'd been saying it long enough that I could almost believe it was true. That I'd never met him. That he'd never seen me. That I'd never fallen hopelessly in love. That he hadn't ruined my entire life.

The only thing I could believe was one undeniable truth: he'd left.

The second we'd graduated high school, he'd taken his beat-up truck and driven straight to LA. One big dream propelling him out to the unknown. He'd been determined to succeed. And he had.

That didn't mean I had to like it.

If I heard "I See the Real You" one more time, I was going to scream.

Blissfully, the final notes of the song faded. Campbell opened his eyes and stared out at the crowd beyond. For a split second, it was as if he saw me again. As if, despite the hundreds of people crammed together in this barn, he found my eyes. Just me.

Probably every other person in attendance felt the same way. He'd probably done it on purpose. Maybe the music industry had taught him how to make it feel like he was eye-fucking the entire room. He'd always had charisma. That special something that said he couldn't be ignored. Even before he was that good of a guitar player with scratchy vocals and piss-poor lyrics, he had *it*. And you couldn't train anyone in how to have *it*. You did, or you didn't. But it had ballooned in the intervening years. He'd taken it from sultry high school heartthrob to the next level of panty-melting rockstar.

Campbell broke eye contact and shot a smile to his adoring crowd. "Thank you and have a good night."

The lights came back up as he disappeared into the

small backstage area. Wright Vineyard was the newest addition to the Wright family royalty. The Wrights owned Wright Construction, a Fortune 500 company and one of the largest construction companies in the country. Their cousins, Jordan and Julian, had moved here from Vancouver, and with the help of Hollin Abbey, they had opened the vineyard. Jordan had gotten it on its feet, Julian kept it running, and Hollin did everything else. It sure helped that his brother was famous and could show up every now and again to draw in a crowd.

Honey swooned next to me. "That was incredible. He gets better every time."

"Every time," Jennifer agreed, dropping her camera around her neck. "Should we go find the guys?"

"Definitely," Annie said.

"Like...backstage?" Honey whispered in awe.

Honey hadn't been around when the winery started and Campbell performed. She hadn't gotten any of the inside scoop yet. She was still too new in our circle.

It wasn't weird for the rest of us. Annie was engaged to Jordan. Jennifer and Julian were talking about moving in together. And despite all of our shock, Hollin and Piper were actually happy. They were still at each other's throats, but I was starting to suspect that it was foreplay.

"Yeah, like backstage," Piper said. She nudged Honey. "That way."

Honey squeaked. She looked back at me with wide eyes and then followed my friends through the crowd.

"Do you think I'll meet Campbell?" Honey asked me. "Do you think...you could introduce me?"

"Me?" I looked at her to gauge whether or not she suspected the same thing as Piper. "Why me?"

"Well, you met him at the concert in Dallas. And I just thought..."

Piper grinned at me. "Weren't we so lucky to meet him backstage at the Dallas show?"

I arched an eyebrow. "You were *so* lucky to see his tour bus."

Piper's cheeks heated. "I sure was."

"Oh my God, backstage in Dallas," Honey breathed. "I couldn't imagine."

"So, Blaire, are you going to introduce Honey or what?"

She was baiting me. She wanted me to decline. But I was done being freaked out by Campbell. I could do this. It wasn't a big deal.

"Sure. I'll introduce you."

Piper's eyebrows shot up. "Really?"

"Why not?"

"Why not indeed," Piper muttered under her breath.

Honey glanced between us, as if just realizing that there was some undercurrent going on. "Is it okay if I meet him? I don't have to."

"It's fine," I lied.

Then we marched backstage.

The guys had beaten us there, lounging around a table, pouring bourbon straight from the bottle. They were selling the new award-winning wine hand over fist. The last couple years was finally paying off for them. They deserved to be celebrating.

But there was no Campbell in sight.

"Hey, where's Campbell?" Piper asked as she slid onto Hollin's lap.

He nuzzled her neck and gestured behind him to the closed door. She swatted at him to stop, but it was half-hearted. She liked when he was handsy.

"Changing," he finally got out. "Why?"

"Blaire's going to introduce Honey to him."

Hollin extracted himself from Piper's neck to look up at me. A smirk was on his lips. I didn't want to know what he was going to say.

So, I brushed right past them, dragging Honey behind me, and raised my fist to knock on the door. But the second I reached the dressing room, the door opened, and I nearly fell forward inside.

Campbell reached out as swift as a viper and grabbed my waist. "Whoa there."

Time froze as we stood, nearly crushed together in that doorframe. The liminal space between two worlds. One in the past, where I had always been allowed past that door, and the present, where I couldn't imagine speaking to him, let alone having him touch me.

I cleared my throat and wrenched backward. "That was...unexpected."

"Sorry. I didn't know you were there," he said, leaning against the doorframe and smiling down at me.

That was another thing I'd forgotten. He was so impossibly tall. Over six feet. And I'd always been a pixie of a thing. Just brushing five feet tall. I had on heels for the show, but still he towered over me. I swallowed. Fuck. Was this the reason I only wanted to date giant men?

"Can I...help you?" he finally asked.

"No. Wait, yes. My assistant wants to meet you."

Campbell cocked his head. I hadn't spoken to him since high school graduation, and now, I was introducing him to someone as if we were friends. Which we were not.

"I'm just so lucky to have met you at the show in Dallas," I deadpanned, arching an eye to see if he'd contradict me.

"So lucky." His lip quirked at our shared joke.

"This is Honey," I said, gesturing to the girl standing behind me.

Still, he wasn't famous for nothing. He knew how to handle fans. He turned up the charm to a hundred and looked toward my assistant. "Honey?" he asked. "Is that your real name, or are you just sweet?"

I tried not to gag at the stupid question.

Honey proceeded to melt into a puddle of goo at his feet. "It's just...Honey. My friends all call me Honey."

He held out his hand, and they shook. "It's a pleasure to meet you. You're a Cosmere fan?"

"The biggest," she gushed.

And then he spent the next fifteen minutes discussing every point of interest with her. It was...genuine. He liked his fans. What guy wouldn't? But he didn't treat her like an annoyance he was desperate to be rid of. He was sincere about the entire interaction. It was better than I'd seen from most celebrities.

As strange as it was, I had some experience with other celebs. I ran a fantastically popular wellness blog, *Blaire Blush*. I had a few million followers on social media, where I doled out relationship advice, preached body positivity, and helped girls all over the world love themselves. I was sponsored by ethically sourced fashion designers and constantly received boons in the mail from people who wanted my influence. It was exciting and kind of crazy that it had ballooned into this with nothing but a blog and my psychology degree.

"So, are you dating anyone?" Honey asked, dropping me square back into reality.

Campbell laughed and ran a hand back through his hair. "That's a personal question."

"I know. I know. I'm sorry. There's just speculation that

you're talking to Nini Verona," Honey said. Just casually dropping the name of one of the hottest models around.

"I know Nini," Campbell said, "but I'm single."

Honey sighed happily. Satisfied that he was still on the market.

Suddenly, his gaze drifted back to me. For those few minutes, I'd thought that he'd forgotten my existence entirely. There was something in those bright blue eyes that made me freeze like a deer caught in headlights. And I couldn't look away even though I knew he was about to ruin my life all over again.

"Unless you want to go out with me," Campbell said.

2

CAMPBELL

*T*he words left my mouth before I could stop them. They were the truth. The thing that I'd wanted to ask. But I'd also known I shouldn't release them out into the world. I was still high on the aftereffects of the concert. Still lost to that buzz that I only got from music. Then, I'd opened my dressing room door, and there stood Blaire Barker.

There was fire in her eyes.

A part of her always looked ready to rip me in half.

But she was stunning all the same. Even more beautiful than the girl she had been when I fell for her in high school. Now, she was a woman with waist-length hair and those fringe bangs that always looked as if she were hiding a secret. Her blue eyes were kohl-rimmed and wide as an animated character. Like a Disney princess in disguise in a green minidress and high heels. Still, she was a foot shorter than me, and I *liked* that in a woman.

So, I'd asked her out. What was the harm?

Besides everything.

Blaire gaped at me in a mask of horror. Her assistant—

the vapid, brainless girl that she somehow let work for her —shrieked loud enough that everyone turned to look at us. Honey resorted to babbling. Something about how incredible this was. And how it wasn't real life.

But Blaire just glared at me as if I had some audacity to ask her that question.

"No," she spat.

I stilled at the word. The heat in it. She wasn't just mad. She was furious.

I knew how she felt about me. I'd known for years. I'd royally fucked up, and then I'd left. I was following my dreams, but I crushed hers at the same time. She hadn't spoken to me in eight years, and I'd been back in Lubbock on and off for the last eighteen months. It was pretty clear that the last thing she wanted to do was go on a date with me. And still, I'd opened my fucking mouth.

"What? Blaire, come on," Honey gasped.

"He was joking," she bit out. She shot me a look that said, *You better fucking go along with this.* "Weren't you, Campbell?"

I nodded slowly, not wanting to incur more of her wrath. "Yeah." I shot Honey a small smile. "Just a joke."

"God, don't do that to me. I almost had a heart attack." Her hand over her heart.

"Yeah, don't do that to her," Blaire practically growled.

I didn't regret it. But I sure as hell hated how upset she was at the notion. Still, I played my part. "Sorry. My bad."

"Honey, go tell everyone we're good over here and you're not being murdered. They're all still looking."

"Yeah. Sure. Sorry," she said and then scampered off.

I expected Blaire to dart off after her. But she stayed next to me until the noise returned and everyone forgot that we were standing alone in the doorway of my dressing room.

"Blaire, I—"

"Stop." She held up a hand. Her voice was ice. Her blue eyes narrowed in anger. "That better have been a fucking joke, Campbell."

I opened my mouth and then closed it. Because it hadn't been a joke. I'd dated since high school. I was a fucking famous musician. So, of course I'd dated and fucked around and all that. I'd gotten good at reading someone's wants. Truthfully, I'd always been good at it, and now, it was just amplified.

But I'd read Blaire wrong.

All wrong.

I'd thought she was finally thawing to me.

She shook her head and then turned to walk away. Part of me just reacted. I didn't want her to go. I wasn't ready. Not yet.

I grabbed her arm and pulled her to a stop. She jerked her head back at me. "What?" she snapped.

"What if it wasn't a joke?"

For a split second, I was back in high school. Back before I got everything I'd ever wanted. All save for one. Because I'd had Blaire Barker. Once upon a time, she'd been mine. And now, she wasn't.

We stood there in that space, and everything else just vanished. Her blue eyes had widened. I didn't know if it was shock or surprise or disgust. She thought so little of me now, and how could I even blame her? The one person I'd cared about the most was the person I'd hurt the worst. I didn't deserve to have this conversation. Eight years wasn't long enough for my penance. Not for someone like Blaire.

I was the asshole in this one. I knew it. I'd known it a long time. It was why, despite returning to my hometown eighteen months ago, I'd hardly spoken to her. I'd hardly even let myself look at her. Because I'd known the second that I did, the dam would break, and I'd be standing waist deep in shit. As I was currently.

Her gaze shuttered. "Don't do this."

"Do what?" I asked as if I were an innocent in this.

"Any of it." She tugged her arm out of my hand. "It's not fair."

"Blaire..."

"Eight *years*, Campbell," she said so low that I almost didn't hear her. But God, I fucking loved hearing her say my name. "It's been eight years. You can't change a single fucking thing that happened." Her eyes narrowed. "And I don't think you'd trade it for what you have."

I gulped. "But—"

"You're used to everyone falling at your feet," she said, continuing right over my protest. "So, stop all your little games and the stupid fucking charisma that works on everyone else. It's *not* happening. Do you understand?"

And I did.

I understood completely.

It didn't matter that I was a famous rockstar. Blaire Barker was out of my league.

"Yeah. Sure." I ran a hand back through my messy hair.

She was still looking at me. As she had purposely not done since I'd returned. "I'm serious, Campbell."

"I hear you. Loud and clear."

She didn't look like she believed me. And I didn't know if I believed me either. When I wanted something, I went after it with all that I was. It was how I'd ended up in Cosmere in the first place. It was how I'd risen so quickly to fame once I settled into the band. Everything had taken off like a jet.

Now, I was looking at her again. At her big blue eyes, filled with concern. That heart-shaped face and those pouty lips and perfectly arched eyebrows. The body and the brain and the smile. Though she hadn't smiled in my direction, I'd seen her radiate with it when talking to other people. And I wanted it pointed at me again. I wanted what I couldn't have. But I wanted it nonetheless.

"Well, well, well, what a show!" a voice rasped.

I jerked my head up in surprise to find my manager, Bobby Rogers, striding toward me. "Bobby?"

"Hey, kiddo," he said, holding his hand out for me. I shook it begrudgingly.

Bobby was insufferable and pushy and the best damn manager in the music industry. He drove me up the wall, but he also fought for me tooth and nail. He'd never pushed for me to go solo. He got us twice as much money as we'd originally been offered. And he drove a hard bargain. The only problem was...he looked like he was about to use those same skills on me.

I'd had no idea he was coming to Lubbock. I'd been home from tour for a grand total of one month, and already, he was here? That couldn't be good.

He ran a hand down his silver handlebar mustache and set his flinty black eyes on me. "Long time no see."

I glanced to Blaire, who had fallen quiet at the silver-haired six-foot-tall giant who had just stridden into our midst in a pin-striped suit more fit for a mobster than someone in Lubbock.

Bobby didn't miss a beat. It was his job to use everything to his advantage. He stuck his hand out to Blaire. "Hello, beautiful. And who might you be?"

Blaire reluctantly put her hand in his. "I was just leaving."

"No need to be shy. Any friend of Campbell's is a friend of mine."

"We're not friends," she said flatly.

Bobby arched an eyebrow at me. I wouldn't hear the end of this. Fuck.

"Well then, any woman as gorgeous as you definitely deserves an introduction. I'm Bobby Rogers, head of Rogers and Rogers Agency. And you are?"

"I'm Blaire," she said uncertainly.

"Any special talents?"

"Shut it, Bobby," I snapped.

He arched an eyebrow at me. "What?"

"Bobby, my manager," I told her. "And he hasn't told me what the hell he's doing here."

"What am I doing here?" Bobby asked. "Kid, it's time to come home. LA is calling."

Blaire glanced between us. "I'm just going to...head out."

"Blaire, wait..."

It was the wrong thing to say. I knew it even as it left my mouth. She had no intention of waiting. And now, Bobby fucking Rogers knew that there was a single girl in existence who could make me utter those words.

She shot me one more glare and then walked away. And my manager was here, so I couldn't follow her. Not that she wanted me to.

"Well then," Bobby said with a shit-eating grin.

I grabbed him by his stupid lapel and threw him into the dressing room. Then, I followed, slamming the door shut.

"What are you doing here, Bobby?"

"I see why you haven't left." He waggled his eyebrows. "Having a little hometown fling."

"No," I ground out.

"Surprised a pap hasn't figured that one out. It'd be good for your image, kid."

"Don't call me a kid and leave Blaire out of this. She's just a friend of my brother's."

"If you say so." His eyes darted back to the door, as if he could see Blaire through the wood, see a way to use her for his own purposes.

"I do say so. Now, cut to the point. You want me back in LA?"

"Not me. If I could, I'd let you have a much longer vacation. The record label wants you to start working on the next album. They need you and the rest of the band in the studio. What you got?"

"I don't have anything," I told him.

"Come on. You always keep your little notebook with you. I saw you jotting down songs on tour."

"They're trash."

"You say that about all your songs. We always figure it out in the studio, and they end up working out."

"Not this time."

He huffed. "Look, kid, you've got to give me something."

I paced away from him and grabbed my notebook out of my bag. "It's all rubbish. I don't want to make any of these songs."

He snatched the notebook out of my hand and thumbed through the pages. "Hey, hey, some of these are good. They can be reworked."

"They're missing something."

"We can figure out what they're missing."

"I'm broken," I told him with a case of melodrama. I was an artist after all.

"Kid, you're not broken."

"Bobby, stop fucking calling me kid."

"You're a kid to me," he said calmly. He was used to

dealing with artists. This was his area. "Tell me what the problem is."

"The songs...they're not *about* anything."

"Is this about the critical reviews of the last album?"

I winced and said nothing. The critics had shredded our last album. Fans fucking loved it. We'd sold out a worldwide stadium tour in under fifteen minutes. But the critics were brutal. They'd called the lyrics trite and boring. They couldn't believe I'd written this album after the last one had so much heart. I could still hear the words of one particular critic saying, "The album is baseless and unimaginative. Campbell Abbey is a one-trick pony."

I should have been able to shake it.

But I was afraid they were right.

"I need more time. It's like I've lost my muse."

Bobby really looked at me. He must have seen the pained desperation on my face. The need to work as an artist and not a machine. The album had to be good enough for me, and with what I had, it wasn't going to be.

He sighed. "All right. I can give you to the end of July."

"That's only a month, Bobby."

"It's all the leeway I can pull for you. You have a month to find your muse." He tossed the notebook back to me. "Either way, you're going to get your ass on a plane to LA to work on the next album."

3

BLAIRE

*C*ampbell was going back to LA.

Good. That was...good. In fact, it was exactly what I wanted. He'd been in Lubbock since Peyton's wedding. The wedding where I had brought a date and purposely avoided Campbell all night. I'd had a good time. But I would have had a better time if he hadn't been there at all.

Then, he'd spent the last *month* in town. A whole fucking month. Hanging out at the winery, spending time with my—*our*—friends, and generally ruining my peace and quiet.

I couldn't exactly tell him to leave. He had every right to be back in Lubbock. And I couldn't tell him to stop hanging out with our friends or at the winery. We were too enmeshed to extricate ourselves from each other's lives. Which was hilarious when I stopped to think about it. Since in high school, we had been so far from each other's lives that he didn't even know I existed until senior year.

LA was where he belonged. It would be better for everyone when he left.

But the last interaction had left me flummoxed. Despite myself, I'd followed Campbell's rise to fame. It was hard not to when he was in every headline. I knew the celebrities that he'd dated, the girls he was rumored to have hooked up with, the songs he'd written about the breakups. So, why in the hell had he asked *me* out?

Should I be flattered? Because I was mostly confused. Campbell Abbey could have any girl on the planet, so why did he want me?

Which brought me right back around to the cynical part of my brain...the realistic part of my brain...which said, of course he didn't want me at all. He'd used the opportunity to fuck with me. To throw me off-balance for ignoring him since he'd strolled back into Lubbock. He'd used his celebrity charm and sexy, messy hair and that panty-melting smile to treat me just like every other girl. But it wasn't going to fucking work.

Fuck. I just wanted to go home.

"Hey, you all right?" Piper asked, dragging me out of my own circle of mental torture.

"Fine," I lied.

Piper arched an eyebrow. "That was convincing."

"Can I have the keys? I'm going to bail early."

"No way!" Piper declared. "We're celebrating. You can't go yet."

She was still seated in her boyfriend's lap. Hollin wrapped his arm around Piper's waist and looked up at me.

"Yeah, Blaire, you can't go. We're just getting started." He nodded his head toward the table. "Bombay and lime."

He winked. It was my go-to drink.

"I just want to go home," I told her, eyeing the drink.

Piper nudged it toward me. "One drink. If you aren't having a good time after you finish...you can go."

I picked up the glass with a devious smile and then downed the entire contents, opening my throat and letting it slide all the way down. Hollin gaped at me as I dropped the glass back onto the table.

"Can you teach her how to do that?" he asked me.

Piper jabbed her elbow into his stomach. "Ass."

I laughed despite myself. "I have a feeling we're not talking about drinks anymore."

"Gag reflexes," Hollin said.

"Shut up," Piper said.

It had been a stunt to get the keys, but already, I was feeling better. It was one night. Campbell would be gone in the morning. He'd forget he'd ever asked me out. There was no reason for me to ditch under those circumstances.

"You win." I took an open seat. "I'll stay."

"Excellent," Hollin said.

"What made you want to run away anyway?" Piper asked. But the smirk on her lips said she knew that something had happened with me and Campbell.

She had been trying to get me to talk about him since he returned. But no one knew what had happened with us, and I'd like to keep it that way if I could at all help it. I didn't even want to tell my best friend.

"It's nothing."

Piper leaned forward. "Because Honey said that Campbell asked you out."

I glared at her. "If you already knew, then why did you bother asking?"

Hollin choked on his drink. "I must have missed that. My brother did what?"

"He was joking."

Piper arched an eyebrow. "Was he?"

"Can we not? I'm not going to date Campbell."

"All right. All right," Piper said, holding up her hands. "Hollin, you need to make your brother behave. We don't want him upsetting my friends."

Hollin grumbled under his breath, "As if anyone could make Campbell do anything."

Which was so fucking accurate.

The thing that had me worried was that not only could no one tell Campbell what to do, but he was also relentless. And I knew this firsthand. If he wasn't leaving on the first plane out of Lubbock, I would be worried that he'd take my refusal as a challenge.

"Y'all," Jennifer said, plopping down into the seat with a huge smile. "Guess what just happened."

We stared at her expectantly. She didn't have a ring on her finger, so Julian hadn't proposed. Though we all assumed it was coming eventually. They had been together for a year and were entirely inseparable. Annie and Jordan had gotten engaged earlier this year, and it felt like another Wright engagement was soon to follow.

"What happened?" I asked.

"Julian asked me to move in with him."

Piper and I exchanged a look. Jennifer had spent the last year living in Piper's house. It was so great, having her there, even if we hadn't actually needed a third roommate. I was going to miss her.

"That's amazing," Piper told her.

"Ahhh," I said, jumping to my feet and throwing my arms around her. "Big step."

"It is," she said. Jennifer flushed furiously at the thought. She was the shyest of our group and only really dropped her introversion when she was behind a camera.

"About time," Hollin said with a laugh. He looked to his girlfriend and winked.

"Don't get any ideas," Piper growled at him.

"Wouldn't dream of it."

But I knew that was only a matter of time as well. Everyone was so happy. Weddings, engagements, and moving in, oh my!

"I'll help you find someone to take my room," Jennifer told us. "I don't want to leave you hanging."

"Hey, don't worry about it," Piper said.

"Yeah, we managed before."

"Worrying is my middle name." Jennifer bit her lip. "Like, I am so worried about the cats. How the hell am I going to move Avocado again?"

We all burst out laughing. When Jennifer had moved in, she'd transported two stray cats, Avocado and Bacon, to our property. They still lived outside and mostly fended for themselves. But Avocado had held it against her for months. I couldn't imagine moving them a second time. It had been hard enough the first go-round.

We discussed possible new solutions for the cats. Even going as far as offering to let her leave the cats at the house. I didn't mind feeding them. They didn't love me as much as Jennifer. But Bacon and I had an understanding. I would be perfectly happy with having them around still.

Annie and Jordan migrated to the table at some point with Julian, who pulled Jennifer into his lap. Honey dropped into the vacated seat next to me. She had been making friends with some other Wright Vineyard regulars. I knew them by face but not name. It had been nice to not have her hovering. She was incredible at her job, but sometimes, she was a little too enthusiastic.

"Oh my God, did you see Nate's new TikTok?" Honey asked. "It already has three million views."

She thrust her phone at me. And there was Nate King in

all of his glory. Nate lived an hour and a half south of Lubbock in Midland, Texas. His family was one half of Dorset & King oil, one of the largest oil companies in the country. We'd met via social media and hit it off. After one date, I invited him to Peyton's wedding. Only part of the reason was because I'd found out Campbell was going to be there. The other part really enjoyed his company. We'd gone on a few dates in the month since then, and our fans *loved* when we did videos together. Both of our followers had gone through the roof since we'd joined forces.

But...I had doubts. Nate was hot and friendly and a really stellar kisser. He just didn't seem like *the one*. And if I preached to my followers that they shouldn't settle, neither should I, right?

"Oh, let me turn the volume up," Honey said, clicking the side buttons so I could hear the song being played.

And I froze in place. Because the song was "I See the Real You" by none other than Campbell Abbey himself. I wanted to throw the phone back at Honey, but I couldn't. I just watched the guy I was sort of, kind of not-exclusively dating start a viral TikTok trend.

The video was good. It was him looking into the camera, wearing a baseball cap, an oversize shirt, and baggy sweats, hiding how good-looking he was. Then, when the chorus dropped, the video seamlessly transitioned to show him shirtless, his eight-pack on display, in low-slung jeans. His hair was done, and he was smirking at the camera like he was going to eat them alive. The caption said, *Show the world the real you.*

I clicked on his hashtag and almost groaned. Already in the twelve hours since Nate's video had gone viral, there were thousands of other people clambering to do the "I See the Real You" challenge. Just my fucking luck.

"We're going to have to do it," Honey said eagerly.

I thrust the phone back at her. "No."

"But Blaire..."

I ignored her. "No."

Piper snatched Honey's phone out of her hand and watched it. She nodded. "Damn."

"Right!" Honey said.

"You could do this easy," Piper said. "It's just a glow up."

Annie's eyes widened. "Quite a glow up. Jesus." Jordan cleared his throat next to her. She grinned at him.

Annie offered the phone to Jennifer, but she shook her head, embarrassed. "I've already seen it."

The girls all laughed.

"Speaking of, where is Nate tonight?" Annie asked.

"He's in New York, visiting his cousin," I told her. "Gavin King, I think."

"You didn't go with him?"

I shook my head. Nate had asked. Though I didn't say that. He'd thought it would be fun to show me around the city with his cousin, who apparently knew all the people. Whatever that meant. But I knew exactly what that would mean for our relationship. We were incredibly casual at this point. New York would have meant defining it. And I honestly thought we made better friends.

"Hey, y'all. What did I miss?" Campbell asked as he exited the dressing room. His manager was nowhere in sight.

Piper glanced up at Campbell with a grin that should have been his first warning. "We were talking about the guy Blaire is dating. You remember Nate from the wedding?"

My jaw nearly dropped at Piper's audacity. But...I had to admit, it was satisfying to see the first hint of jealousy on Campbell's face.

4

CAMPBELL

*M*y eyes shifted to Blaire and back to Piper. "Sure," I ground out. "I remember him."

I remembered coming home from tour, jet-lagged to hell and suffering through a wedding when all I wanted to do was sleep, only to find Blaire had an actual date. I'd been back for over a year, and she hadn't had anyone else in her life. A five-month tour had fucking ruined that for me.

I hadn't actually met her date. I'd hated him on sight. But maybe that was bias? Or jealousy? The fact of the matter was that I didn't care about him in the slightest. Only that he was standing in my way.

"He just started a viral video, using your song," Piper continued. She pushed a phone into my hand, and I watched him essentially take his shirt off and smolder at the camera.

"Uh, great?"

"You think so?" Piper asked, and I could hear the first trace of sarcasm in her voice. I was happy for my brother because she matched him perfectly. But he was also such a shit that I sometimes didn't know if he was making fun of me or not.

I handed her back the phone back. "I didn't realize that passed as entertainment."

Hollin snickered. "Ass."

"It's a thirst trap," Honey provided helpfully.

"Campbell doesn't care," Blaire said, snatching the phone out of Piper's hand and all but throwing it at Honey.

I *didn't* care. That was entirely accurate. But she looked embarrassed that the phone had gotten into my hands. And I couldn't see why. She was the one dating the guy—the *thirst trap*—after all. Interestingly, she hadn't mentioned him when she turned me down. Not that she was obligated to. We had enough issues without her dating someone else.

"Yeah, but it's his song," Honey continued.

"That it is," I said, smoothly taking the seat next to Blaire. "I'm sure the record label will appreciate it being used."

Blaire jumped to her feet. "I need to get another drink."

"I could go with you," I offered.

Her eyes widened fractionally. "No thanks. Honey will come with."

"Uh, yeah. Sure," Honey said, standing beside her boss. She looked down at me. "Did you want something?"

"Sure. I'm not picky. Whatever you're having."

"Okay," she said with a wide smile.

Blaire rolled her eyes and tugged Honey away. They dipped their heads together and were speaking furiously. I could only guess at what.

Piper hopped off Hollin's lap, patted him on the shoulder twice, and then walked around the table to chat with Annie and Jennifer. Hollin shot me a brotherly look that I knew all too well.

"What?" I asked.

"You asked out Blaire?"

I shrugged. "It was a joke."

"Bullshit."

Despite myself, I laughed. Leave it to my brother. "Fine. It wasn't a fucking joke."

"She's dating someone else."

"Yeah, well, she didn't mention that."

Hollin shrugged. "Probably because it's not serious. Or so Piper says."

"So, why are you up my ass?"

"Look, I don't give a fuck if you want to make an absolute fool of yourself. But Blaire is Piper's best friend. I think she'd actually kill you if you hurt Blaire." Hollin seemed to consider before adding, "Again."

"You don't know shit."

Hollin smirked. "Don't have to. I know your stupid ass."

"Yeah," I said with a chuckle. "Well, you're not wrong anyway."

"Of course I'm not wrong."

"Shut up."

Hollin crossed his arms over his chest and leaned backward. "I'm just saying that you're a dipshit and you need to be on your best behavior with Blaire. I will not be held responsible for how my girlfriend responds otherwise."

"Best behavior," I grumbled. "Fine."

"Good."

"But can we talk about how that fucking video was a piece of shit?"

Hollin barked out a laugh. "It's terrible. If I took my shirt off and leaned into the camera, I could get a few million views, too."

I arched an eyebrow at him.

"Yeah, yeah, you'd probably get, like, fifty million views."

"I don't take my shirt off."

"Fine. Twenty million views with your shirt on."

"I'm offended," I said with a smirk. "I think I could get fifty with my shirt on, too."

"Whatever, dude. What did the infamous Bobby Rogers have to say?"

I blew out a breath. "He wants me back in LA to start recording the next album."

"Fuck. Already?"

"He said I could have another month, and then I needed to figure my shit out. I don't have any music though. The lyrics are all shit. What the fuck am I going to do?"

"You're a professional. You'll figure it out in the next month," Hollin assured me.

I nodded reluctantly as Blaire and Honey returned from the bar. Honey plunked a glass down in front of me. It was pinkish orange with a slice of orange attached to the rim. If I had to guess, based on those few shit years of bartending to survive LA, the drink was a Sex on the Beach. Honey had one in her hand as well. While Blaire's drink was entirely clear with a lime in it. Why hadn't I gotten *that*?

Blaire arched an eyebrow at me. "You said you weren't picky."

Ah. Ah, okay. That was how she was going to play it.

Hollin's words were still in my head. I needed to be on my best behavior. Not that Hollin had ever been on good behavior in his life. But I'd hurt Blaire even if he didn't know what I'd done. I didn't want to push her away.

I raised the drink to her. "I'm man enough for Sex on the Beach."

Honey giggled. Blaire just rolled her eyes as I took a good, long sip of the sickly-sweet drink. Under normal circumstances, I would have sent the drink back and gotten a bourbon and Coke or a beer or something, but I couldn't now. Even if this would bite me in the ass later.

Blaire had just plopped into the seat next to me and turned to talk to the girls. Honey looked torn on whether to talk to me or her boss but inevitably ended up hovering over Blaire. That was a relief to me. I loved my fans. I just hadn't planned on dealing with any tonight. It took a good amount of mental energy to be on like that. I usually had to prep for it.

"What the fuck are you drinking?"

I turned back around and found my sister, Nora, striding toward me. She wore outrageously tall high heels everywhere she went. She was the event planner for Wright Vineyard and had orchestrated the entire evening. If she was back here already, that meant the night was coming to a close.

"Sex on the Beach. Want one?"

"That's disgusting," Nora said. "I thought you had taste."

Hollin chortled. "Why would you think that?"

"Ass," I grumbled.

Nora's eyes darted around the backstage area. I thought on some level, she was looking around, still expecting to see August and Tamara—her ex-boyfriend and ex-best friend. She'd dated August for three years and been friends with Tamara almost her entire life. But then she'd found them hooking up last month and lost everything in the blink of an eye. She'd had to move out of her apartment with Tamara and into Hollin's guest bedroom.

I was slightly disappointed that I hadn't seen August since then because Hollin busting August's nose wasn't enough for me. He deserved a few broken bones for what he'd done to my sister.

"Are you still good for helping me move tomorrow?" Nora asked.

I groaned. "Can't we hire movers?"

Hollin smacked the back of my head. "That's what pickup trucks are for."

"Yeah. Stop being so pretentious," Nora said with a grin. "I don't have that much stuff, and I need to get the fuck out of Hollin's house."

"Hey, it's not so bad!" Hollin said.

"The walls are thin," Nora told me with wide eyes.

Which meant Hollin and Piper were *not* quiet.

"Yeah, yeah. I'll help move you out of the sex house."

Hollin just leaned back with a self-satisfied light in his eyes and a smile on his face. He was so fucking happy. And I didn't begrudge him for an instant.

"Bright and early," Nora said, pointing at me. "Eight a.m. I want to get this done before it's too hot."

"I'll be there."

"Which means finish your girly drink and go home. I don't want either of you hungover either."

"It'd take a lot more than this," I said, picking up the Sex on the Beach, "to get me drunk enough for a hangover."

"That was not a challenge," my little sister said.

I glanced at Hollin, and he nodded at me.

We raised our glasses together and said, "Challenge accepted."

5

BLAIRE

I might have had too much to drink.

After Campbell had asked me out and then I had to sit around and pretend that his presence didn't bother me *all night*, I'd maybe gone a bit overboard. I could drink like a tank even though I was only about five feet tall. My tolerance had always been high. I thought it was because I'd started drinking with my mom at a young age because she had all these psych reasons for avoiding binge drinking by not making alcohol taboo. It had mostly worked —I'd give her that.

Tonight was a different story.

Honey had left a half hour ago, and I was on Piper's arm as I stumbled back to her Jeep.

"Do not throw up in my car," Piper said. She was completely clearheaded. She'd only had one drink early in the night.

"I'm not going to...throw up," I said with a hiccup. "I'm blackout girl, not throw-up girl."

"Great," Piper grumbled. "It's been a few years since I've seen you this drunk."

"Shh," I said, putting a finger to her mouth. "It's *fine*."

Piper leaned me against the Jeep and then patted her pockets down for the key. She wasn't carrying a purse. "Fuck. I gave the damn key to Hollin when I first got here. I'm need to run back inside."

"I'll be fine right here."

She looked at me with pursed lips, as if she didn't believe me. Then, her eyes darted around. "Hey, Abbey!"

I glanced up and saw that it was not in fact her boyfriend, but the other Abbey brother. Campbell's head popped up at the sound of his last name. Piper waved him over, and he came forward almost reluctantly.

"I need to run in and get my key from Hollin. Can you make sure that Blaire doesn't pass out or do anything really stupid?" Piper asked.

"I don't need a babysitter." I put my hands on my hips to try to look indignant but pitched forward. I would've fallen on my face if Piper hadn't been there to catch me and leverage me back against the Jeep.

"She's drunk. And she does need a babysitter."

Campbell frowned. As if he'd just realized that I was a wasted mess. "Yeah. Sure. I'll stay with Blaire."

"Good. Be nice," Piper growled. Then, she was stomping back inside with a huff.

"You don't have to stay," I told him. "You should just leave since it's the only thing you're really good at."

Damn my drunk mouth.

Campbell winced slightly. "I'll stay right here actually. If I left, I think Piper would hunt me down and kill me."

I rolled my eyes dramatically. "At least my best friend can scare you into being a gentleman."

Campbell took a step forward until he was nearly in my personal space. For a second, I couldn't breathe. Not even a little. I was captivated by him. I could remember the smell and taste of him. The *want* of him. It clouded my already-addled brain.

It would be easy to want Campbell Abbey again. So easy.

"I want to apologize," Campbell said evenly.

"What?" I asked, jolted out of my runaway thoughts. "Why?"

"For how I acted earlier. When I asked you out," he clarified. "I know we have history. I know that you're...seeing someone else. Though I suppose I didn't know it was serious when I asked you. But I didn't intend to make you uncomfortable."

"I wasn't uncomfortable. I was mad."

"Then, I'm sorry for making you mad," he said evenly. He stuffed his hands in the pockets of his ripped black jeans, as if it was the only way to keep himself from touching me.

"Well, it doesn't matter anyway."

"Why is that?"

"Because you're leaving again. So, just run on back to LA. Go live your big, glamorous life. It's what you always wanted."

His face was like stone when I delivered that one-two punch. It had been eight years since I'd had to read Campbell's expressions. And it should have been difficult to discern what he was thinking, but somehow, it wasn't. Even tipsy, I could tell that he didn't want to say whatever was about to come out of his mouth.

He glanced down at the ground and kicked a stray rock. "I'm not."

"You're not what?"

Our eyes met again.

"Leaving."

My jaw dropped. "But your manager said..."

"Yeah, well, he doesn't call the shots. They want me back in LA to record a new album, but I don't have any songs worth recording right now. So, I decided to stay in town and try to relax." He shrugged. "Find a way to get my music back."

"No," I whispered. His face darkened at the word. "Well, I guess it'll just be like the last eighteen months then."

A smirk crossed his lips. "Except that you're speaking to me now."

Damn it, he was right. If I'd just not talked to him, it would have been so much easier to continue. But now, we'd broken the dam, and I didn't know how to stop. Already, we had been alone twice in one night. Only now, we were *really* alone. There was no one outside within a hundred yards of us. Piper should have been back, but something told me she was purposely taking her sweet time.

My eyes darted to his lips. Those perfect lips. God, I was too drunk to think coherently. There was no other explanation for why I was suddenly thinking about kissing Campbell Abbey.

"So?" I finally got out.

"So, I guess it will be different than the last eighteen months."

"I spoke to you before."

He chuckled and took another step in closer. "Oh, I remember. You said, 'Got something to say?' and looked at me as if the world could swallow me up and eat me whole."

I flushed at that memory. It had been a few months ago, when all of us had flown to Dallas to see Cosmere perform. Campbell had given Hollin backstage passes and seats in the Owners Club. It had been incredible...until we went backstage at the end of the show to hang out with the band.

I hadn't even wanted to go to that damn show. Piper insisted that I attend, and some part of me *wanted* to be there, doing cool things with my friends. The only problem was Campbell...and the fact that it was exactly what I'd thought it would be. Campbell, surrounded by gorgeous groupies, all vying for his attention. Then, he had the nerve to get upset when Santi, the drummer for Cosmere, put his arm around me. It was an actual joke—unlike the bullshit Campbell had pulled tonight. Santi was boisterous and overly friendly and ridiculous. He wasn't hitting on me.

And the whole thing would have been funny, but as soon as Santi dropped his arm around my shoulders and asked me if I was taken, Campbell jumped to his feet. Santi was incredulous. Everyone in the room had looked at us. It was one thing for Campbell to get mad that someone was hitting on his little sister. It was quite another for him to be *madder* that they were hitting on me.

I'd spent the last eight years making sure not a damn person knew that I was the girl behind "I See the Real You." Then, he had almost ruined the entire thing in one go. It was bad enough that Hollin and Piper had figured out that we had history. The last thing I wanted was for the entire world to know.

"Well, you were the idiot who jumped up, as if you were protecting my virtue," I snapped at him.

He rocked back on his heels and nodded. "Yeah. I... wasn't really thinking."

"Whatever," I groused.

Silence lingered between us. As if Campbell didn't know what to say to not make me upset. And I had nothing left to say to him. I was beginning to sober up, and I just wanted Piper to hurry the hell up.

"We could...try to be friends." He looked up at me under his long, dark lashes.

"Friends," I said with a sardonic laugh. "In what world?"

"All of our friends are friends. It might be easier if we... acted like we were, too."

"We've *never* been friends, Campbell."

"That's not true," he said with a frustrated sigh. "We were friends in high school."

I laughed right in his face at that. "You're unbelievable. Please do not try to give me revisionist history. I was there. You were the most popular boy in school despite not giving a single fuck that you didn't dress or act like any of the other popular kids and you played no sports. You just had *it*. You always have. And I was nobody."

"You weren't nobody."

I glared at him now. The alcohol only fueling my rage. "Shut up. I was absolutely nobody. I was the weird smart kid. I wore giant glasses and had a bob haircut that my mom did herself. I was in chorus but was way too shy to ever audition for a solo. And I played soccer but not for the high school team because the girls were *horrible* to loser me."

"And now, you have a million followers."

"Three and a half million," I corrected him.

He tilted his head at me. "Proof that it doesn't matter who you were in high school."

"That is a fact, but again, we were never friends. You weren't friends with the loner girl." I crossed my arms over my chest. "I was invisible to you...to everybody."

"Until you weren't."

"Yes," I whispered. "I was either invisible or everything to you, and I'm not going to be satisfied with a middle ground. So...just pretend you can't see me anymore."

Campbell was silent for a few seconds at my proclamation. Then, he said, "That sounds like a song."

I groaned. "Fuck you, Campbell."

He blinked at me in confusion, as if coming up from underwater. "What?"

"I'm tired of being the girl with a song."

He opened his mouth to say something, but I didn't want to hear it. I was tired of waiting on Piper. I didn't want to stand here any longer and listen to Campbell's bullshit. One thing was clear: we were never going to be friends.

So, I pushed off the Jeep and strode back toward the winery. And I was glad that Campbell didn't follow me or try to change my mind. It made all of this easier.

PART II

INVISIBLE GIRL

6

CAMPBELL

*T*he next morning, I slept through three alarms and two angry phone calls.

"Fuck," I spat as I raced out of bed and threw on a pair of ripped jeans, a black T-shirt, and tennis shoes.

I was staying in a hotel ten minutes from Hollin's place. He'd told me to just fucking move in for however long I was here, but I was used to my own space and my own stuff. I wasn't sure how comfortable I should get in Lubbock. And considering Bobby's appearance last night, it seemed like I'd made the right call.

I drove across town in the Range Rover I'd purchased when I got into town. Sharing Hollin's house was one thing; not having my own wheels was another. Truthfully, I'd thought I'd be here longer. It hadn't felt frivolous at the time.

Hollin's truck was parked in the driveway. My dad's car and my aunt's classic orange VW bug that she'd refurbished herself at the mechanic shop she worked at were parked on the street. They must have been inside because when I pulled up behind them, only Hollin was in view.

"Where the fuck have you been?" Hollin asked, carrying a giant box on his shoulder.

"Overslept." I swiped sleep out of my eyes. "Sorry."

"You look like shit."

I ran a hand back through my mussed hair. It was not artfully done. It was just a wreck. "Thanks."

Hollin dropped the box into the back of his pickup and turned to face me. "You left before I did last night. Why are you so tired?"

"Couldn't sleep."

Which was true but not the real reason. Something had happened last night. After that very angry conversation with Blaire, a light had flickered on in my head. All those months on the road, all that time I'd been struggling with my lyrics, even while writing the last album, and last night had just changed it all.

One minute, I had been talking to Blaire about high school. The next minute, I was in another world, where words rushed across my mind. Almost like I was too slow to reach out and grab them all. I blinked back to awareness and uttered the completely senseless and rash words that sounded like a song. And I lost her. Blaire stomped away faster than I could hope to apologize a second time.

So, I drove back to the hotel. I'd planned to call it an early night. Instead, I'd taken out my notebook and stayed up until four in the morning, working on a new song. And it was...good. It was maybe the best thing I'd written in years.

"Invisible Girl" was going to be on the new album. Though...I'd probably have to warn Blaire. Since she had gotten so mad even at the notion that I might write another song about her. But, fuck, I couldn't help it. When creativity struck, I wasn't stupid enough to ignore it.

"So, what's her name?" Hollin asked.

I jerked my head up at him. "What?"

"The girl who kept you up all night."

Blaire. Though I could hardly say that because it had absolutely nothing to do with what he was insinuating. But it was her words that had weaseled their way into my subconscious and forced me to write all night.

So, I chuckled. "I wish."

"You wish? You could have practically any single girl in a twenty-mile radius."

I was fairly certain that the radius was larger than he was giving me credit for. But that was beside the point.

"I started working on a new song," I confessed.

Hollin arched an eyebrow. "Yeah? I thought all your music was shit?"

"It was. But not this one."

"Well, that's a relief, isn't it?" Hollin asked as we headed back toward the front door, where a peeved Nora stood with her arms crossed.

"Are you two done?" Nora asked. "We have more boxes to move."

"I still think we should have hired someone, shrimp."

She rolled her eyes at the nickname I'd been using for her since she was a kid. "You were late. I thought you might not even come. Can't get your pretty hands dirty."

I glanced down at my callous hands from years of guitar work. They were hardly pretty, but they were fucking useful. "Just wanted to make Hollin do most of the work."

"That seems fair," she said, pulling me in for a hug.

"Dad is inside," Hollin said before we walked in.

"Yeah, I saw his car."

Hollin shot me a look. "Behave."

I rolled my eyes. "It'll be fine."

"We've heard that before," Nora grumbled.

I sighed as they stepped inside.

My dad and I had a...complicated relationship. Even before my mom had died. When I'd been young, I was Mom's favorite. But Mom and Dad always fought. One day, it had been too much, and she left. I begged her to come back. And she did. She had come back just to get me to go with her. Dad threatened to call it kidnapping. Everything fell apart after that.

We came back to live with Dad, Hollin, and Nora. She stayed for me. And I bore the brunt of that. Especially since they never stopped fighting. Then, two months before I met Blaire, one of those routine arguments sent Mom flying out of the house in a rage. She was in a hit-and-run and died on-site.

I was irrational and utterly inconsolable. I blamed my dad for the fight and their arguments, which had always been rough but turned worse than ever after we came back. All I wanted to do was get the hell out of that house, away from my dad. All I had for an escape was my guitar and Blaire. She was the person I turned to when the fighting with my dad became too much. I snuck into her house when I couldn't handle it anymore—the loss, the fighting, the pain.

She was everything. Until I finally left.

So, it was no wonder that my siblings were worried that Dad and I would start fighting again. We'd always been a powder keg, ready to explode. I'd been working on it, and I wanted a relationship with him. I just didn't think anyone would stop being wary.

I followed them inside to find my dad, Gregg, organizing boxes by size for Hollin to move. He was dressed in practical khaki shorts and an old T-shirt with a beat-up baseball cap on his head. He shouldn't have even been touching the boxes with the knee problems he had. Sometimes, he had to use a cane to get around.

"Dad, don't," Hollin said, hurrying over.

"Hey, Campbell," Dad said.

I nodded my head at him. "Dad."

Aunt Vail's smile lit up. "Hey, kid!"

We hugged. She'd married my aunt Lori in Colorado after the local church ran them out. They'd only come back when a new pastor had been hired and my other aunt, Helene—Jordan and Julian's mom—had returned from Vancouver after leaving her husband, Owen. Things were better for them now. But I didn't understand how they didn't hold it against the whole church.

"Good to see you."

She crossed her tattooed arms. "You're late."

"Yeah, yeah. I've heard it."

"Oh good, Campbell is here," Aunt Lori said. "You can help me clean."

I laughed and hugged her. "I think I will be *carry the boxes* guy."

Lori shook her head at me and then drew me in for a hug. She was night and day compared to Vail with burnished hair past her shoulders. Normally, she wore sundresses, but today, she was in high-waisted shorts and a Lubbock High cheerleading shirt she'd had since high school. Her hair was pulled back with a headband, and she wore thick yellow gloves.

"How do you live like this, Hollin?"

Hollin guffawed. "It's not that bad, Lori!"

Nora snickered. "It's not *great* either. How does Piper stand it?"

"Jesus, y'all, I'll get a housekeeper."

Dad pulled in closer to me. "You look like you're not sleeping."

I ran a hand through my hair. "So I hear."

"Campbell is writing again," Hollin pitched in. Always the intermediary.

"Really?" Dad asked.

I nodded. "Yeah."

"And it's not shit?" Nora asked with an arched eyebrow.

Dad laughed. "Nory, language."

"Hey, those were his words!"

"True," I agreed. "But no, not this song."

"What changed?" Nora asked. She tugged me away from Dad and into the spare room she'd been staying in.

I knew exactly what had changed. But I just shrugged. "Don't know. Maybe the threat of returning to LA kicked me in the ass. Procrastination until under deadline."

Nora narrowed her eyes at me, as if she could hear the lie in my voice. But she didn't call me on it for once. She just put me to work. She didn't actually have *that* much stuff. A bed, dresser, and love seat were the largest items. And with everyone's help, we loaded up the cars and were on our way across town in no time.

Nora's new place was a three-bedroom house on the south side of town that she was sharing with Weston Wright. Hollin had flipped his lid when she suggested moving in with the newest Wright to Lubbock, but it made sense at least. They both needed a roommate, and she couldn't exactly stay with Hollin forever. Not that I let her know I approved. I could play the big-brother gig just as well as Hollin.

But West seemed cool. Even if the situation that had brought him to Lubbock was unorthodox.

Last year, Jordan and Julian had received an email from

Weston, saying that he thought they were his brothers. Then, it all came out. Their dad, Owen, had had a relationship with a woman in Seattle while he had his family in Vancouver. They had *three* siblings. Weston, who was most interested in meeting them; his twin brother, Whitton; and their younger sister, Harley. Jordan and Julian had flown up to Seattle to meet Whitton and Harley and to try to get to know this new side of their family, but none of the Wrights had returned to visit Lubbock.

Then, Weston's job as part of a backup band had fallen apart somewhere in Eastern Europe, and he'd said fuck it and come back to the States. He'd decided to try it out here rather than in Seattle. Especially since Harley had just gotten into Texas Tech as a National Merit Scholar. He thought it was only a matter of time before Whitton followed them here, but he was stubborn. And I could hardly blame him when his entire life had been upturned in a matter of months.

"Hey, you made it," Julian said, shaking hands with me after I hopped out of the SUV.

"We made it. I might have overslept."

"No problem. We got most of West's stuff moved in already. You need a hand?"

"Julian, are you offering our help?" Jordan asked with a look.

He just grinned. "Some manual labor would do you good."

I shook Jordan's hand when he approached. "Don't worry. I fucking hate it, too."

"There'd better be beer after this," Jordan grumbled. "That's all I'm saying."

Hollin's ears perked up at that. "Did someone say beer?"

"After," Nora said. She pushed him along and into the house.

I grabbed a box and lifted it onto my shoulder before following her inside. The house was skinny but long with the living room, dining room, and kitchen in a stretch on one side. There was a hallway to the other side of the house, which had the three bedrooms and two bathrooms.

Weston stepped out of the room at the front of the house. He looked so much like Jordan and Julian that sometimes, it was disorienting. Especially since he'd recently cut off his floppy hair into a short hairstyle that resembled the rest of the Wrights.

"Hey, you made it," Weston said, leaning against the doorframe.

"We did. This one overslept." Nora threw her thumb back at me.

Weston grinned and offered his hand. "Hey, man."

"How's it going?"

"Good, I guess. Mostly surreal."

"I could see that."

Weston's eyes tracked past me to Nora. "Hey, Nor, I took the front room, so you could have the en suite bathroom."

She grinned like a fiend. "You sure? It's only temporary. Don't you want your own space?"

"Don't worry about it. As long as you need to be here. Plus, I figured you should have your privacy."

"All right," she said with a smile. "Thanks."

I arched an eyebrow at him. "Did Hollin talk to you?"

Weston crossed his arms. "Yeah. Are you going to give me the same speech?"

"Do I need to?"

"No."

"Then, we're good," I told him. "Just don't touch my sister."

He blanched. "Hollin went into detail."

I laughed. "I bet he did."

Hollin was intimidating enough for the both of us. West had clearly gotten the picture.

I glanced into the spare room as I went to get another box and froze. "Oh, is that a vintage Fender Strat?" I asked, ogling his collection.

Weston lit up. "Yeah, dude. It's my favorite guitar. I have a few others, but I almost always play the Strat."

I could see why. It was in pristine condition. They didn't even make guitars like this anymore. As much as I loved the latest and greatest, I had a huge affinity for the original trailblazer guitars. They just had something to them.

"Do you mind if I..."

"Not at all," Weston said.

I stepped into the music room. He had every manner of instrument set up inside. He had just moved in this morning and this room looked like it was the first thing he'd put together. Which meant he and I were very alike. Instruments were the first thing I cared about, too. There were two keyboards and an upright piano against the long wall. Then, three electric and two acoustic guitars, a bass, an electric drum set, a saxophone, trumpet, and harmonica.

"You play all of these?" I pulled the strap of the Fender over my head and began to tune her. She was already almost perfectly in tune. Oh, yes, I liked her.

"Yeah. I prefer keys, but I can do a bit of everything. When you play backup, it helps to be able to jump in wherever they need you."

I experimentally plucked a few chords. The ones I'd been working on for "Invisible Girl" last night. "That's a fact.

You must have an ear for it to be able to play them all well though. I've been working on keys the last couple years, but guitar is always going to feel like home."

"Yeah, that's how I feel about the piano. My mom started me in lessons when I was five."

Nora poked her head in. "What is going on in here?"

I shot her a grin. "I found the guitars."

"Dear God," she groaned. "I'm never going to get you out of there, am I?"

I affectionately looked down at the Strat. "I'll come back for you later."

"You are outrageous," Nora grumbled. "Come move something."

I pulled the guitar back over my head and handed it off to Weston. "Thanks for letting me try her out. I dig it."

"What was that you were playing?"

"New song that I'm working on."

"Thought it might be," he said with a nod. "I think I know all of Cosmere's chords, and it didn't sound familiar."

"Yeah? That's cool," I said. I forgot that I was a celebrity and that, yeah...someone this into music probably new my catalog. It was the sort of thing I had done with Weezer, Green Day, and Nirvana before I rose to fame. Sometimes, it was still surreal to think that my band could even exist beside those greats.

We headed out of the music room and back to grab more boxes for Nora.

"So, Julian said you got a job at a local studio in town?"

Weston nodded. "Yeah, it's just part-time. But I figure something is better than nothing."

The wheels were moving in my mind. "Any chance I could stop by and get some studio time in?"

Weston's head jerked to me so fast that he was going to

have a crick in his neck. His eyes were wide. He tried to play it cool after that, but he didn't quite manage it. "Uh, yeah. I think...you know, I think anyone would want you in their studio."

"I couldn't use any of the recordings, but it might help me get some of these ideas out of my head."

Weston nodded emphatically. "You let me know when, and I'll be there."

I laughed and reached for another box. "Sounds good."

Already, ideas were swirling away in my mind. Studio time without the band, without my manager, without the record label breathing down my neck. It might be just what I needed to figure out what I wanted to bring to the table and where I wanted to take Cosmere.

There was only one problem.

If I was going to record "Invisible Girl," I needed to talk to Blaire first. Fuck.

7

BLAIRE

*H*oney held up my phone. "All set. Ready when you are."

Nate King stood at my side, looking as scrumptious as ever. He'd come back from New York City yesterday and driven straight into town. Before he'd left, we'd agreed to film this dance sequence together. It was a newer trend, where you walked down the middle of the street, performing this specific dance number. Soccer and track were more my forte, but apparently, I didn't have to be a great dancer to do this kind of dancing. My followers didn't seem to care. And they cared even less when a hunk was dancing next to me.

"You ready?" Nate asked with a wink.

He had on dark jeans, a gray T-shirt, and sneakers. I'd changed out of my everyday workout kit and into a complementary outfit—jean shorts, a gray crop top, and matching kicks. The company had sent us the same pair after we mentioned them on one of our videos last month.

"Sure," I said, nodding at Honey. She was taking behind the scenes

"Here we go. I'll count you in," Honey said.

I turned away from Honey where she stood for behinds the scenes footage and faced the videographer we'd hired for this job. I took a deep breath and released it.

Showtime.

"Five, six, seven, eight."

And then I couldn't focus on anything but the choreography I'd crammed into my head the last few days. This was take six. One of us kept fucking it up and breaking down into laughter. We were going to have some amazing bloopers, but I was ready for this to be over.

The music started, and we strode forward. My arms and legs moving almost of their own accord. I skipped backward a step. Nate caught my arm, and I did this little jump-hop thing where I landed on his other side. We looked at each other, smiled, and walked back toward the camera. We'd added the look after one of our mess-up runs. Honey had thought it looked too good and we needed to add it in on purpose. She wasn't usually wrong about these sorts of things.

"And that's a wrap," Honey called after we finished.

I laughed and bent forward to get air into my lungs. I could sprint through an entire soccer game, but walking toward a camera for one minute left me winded.

"That was the one," Nate said. "Even that smile was perfect."

He touched the side of my mouth, and I stepped backward. Yeah, I needed to talk to him.

Honey rushed over to show us the behind-the-scenes footage. We watched side by side and then agreed on the one that we were going to use. Everyone packed up, leaving me and Nate alone.

"Coffee?" I asked.

"Or…we could go back to your place," he suggested with a wink.

I laughed softly. His *thirst trap* stuff hadn't actually worked on me. It was the fact that underneath the persona, he was a real person I enjoyed being around. But sometimes, he forgot and tried to use his charm on me. I was sure he used it on anyone who was within range. It wasn't on purpose. I just…wasn't interested.

"Coffee," I said instead.

He nodded, not seeming to care that it hadn't worked. "All right. I'm down."

We drove separately to my favorite local coffee shop, Monomyth. Luckily, it was the middle of the day in the summer, so it was relatively empty. Students normally filled all the available spaces with their laptops and notes. I ordered a dirty chai latte, and Nate got a large black coffee. Then, we took our drinks to a seat by the large window in the converted old house.

"I think this video is going to be a huge success," he said.

"Me too."

"While I'm here, we could do the 'I See the Real You' challenge."

"Oh yeah, I was so happy for you when I saw that go viral."

"I've done a few of them now because people asked. You know how it is."

"Yeah," I agreed. "The *can you do that again because I blinked*?"

He laughed and nodded. "Stuff like that. But it'd be fun to do it together." He looked me up and down. Though he'd seen me in a lot less, I still flushed at the attention. "You'd barely have to do anything for the glow-up."

"I don't think so," I said, taking a sip of my drink.

"I could even film for you."

"I don't want to do the challenge."

"Why not? Don't you know the guy?"

"Which is why it'd be weird," I told him. Though, of course, that wasn't the reason at all. I couldn't imagine doing any videos to Campbell's songs. Let alone to the song written about me.

"We wouldn't have to do a hot glow-up. You know people have taken it to a whole new level already. Some people are switching the camera to show themselves in a T. rex costume or going from, like, a slob on the couch to still a slob on the couch. Like, that's just who they are." He snapped his fingers. "A perfect *Blaire Blush* version might just show you in your workout outfits and then switching to a different color. We could do a bunch of them and change out your hats. Obviously, you already are who you are. You don't have to change for the camera."

"Or get naked for it," I teased.

He grinned. "Just for me, love."

I snorted. "Awfully full of yourself."

"Should I not be?" he asked, leaning back in his seat and putting his hands behind his head. His giant biceps flexed, and he raised his eyebrows.

"You should be," I agreed easily. He was attractive, and he knew it. "But Nate, I don't think this is working."

"What is this exactly? Because I think our followers would disagree."

"The business arrangement is working out great, but I don't think I want more than that."

He dropped the chair back down on all fours and leaned his elbows on the table. "Strictly business?"

"Yeah. I mean, I want to stay friends. I like hanging out with you and shooting videos. I think you're right that our followers love when we collaborate. I just don't feel anything...more than that."

He squeezed my hand. "Hey, no problem. It's not like we ever defined what we were doing. I always assumed this was casual for the both of us. It worked when it worked, and if it isn't for you, we can keep it business."

I blew out a sigh of relief. I hadn't thought that Nate would be upset, but I hadn't dated all that much, and the breakups that I'd gone through were not this chill. "Good. I wouldn't want to hurt you."

"Blaire, you don't have to worry about me."

"Friends?"

"Definitely friends."

We chatted for another hour about our videos. He kept trying to get me to do the "I See the Real You" challenge, but I had no interest whatsoever. So, we brainstormed other videos we could do together. Figured out a way for one of us to travel to the other to do them. We'd done some stitch and duet videos, but they never performed as well as when we were in the same space. So, it was worth it to make the drive.

When we finished our brainstorming session, he kissed the top of my head and let me go. I felt lighter as I drove home. Nate King was going to get an amazing girl. But it wasn't me.

Jennifer's car, Cornelia, was parked in the driveway when I pulled in. Piper's Jeep was gone. She must have still been at work or with Hollin.

"Honey, I'm home," I called to Jennifer, who was slumped over her computer at the dining room table, clicking incessantly. She was the best photographer I knew, and she spent *hours* editing her images to her perfectionist specifications. I was worried, one day, she'd have carpal tunnel from all the micro-clicks.

"Hey!" She met my gaze over the top of her computer.

"Get any packing done?"

She gestured to the half-filled boxes. "A little. Julian wants to hire someone, but I think it's a huge extravagance."

"Aren't you behind on editing though?"

Jennifer bit her lip. "I mean...yes. I feel like I always am."

"How far behind will you get if you pack up all your stuff on your own?"

"I did it last time."

"Last time, you weren't dating a Wright."

She huffed. "That doesn't mean anything."

"They're Texas royalty, Jen," I said with a laugh. "If your boyfriend wants to make your life easier, why not let him?"

"I don't know. I was taught the value of hard work and... all that."

I laughed and plopped into the chair next to her. "You work hard enough on your actual job."

"Yeah. True." She yawned and closed her laptop. "How did the shoot go with Nate?"

"Good."

Jennifer waited. "And?"

I glanced down at my chipped manicure. "We broke up."

"Oh, Blaire."

"No, it's not sad. I mean, technically, we weren't even official. We'd never defined our relationship. But I decided that he wasn't the one, and I didn't want to settle. He was cool about it. We're still going to work together."

"Well, that's...good. Very grown-up of you," she said, but I wasn't sure if it was a compliment. "Why the change of heart?"

"No change of heart really. I'd been trying to feel something and decided it wasn't there."

"And it has nothing to do with Campbell salivating over you this weekend?"

My eyes widened. "He was not!"

"I thought it was obvious," Jennifer said with a small smile.

"Ugh," I groaned. "Not you, too."

"You don't have to tell me anything you aren't comfortable with, Blaire, but I have eyes. I see the way you two look at each other."

I blew out a harsh breath. "We knew each other in high school. That's why anything with Campbell is a big no."

"If you say so."

She grinned knowingly at me and then returned to her work.

I wished it were as easy as snapping my fingers and declaring all the stuff with Campbell in my past. That I could just say it didn't matter and we could go on that date he'd asked me out on—very clearly *not* joking. But there was no magic wand to wipe away our history. There was no fairy dust to make the world reshape itself around us. And going on a date with Campbell would be like asking for my heart to be ripped out of my chest and shredded.

Nate might have been the safe choice. But Campbell was absolutely the most reckless decision I could make.

8

CAMPBELL

There was one of many problems with telling Blaire about the new song. The first being that I didn't have her number. The one that she'd had in high school no longer worked, and I had no interest in asking Hollin for her current one. I could just imagine how that conversation would go. The last thing I wanted was for other people to know anyway. So, that was out.

I also didn't use social media. I had accounts that my publicist sometimes updated. She wanted me to post more, to be active, but it hurt the creative process. Pretty much everything online was utterly draining. Not that I could imagine sliding into Blaire's DMs. That felt too casual, even for us.

The one thing I *did* have was her email. Mostly because it was readily available on her website. I felt ridiculous, sending her an email, but besides just showing up at her house, uninvited, or waiting until I saw her in person again, I thought this might be the easiest route.

I hardly checked my own emails since they were constantly inundated with fan mail. Even though I had a personal private address that only the record label was supposed to have, it didn't keep people from figuring it out. But it was the best that I had. So, here I was...writing Blaire an actual fucking email and hoping it reached her.

To: blaire@blaireblush.com
From: campbellsoup@cosmere.com
Subject: Don't hate me

Blaire,
I know you don't want to talk to me but...

Nope. That wasn't going to work.

To: blaire@blaireblush.com
From: campbellsoup@cosmere.com
Subject: A quick request

Blaire,
It's Campbell. I...

Yeah, she would see my email address. She wasn't stupid. Fuck.

To: blaire@blaireblush.com
From: campbellsoup@cosmere.com
Subject: I'm a fucking idiot.

Blaire,
I'm probably the last person on the planet you want to talk to. After all, I was the douche who broke your heart. But still, won't you be so kind as to spare me a few minutes of your time because I'm a selfish asshole?

Fucking fuck fuck. Just what I wanted typed out and sent into the ether. One tip-off to any tabloid, and I'd be *fucked*. I needed to get it together. This wasn't personal. I didn't have to make it about what had happened before. It was just meeting up to discuss something. Business, not personal.

To: blaire@blaireblush.com
From: campbellsoup@cosmere.com
Subject: Meet up

Blaire,
Can we meet up sometime this week to talk? I want to run some-thing by you. I'm free anytime this week.

Best,
Campbell

Best. Fuck. Was I really going to sign it *best*? I guess I was because what else could I put there? Fuck it. Good enough.

I pressed Send.

If she even looked at her emails, she wasn't going to respond. She had made it perfectly clear last weekend that she wanted nothing to do with me. I'd actually fucking tried to stay away from her. I'd given her the space she so clearly wanted. It had just all unraveled. And with it had come back my creative process.

Now, it felt like a flood had been opened in my mind. I hadn't written another song, but over the last couple days, there were at least snippets that I'd been able to jot down and not hate.

Sometimes, songs came to me fully formed, like "Invis-ible Girl" had, but most of the time, it was just a bunch of lines that became a bigger idea. I could feel all of these smaller catchy lines coalescing into something, and it was going to be great. When I found the key, it was going to shine.

And that was because of Blaire.

Not that I intended to tell her *that* exactly. If she hardly wanted to look at me, then she wasn't going to want to know that one conversation with her had clicked something back into place inside me. I didn't even know how I could explain it to anyone else, let alone her.

I swiped down to refresh my phone, not expecting anything, except more fan mail, and then there it was. A response.

I clicked on the email, momentarily stunned.

To: campbellsoup@cosmere.com
From: blaire@blaireblush.com
Subject: Re: Meet up

Campbell,
Sure. I could do this afternoon. What time is good for you?

Best,
Blaire

I blinked and blinked again. That was the most innocuous...almost-*nice* response I had ever thought I'd get from her. Should I have read condescension in every syllable? Was her *sure* more of a *surrre*? Did it matter?

She'd said yes. She'd meet me. I could tell her about the song.

A pit opened in my stomach. Well, fuck. Now, I had to tell her about the song. In abstract, it had seemed like a good idea. The right thing to do. And now, it felt daunting.

But I had to do it anyway.

To: blaire@blaireblush.com
From: campbellsoup@cosmere.com
Subject: Re: Meet up

4pm? I'm coming from a much needed haircut. The Wrights hooked me up with their hairdresser, Lisa. Work for you?

No backing out now. Not unless she decided to change her mind.

To: campbellsoup@cosmere.com
From: blaire@blaireblush.com
Subject: Re: Meet up

4 it is.

Oh, and while you're here...do you think we could do the I See the Real You challenge? It wouldn't take long to film. My followers keep asking me to do it, and I think it would be a big surprise.

A big surprise.

Fuck me. Just seeing that she'd written that was a huge fucking surprise. She *hated* that song. People must have really been hounding her to do that fucking challenge if she was desperate enough to ask me to be in the video.

But shouldn't she be doing it with *Nate*?

I might or might not have stalked her videos and seen that he'd come into town to see her. She'd posted a few videos of them walking around downtown Lubbock, dancing like they were in some high school musical number. They were charismatic. If the effect wasn't a bit cheesy. Or maybe I just didn't like the part where she'd put her hand in his and smiled at him like they were a hundred percent an item.

But she was asking me to do this one. Not him.

Which had to count for something, right?

After all, it was her song. I'd written it for her. It only made sense for us to do it together. Except for the fact that I'd spent the e years since the song released protecting her identity. If I showed up in a video with her, there was bound to be speculation.

She must have already done that math and decided it was worth it. And if she thought it was, then who was I to deny her? It was Blaire. I couldn't say no anyway.

To: blaire@blaireblush.com
From: campbellsoup@cosmere.com
Subject: Re: Meet up

Yeah, I'll do the challenge. Need me to bring anything for it?

Fuck. It was happening.

To: campbellsoup@cosmere.com
From: blaire@blaireblush.com
Subject: Re: Meet up

Great! Just you and your guitar. On second thought, your leather jacket too.

Well, this was going to be interesting.

9

BLAIRE

*A*fternoon light streamed in through the living room windows. I yawned from my perch on the couch as Honey went through the list of videos we needed to record for the rest of the month. I had my main videos for most of next month already planned out, but there was always room in my schedule for new trends and responses to questions in my videos. Sometimes, it was easier to video-respond to personal questions than to try to type it out.

It was really what I was most comfortable with anyway. My following had grown so much from trends and that sort of thing, but *Blaire Blush* was my baby. It was the place I'd invented for other women to feel safe to discuss their issues and to show that our bodies were normal just how they were. Stretch marks, hip dips, skin folds, skin textures, and more. All of those things that the media Photoshopped away, I tried to bring awareness to their normality.

Women were beautiful in every form and were always a cause for celebration.

I made sure that enough of my videos showed who I was without the glitz and glamour of makeup and Photoshop and editing. Sometimes, those things were fun. But not at the expense of a woman's heart.

"I can't do another one today, Honey," I told her. "I am wiped."

"All right. No problem. I have a full list here." She glanced at the Apple watch on her wrist. "It's almost four o'clock anyway."

I breathed a sigh of relief. Four o'clock. That was when I clocked out for the day. Metaphorically.

My job was twenty-four/seven, but I had some boundaries. And four was usually my time to send Honey home, stop looking at social media, and try to be present in the real world. If it wasn't the summer, I'd go for a run outside. But it was currently a hundred degrees outside, so no, thanks.

A knock on the door jolted me from my thoughts of finally relaxing. Honey's leg bounced energetically from her spot at the table.

"Want me to get that?" she asked.

I groaned. "No. I got it."

I came to my feet, pushed my bangs out of my face, and headed to the door. I yanked it open, prepared to see a package had been delivered.

But in the doorway stood Campbell Abbey.

My heart lodged in my throat at the sight of him. He'd cut his hair since the last time I'd seen him. It was still long on the top but shaved closer on the sides. His eyes were the light blue of the Caribbean Sea, and his jaw had been chiseled from marble. And I should have hated the same ripped black jeans he always wore and the distressed black T-shirt, but it all paled to how he looked in a leather jacket with his goddamn guitar at his side. It was the Campbell Abbey I'd fallen head over heels for in high school. Almost a vision of the past. As if no time at all had passed between us.

Then I blinked, and the vision was gone.

"What are you doing here?" I gasped.

His brow furrowed, and he stilled, as if struck. "What? What do you mean? You invited me over."

"I did no such thing."

Campbell's eyes darted away and then back to me. "I wouldn't be here if you hadn't responded to my email."

"What email?" I asked, dumbfounded.

Now, he looked thoroughly perplexed. He stuffed his hands into his pockets and rocked back on his heels. "You really have no idea what I'm talking about."

"No, I don't. I don't even check my emails. I..."

Then, the thought occurred to me. *I don't even check my emails.* But someone else did.

I saw red.

"Honey!" I yelled, whirling around.

Honey jumped out of her seat and came running. She was chewing on a lock of her long blonde hair. A sure sign that she was in distress. "Hey, boss. Gah, I meant to tell you."

"That you emailed Campbell?"

"He emailed me!" she cried. "Um, you. He emailed you."

Campbell's jaw dropped open as he came to the same realization that I had. Honey had invited him over to the house at four o'clock when she knew we'd be wrapping up for the day.

Fuck. What else had she learned by pretending to be me?

"Did you email me?" I asked him.

He nodded. "Yeah, I did."

I exhaled slowly, trying not to rise to the anger boiling up in my chest. "Could you wait here a minute?"

"Uh, sure."

Then, I latched on to Honey's arm and dragged her away

from the front door. I didn't stop until we were out of range for Campbell to hear what was about to come out of my mouth.

"What were you thinking?" I hissed.

"I know. I'm so sorry. I should have told you. But you hired me to help grow your business, and *this* will help you grow your business."

"Campbell?"

"Yes. He agreed to do the 'I See the Real You' challenge with you."

I nearly blew a gasket. "I'm *not* doing that challenge. And Campbell would never agree to do it with me. He doesn't even get on social media. He barely knows me."

Honey shrugged. "He said he'd do it."

"And what else did he say?"

"Nothing. Just that he wanted to talk to you. And then...I asked if he'd do the challenge."

"Honey," I said, squeezing the bridge of my nose.

"He said yes though."

Well, at least it hadn't been anything personal. I'd have to read the entire exchange to make sure she didn't know anything more private. But, Jesus Christ, I'd thought it would be a blessing to get Honey to take over my always-inundated inbox. Now, I was wondering if it was a nightmare.

"This is crossing a boundary, Honey," I said, looking her in the eye. "You know that any personal emails that come through are to be flagged for me, unopened. You know that it's an invasion of my privacy to talk to my friends on that account as me."

"I know but—"

"And furthermore, all decisions about the business go through *me*. I have the last say on what videos we're making, what pictures we're using, what questions I'm answering. I'm *Blaire Blush*. You don't get to unilaterally decide what I am doing."

"You're right," she said automatically. "I just did it for you. I see now that it was too much."

I exhaled. "You should go home."

Tears welled in her big brown eyes. "Are you firing me?"

"No," I said. "But you can't do anything like this ever again."

"I won't. I promise."

"I'm giving you the rest of the week off. We'll start again on Monday."

She nodded, mollified by my words. "Okay. I am so sorry, Blaire. You know that I'd never do anything to hurt you. I only want what's best for you and the company."

"I know."

She gulped and then slunk out of the room. I braced an arm against the door when she was gone. Because this wasn't over. I still had to face Campbell.

And the worst part of all of it was that Honey was right. As mad as I was with her for how she had gone about it, Campbell was exponentially more famous than me. We knew each other. As far as Honey knew, we were even friends on speaking terms. A guy who could joke about asking me out. From her perspective, why wouldn't I film a video with him?

If only it were that simple.

I tucked my hair behind my ears, mussed my bangs, and then headed back toward the door. Campbell still hadn't come inside. He was leaning back against the doorframe, staring down at his phone.

"Hey," I said. "Sorry about that."

"Did you fire your minion?"

"I didn't. This is the first time anything like this has happened. So, I'm giving her another chance. You have no idea how hard it is to find good employees."

"I thought the emails were suspicious," he admitted. "I guess I just wanted to believe that you were that comfortable with seeing me again."

"God, what was in those emails, Campbell?"

He met my gaze evenly. "Nothing. I just asked if we could meet up, and then you—*she*—agreed. I never mentioned anything about the past, and clearly, she doesn't know that we know each other."

"Well, that's a relief at least."

"Yeah," he said, his gaze darting away again. "I guess I should go then. I can't imagine you actually wanted to see me today."

I hadn't. And...I had.

I absolutely would have told him no if I were the one who had gotten the email from him. But now that he was here, I just couldn't send him away either.

"Might as well come inside."

"Really?" he asked, straightening in surprise.

"Yeah." I opened the door wider. "You said you wanted to talk to me?"

"I do."

"Then, come on in."

Campbell glanced at me uncertainly one more time before stepping across the threshold and into the house. I closed the door behind him, releasing a quick breath. I was doing this. I was *inviting* Campbell into my house when no one else was home. It felt like a recipe for disaster or just a remembrance of that girl who had been wild enough to sneak him into her bedroom every night. Carefree enough to fall in love.

"Sorry about Honey again," I said, suddenly self-conscious with him so close.

He propped his guitar against the dining room table. Then, he shucked off his signature leather jacket, draping it across the back of one of the wooden chairs. I couldn't imagine how he could have been comfortable in this heat in that jacket. I knew it was what he always wore, but still.

"I probably should have guessed. I don't usually check my email either unless my publicist tells me to," he admitted.

"What a life."

"Yeah." He shrugged.

"Why were you wearing that?" I blurted. "You do know it's a hundred degrees outside."

"A hundred and two actually."

"That's outrageous. You don't have to live your LA life here in Lubbock. No one cares if you survive by wearing shorts."

His eyes finally found mine. "You—well, I guess, Honey —asked me to wear it."

"She did?" I asked, horrified. "Oh God." I sank into an oversize armchair. "I am so sorry."

He brushed it off. "It's no big deal. I wear it onstage until I'm sweating through it most shows anyway. I've kind of gotten used to it."

"Still." I shook my head. "Why did you even agree to any of this? I thought you weren't even on social media."

"I'm not. Not really. I have it. It's mostly managed by someone else, but I find it difficult to navigate and be creative."

"No kidding." I exhaled harshly. "So...why would you film this challenge?"

He stared fixedly at the floor. As if he couldn't even meet my eyes. Couldn't get the words past his teeth.

I crossed my arms across my stomach, bracing myself for his answer. It couldn't be good. There had to be a catch. Something that was going to hurt me. I didn't know what, but he was silent for a reason.

Then, finally, with a practiced slowness, he looked at me. "For you, Blaire? Anything."

I swallowed around those words. Dear God, those *words*. If only they were true. If only he had been willing to give me everything. We wouldn't be sitting here in this hollow moment, aching for something we could never have.

I jumped to my feet. "Fine. Then, let's do it."

"What?" He stumbled over the word. "Do what?"

"Record the video."

Confusion clouded his features. "I thought you didn't want to."

"Well, I don't, but Honey, as wrong as her actions were, was right. The followers are clamoring for me to do this challenge. I've been avoiding it—for obvious reasons. But you're here." And he was here. So close to me. Closer than he had been in years. I had no idea what he wanted to talk to me about, but I just knew that I didn't want him to go. "So, we might as well."

"What do you want me to do?"

And that was all the answer I needed.

10

BLAIRE

*T*he challenge itself was simple. Especially how Nate had started it out as a glow-up to "show the real you." But that wasn't my message, and I knew that it wasn't what Campbell had meant when he wrote the song. He'd meant that I wasn't the girl I showed everyone else. I was *his* girl. He had seen the truth.

Which meant that in the video...Campbell had to see the real me again.

I set up the camera with him out of sight. Just me in the first frame, staring off into the distance. I pulled my hair up into a high pony and brushed my bangs out of my face. Campbell strummed the tune of his most popular hit, and I lip-synced the words to the camera. Coy and distant. The girl I'd been in high school.

Then, I cut the camera. I didn't even watch it to see if it needed a second take. I didn't know how many times I could hear him sing that song. Let alone on an acoustic guitar with just his rich vocals a foot away from me. It ripped through every layer of the walls I'd put up around myself.

No. One take was going to have to do.

"I have to get changed for the second shot."

"All right," he said, strumming a different tune. One that I'd never heard before. His eyes focused on the strings. "What should I do?"

"You're going to be in this one with your guitar, singing. Maybe put your leather jacket back on."

"And you?" he asked, meeting my eyes, still playing that strange melody.

I liked it. It was catchy. Not like anything I'd heard from him before. I wondered what it was.

"You'll see."

I hurried into my bedroom and leaned back against the door. This was harder than I'd thought. Frankly, I hadn't had much time to think about how it would affect me. I'd pay for this later.

But I didn't have time now.

So, I pulled on my big-girl panties and got to work. I curled my hair into long, voluminous waves and worked my signature fringe bangs for all they were worth. My makeup wasn't heavy, but it was still statement makeup. Smoky eyes, winged eyeliner, a cherry-red lip. I considered wearing a sexy outfit to complete the official glow-up, but that wasn't what I was going for. Instead, I reached farther back in my closet and pulled out a long, flowy black skirt with a million pleats and an ash-gray crop top. I tugged on my Docs just to give it enough of an edge. It wasn't *sexy* in the traditional sense. But it was me...and it matched Campbell.

I swallowed hard before stepping out of my room to find Campbell had added lyrics to the tune he was messing with. I didn't catch them before he came to an abrupt halt, his eyes fixed on me.

He didn't say a word. Just devoured me with his eyes.

I turned in place. "You think this works?"

"It looks like what you wore in high school."

"That's the idea," I muttered. I hated the next words that came out of my mouth. Even though I knew they were what I should do. "I thought we could record it a couple of times in a few different outfits, and then I could cut them together. To show I'm always the same girl. In this, in my athleisure kits, in my soccer uniform, that sort of thing."

"And I'll just be like this?"

"Isn't that *exactly* who you are?"

He could barely drag his eyes away from me long enough to look down at himself. "I'd probably change the guitar."

I laughed, a soft, melodic thing, and he jerked his gaze back up to me.

"What?" I asked warily.

"I just...haven't heard you laugh in a while."

"I laugh," I said defensively.

"Not around me."

I bit my lip and hurried toward the camera. Well, if I didn't laugh around him, I had good reason.

"Let's do a test run, yeah?" I said, going straight back to business.

"Sure. Whatever you want."

He adjusted himself on the stool I'd brought over for him so that he was in the shot. I set up right where I had been, and he drew in tight next to me. I swallowed at his nearness. Fuck, he was so close. And I'd signed up for this.

I could back out. I could bail on what was happening. But, damn, it *would* be good for my career.

So, I gritted my teeth and ignored the yawning, gaping need that had formed in Campbell's presence. The want that millions of girls worldwide felt around him. And I was only different in that I'd had him before he was famous. I needed to keep reminding myself of that fact. It wasn't real. This wasn't real. It was just history. Nothing more.

"Okay. We're set up. We'll try this take."

"Start over from the chorus?" he asked, settling into the stool.

"Sure. Or right before the chorus."

He nodded as his fingers moved effortlessly across the guitar. I pressed the red circle on my phone to record and then stood next to him. For a moment, I let my eyes drift up from the guitar and to his face. His eyes were fixed on the guitar as he hummed the lyrics to get us into position.

Then, he started to sing, and everything in the entire world fell away as I catapulted back in time.

My body might have been in the present, standing before Campbell as he sang "I See the Real You." But I was no longer there.

I was sitting on my bed, back at my parents' house. Campbell waited outside in the cold, frantically texting me to see when my mom would be gone. Then, he tumbled in through the window, laughing as he worried more about his guitar than the gash at his knee.

"Shh," I whispered even though I had the house to myself.

He sat up and drew me to him, kissing my lips so hot and fierce and needy that I almost forgot what he was doing here. His hands were halfway up my sweater before I giggled and shoved him backward.

"You said you wrote a song."

His eyes were on my breasts, and then they jerked back up to my face. "I did. But I think I want to kiss you again."

His hands slid up into my stupid brown bob, and then he was kissing me for real. Slow and languid, as if we had all night to explore this. Rather than the few hours that my mom was away on her girls' night out. I wanted to live in this moment forever. But I was scared. We hadn't gone all the way yet. We'd barely done anything, and though I wanted it all with him, could see our entire future, I still hadn't agreed to it yet.

"Okay. Okay," he said with a laugh as I scooted back again.

I lay down on my bed and watched as he tuned his acoustic guitar. He shot me one heart-melting grin and began to play. The words falling from his lips.

Tears welled in my eyes as I realized that this wasn't just a song; this was a song about me. This was about him seeing me. Really seeing me. Not just the weird girl at school, but the girl I was when I was with him. The girl that belonged to him.

His eyes left the guitar and fixed on my face. As we stared at each other across the short distance, I knew with teenage certainty that I would love him forever.

I blinked, and the memory dissolved in my mind. Campbell was still singing, but he was looking at me as if he knew exactly where my mind had gone. The same unshed tears that had come to my eyes at seventeen were there again today.

He ended the chorus and let the rest of the music fade away. He still stared at me. Waited for the moment to break or to see if I would give him exactly what I had given him that first night. My whole heart.

Except that my heart was no longer whole. It was a broken, shredded thing that he'd destroyed all on his own. So, though the music was a spell that lingered between us, it was also a lie. Because no matter how much he had seen me then, he didn't even know me now. And he couldn't fix any of that.

"Blaire," he said with concern, reaching out for me.

I yanked away from him on instinct. I swiped at my eyes and rushed to the camera. I ended the recording and breathed heavily as I tried to get myself back under control.

"Do we need to do it again?"

I watched the video to see what in the hell had even happened. I hadn't been singing or even lip-syncing. I didn't even look at the camera. In fact, neither of us looked at the camera. He was playing, and then all of a sudden, he looked up at me, sang to *me*, existed for *me*. We had eyes only for each other. And then the moment ended. He'd finished singing, and a look of terror had come into my eyes. A rabbit seeing a fox.

"Fuck," I whispered.

"That bad?"

I turned off my phone. "No."

"Can I see?"

I dipped my chin to my chest, and then with a sigh, I handed him my phone to watch it.

After a second, he said, "Oh."

"Yeah."

"We can do it again."

I shook my head. There was no point. I couldn't handle trying one more time. I probably couldn't even use this. No one could look at that video and not see emotions swirling between us. Even if I were a great actor, which I was not, people would still say there was too much chemistry for us to fake all of it.

"It's fine."

"Blaire..."

"What did you want to talk to me about?" I asked to change the subject as I took my phone back.

"I wrote a new song," he said slowly.

I turned finally to face him. "Okay."

"It's based off of what you said to me. About how, to me, you were only ever invisible or everything. That there was no in-between."

"You wrote another song about me?" I said incomprehensibly.

"Yeah." He ran a hand back through his hair. "I haven't been able to write. Critics hated the last album, and I think they got into my head. Everything I've written since, I have absolutely hated."

"They can't all be bad."

"My manager thinks they're good, but what does he know? They all sucked...until this song." He sat back down on the stool, fiddled with the guitar, and began to play.

It was the melody that he had been playing earlier that I thought was catchy. I'd missed the lyrics then, but I immediately decided the tune was going to be a hit. And then when he started singing, I actually sat down because it was so good.

I tried really hard not to smile as he belted out about the invisible girl who was everything to him. I tried to remind myself that it was just a song. I'd just happened to be the inspiration for it. It had nothing to do with me. But it was hard to differentiate. It was hard to hear him sing words that I'd said to him in hate sang back to me in love.

"That's what I have so far," he said, stilling his fingers and looking at me warily. "What do you think?"

"It's amazing."

His eyes lit up. "Yeah?"

I nodded slowly. "Better than the last album."

"That's what I thought!" He got up and paced around like the excited fool he was. Then, he turned back to face me with fear and uncertainty. "I didn't give you a choice with the last song, Blaire. And I didn't think it was fair to just record this, knowing how you felt about the last one."

"What are you saying?"

"I don't know. I wanted to make sure you were okay with it."

"You don't get to choose when inspiration strikes, Campbell."

"I know but..."

"It's okay," I finally said. I looked down at the phone in my hand. The secret that was hidden in that video. He'd done that for me just because he'd thought I'd asked. For no other reason. Could I really deny him a song that would help his career? I met his eyes again. "You can record it."

He blew out a relieved breath. "Oh, good. I was going to lay it down with Weston later this week if you were okay with it."

"Weston? Really?"

"Yeah, we've been hanging out. He's a cool guy. Plus, he works in a local studio. You can swing by to hear it if you want."

I gulped and drew back. I couldn't fall further for this man. He'd hurt me once, and he was surely leaving again. No matter what he thought. LA was his home now.

"Maybe."

He heard my refusal in the word and just nodded. "Well, if you change your mind," he said, taking my phone out of my hand and typing into it, "here's my number."

Then, he smiled down at me, and it took everything in me not to reach up onto my tiptoes and drag his mouth down to mine. He was gone before I could do something stupid, and I flopped back on the couch.

"I am so screwed."

11

CAMPBELL

"What do you think about this?" Weston asked. His fingers moved effortlessly across the keys. He pulled sound from the instrument in a way that I'd never encountered. Cosmere's keyboardist, Michael, was good at keys, but Weston had a completely different ear. He wasn't playing for mainstream music. He was just a professional who had done a lot of work. Thus, the sound was so much more dynamic.

"Fuck, man. That's it."

"Are you sure?" Weston looked back at me. "I could do something like this."

Then, he tried a slightly modified rhythm that I also liked, but it wasn't quite right for this song.

"No, the first one. But hang on to the second. I have an idea for that one."

"Okay. I'll record it, and we can lay it over what we have so far."

I nodded at Weston as he set up the recording for the keyboard section. It felt fucking good to be back in the studio. Especially this studio. Even though it made no sense.

I'd always wanted that LA studio, where everything was moving fast and my career was on the line. I'd wanted that life.

Now that I had it, being in this small space—at LBK Studios, in downtown Lubbock, where the only thing that mattered was the music—felt revelatory. How had I ever worked out my songs in LA? It was exhausting and hardly the best place to get out of a creative rut.

It'd made sense with the first album when we walked in on a creative high, but now, we were exhausted from tour, and the record label was demanding more and more from us. We were superstars with everything we'd ever wanted, and suddenly, I wished for just a sliver of downtime. An ounce of breathing room to rediscover what I loved about all of this.

Sitting in Weston's small studio was giving me that feeling again.

Weston finished playing and then headed back into the booth. A few minutes later, his voice came through the speakers. "Hey, dude, your phone has been ringing nonstop. Looks like it might be an emergency."

I furrowed my brow. What kind of emergency could be happening?

I left my guitar, grabbed my phone, and saw that the missed calls were all from LA. My manager, publicist, a guy at the record label, Santi, and Viv had all called in the last half hour. What the hell was happening?

"Uh, maybe it's because of this," Weston said.

"What?"

He passed me his phone. "Someone sent this to me while we were recording."

I took the phone. On the screen was Blaire's video of us

doing the "I See the Real You" challenge. Already, the views were in the millions.

It had been two days since we'd recorded the video in her house. Two days that I'd been waiting for her to post it. Two days that I'd thought maybe she'd changed her mind.

After all, I'd spent years keeping her out of my spotlight. I'd never confessed who the song was about. I'd hinted, but I respected her privacy. And she never said that she wanted to be known for it. Now, here we were, with this video. It was incriminating, to say the least. It looked like we were half-ready to rip each other's clothes off. And I'd considered it. If she had looked at me like she was half-interested, I would have. But instead, I had seen fear and hurt, mixed with desire. Those were things I couldn't...wouldn't touch.

So, I'd assumed that she'd seen what I saw in the video and decided to just trash it. It would certainly be safer. Blaire was in the public eye, but there was a difference between a social media influencer and...well, me. That wasn't even bragging. It was just my life.

It appeared that it'd just taken her a few days to work up the nerve.

A quick glance at the comments told me two things: everyone thought Blaire and I were dating and that this was a not-so-subtle hint at a new album.

No wonder everyone and their mother was calling me. I hadn't prepped anyone that we were doing this. I hadn't told a soul that it was going live. And now, everyone must be scrambling because of the attention. Because of the apparently not-so-subtle hint that I hadn't meant to give.

Bobby Rogers flashed on my screen again.

With a sigh, I answered it. "Hey, Bobby."

"Campbell, Campbell, Campbell. What have you gotten yourself into?"

"I did a video. It's no big deal."

"Well, I have been on the phone all morning since it went live. Where have you been?"

"I'm in the studio."

"You're in LA?"

"No," I said warily. "I have a friend in town who works at LBK Studios. I'm just laying down some ideas for new songs."

Bobby's skepticism turned to enthusiasm. "You found your muse!"

"Sort of."

"Look, this is great, Campbell. I wasn't sure about you staying in bumfuck nowhere, but it's clearly working. This girl is good for you. She is helping you write, getting you on social media, and—"

"Leave Blaire out of this," I said, my voice like ice.

Bobby sighed. "She put herself into it, kid."

"What do you want, Bobby?"

"If you're writing new music, then absolutely nothing. I talked to Barbara." That was my publicist who I hadn't answered because I knew she'd be pissed that I'd done this without her. "And she was mad at first that she'd had no warning, but now, she wants to send a team down to Lubbock to help make more of these videos. It could really ramp up the new album."

"No. No team, Bobby. I want to be alone to figure this shit out, or there will be no new album," I told him as I paced away from Weston.

"All right, all right. I thought you might say that. So, I told her to wait on it. But," he said as if he had plans B, C, and D waiting for my refusals, "I want to send the rest of the band there."

"Wait, what?"

"The band! You write better music when you have everyone there. You said it yourself. If you're writing new songs and even inadvertently promoting it, then we'll set you up in Lubbock until it's time to record."

"You're going to send the entire band to me?"

"Yep. I can even hook you up with recording space. We'd still have to lay down masters here in LA, but you could get some time in to practice."

"I already have a place." I glanced over at Weston, who had his headphones on to listen to what we'd recorded. "And a guy that I like. We can use LBK Studios."

Bobby sighed, as if he was suffering. "Fine. Your call, Campbell. Just get us an album. You'll have Viv, Santi, Yorke, and Michael there to make it all come true."

"All right." I couldn't deny that having them here would certainly help the process. I just hadn't thought they'd want to travel to Lubbock to do it. "You sure they want to?"

"They're on board. Just say the word."

"Fine. But, Bobby, I'm serious about leaving Blaire out of all of this."

"I heard you the first time, Campbell."

"Promise me."

"You know I never make promises that I can't keep."

I exhaled in frustration. *Oh, Bobby.* "Just do your best to control it all."

"Fine, fine. Can't wait to hear the new songs."

Weston pulled his headphones down after I hung up. "Everything all right?"

I stared at the exposed brick wall. I should be happy about all of this. The rest of Cosmere was coming to Lubbock to help me figure out my shit. That was a good thing. Especially because we'd have Weston Wright recording and not some soulless LA schmuck.

Yet I couldn't stop worrying about Blaire. I thought she'd known what she was getting into, and now, I was starting to wonder if I even knew what she'd gotten herself into.

"Yeah," I finally said. "The rest of Cosmere is coming into town. We're going to figure out the songs for the album."

"That's great."

"You're going to record them."

Weston blinked at me. "What?"

"Masters will be done in LA, but I want to keep working with you. I like the direction for 'Invisible Girl.' I told my manager we'd be working here."

"Holy fuck," West said. "Are you sure? There are probably better people for this job, Campbell."

"Yes, I'm sure, but if you want to bail..."

"No," he said at once. "Absolutely fucking not. I want to do this."

"Great. Then, you're hired." I nodded at him. "Let's take a break."

"Sure." Weston looked dazed for a few moments and started typing on his phone. Probably telling other people what had just landed in his lap.

I should call Santi or Viv to make sure this was all right with them. Santi would bullshit his way through it, but Viv would tell it to me straight. Instead, I pulled up another number.

Blaire had texted me her number after I gave her mine. I wanted to call her and see where her head was, but even though we currently had a video that was going viral, I couldn't seem to push myself to hear her voice over the phone. How did a phone call feel too intimate? *How?*

So, I shot her a text.

Saw you posted the video. My phone has been ringing off the hook. My manager is sending the rest of the band to Lubbock to figure out the album now. So, I guess I have you to thank for that.

What? He's sending the whole band because of one video?

Probably just an excuse. I'd guess he already wanted to, and this gave him the leverage to make it happen.

Is this a good thing? It sounds like a good thing.

Yeah. I'll get more done with the five of us than just me.

I'm glad.

I wasn't expecting the video to do this.

I've had videos get a few million views. But we're at fifteen already, and it just released a few hours ago.

I had in fact expected it to do this. I thought it would reach way more than fifteen million views by the end of the day. The rest of this happening was what had surprised me.

Are you...cool with it?

I guess. I can't take it back now.

No, we couldn't. It was out there for all the world to see and judge. And somehow, all I could think was how I would get to see her again.

What are you doing this weekend?

For a very long time, nothing happened. The three dots that said she was typing kept appearing and then disappearing. As if she couldn't quite decide if I was going to ask her out or not.

It's Fourth of July weekend. I'm going to the festival and then fireworks. Do you want to come with all of us? Hollin will be there with Piper.

Right. The Fourth. I'd forgotten about that. Holidays weren't a fun thing for musicians. We were always booked for those dates. Unlike normal people who got to experience them, we got to entertain. Since Cosmere had just gotten off a huge tour, we'd refused any Fourth of July events. Though Bobby had been pissed. I was kind of glad now.

It didn't mean that I could go gallivanting around a summer festival though. Not without security.

I don't think it's safe for me.

Oh. I didn't think about that. If you change your mind, I bet we can get you to the fireworks incognito. I'm sure someone has a Hawaiian shirt and cargo shorts for you.

I laughed at the thought. Yeah, no one would expect me to be in that kind of getup. And she must have known it would make me laugh and shudder, all at the same time. The other thing was...she was giving me another way in. She was even offering it. It still wasn't safe for me to go, but maybe she'd say yes if I asked her out this time. Or at least, not an immediate no.

Though I didn't know what was happening with her and Nate. What could I lose from asking?

Have to pass. But have fun.

Is Nate going to be with you?

There was another long pause. She hadn't mentioned him when we were alone at her place. She still posted videos of them together, and they commented on all of each other's stuff. But she had been perfectly quiet about him.

No. He's in Midland.

Another long pause.

And we decided to stop seeing each other.

My head spun at that news. Well, thank fuck. That certainly made what came next a lot easier.

I see. Well, I'm going to watch the fireworks from the top of my hotel. You can join me if you want.

That's a good view.

But I think I'll watch from the park.

I hadn't expected her to say yes. But we were talking, and that was a start. She was right about one thing: she was either invisible or everything to me. And she wasn't invisible to me any longer.

12

BLAIRE

The girls giggled behind me as we walked around the Fourth of July festival in Mackenzie Park. Fireworks would be set up down the hill in an hour or two. Already, cars were filling the parking lots to get prime locations. But the festival was still full of college students who were unlucky enough to be taking summer classes, teens holding hands and sneaking kisses, and families full of toddling children, happy to eat cotton candy and ride precarious carnival rides. A band blared music from the stage, and booths were set up with food and crafts and a market to sell wares. It was a delightful summer evening despite the heat. But at least Lubbock was part desert, so the nights were windy and cooled down to almost a reasonable temperature.

"Are you watching it again?" I grumbled.

"Just one more time," Annie said.

"Fine. *One* more time."

Annie, Jennifer, Honey, and even Piper crowded in around Jennifer's cell phone and pressed play on the viral video of me and Campbell. Which, at my last check, had twenty-seven and a half million views.

"You crossed thirty!" Honey squealed.

I couldn't help it; I jumped to look at the screen. And, holy fucking shit, I was at thirty *million* views of this one video.

I'd stopped reading the comments after the first hour when it went past my followers to everyone else in the world. Honey had taken over from there. It was safer for my sanity. The first few comments—from those who were mad that I was in the video with Campbell or who thought it was a publicity stunt—were enough for me to quit reading for...pretty much ever.

"That's nuts."

"It's incredible," Piper said with a smile. "I love to see your success."

I shrugged. "I mean, I posted a video. Campbell did all the rest."

Annie exchanged a glance with Jennifer. "Campbell might have supplied the audience, but they're sticking around because of you. For the content you already have in place. Now, they know who you are."

"I guess."

"It's brilliant," Honey said. She smiled at me with her wide brown eyes. She'd gotten her hair cut to have bangs yesterday, and I still wasn't used to it. She kept brushing them out of her eyes, as if the fringe was bugging her. "We've had so many engagement requests for your work."

"Yeah. Who cares how they got here?" Piper asked. "You should milk it for all it's worth."

She was right, of course. I'd always gotten exclusives and free clothes for my minor celebrity status, but everything had blown up in the last couple of days. Among the most exciting was a speaking tour for *Blaire Blush*, a potential book contract around my wellness initiative, and a spot on the *Today* show. I couldn't freaking believe it. All because of one video with currently thirty million views and counting.

I didn't know what I was going to do. Or if I was going to do any of it. I needed representation. I'd been overwhelmed before this video. Now, I needed someone in my corner to figure out which of these offers was real and how to capitalize on them. Which meant...I probably needed to talk to Campbell.

And I hadn't talked to Campbell since I'd invited him to see the fireworks today. Which still made me blush. I'd asked it innocuously. His brother and sister were going to be here regardless. But it was *me* asking. I didn't know what had come over me, but some barrier had been broken down between us after that video.

It was better that he wasn't here though.

I bit my lip and looked down at the video that was playing *again*. We looked so *real* there. As if that were reality and this disconnect and anger between us were fake. It was better that I didn't see him right now.

"Marie?" a voice called from a short distance away.

I grimaced and froze. I knew that voice. I purposely avoided that voice at all costs.

I turned around, and there she was. Almost five feet tall with a short blonde bob that was dyed that color every three weeks like clockwork. She wore a sensible red blouse tucked into mom jeans with sneakers that were two decades out of date. She was lucky that all her old clothes were coming back into fashion. She didn't look quite as embarrassing as she had when I was in high school.

"Hello, Mother," I said with a vengeance. If she wanted to call me Marie, then I'd be sure *not* to call her

Pamela, like she'd asked me to call her since I was seven.

My friends glanced at each other in confusion. Yeah, I never mentioned that Blaire was my middle name. I'd never much felt like a Marie.

"I'll meet up with y'all at the fireworks display. Same place as last year, right?"

"Definitely," Annie said.

"Let us know if you need us," Piper said warily.

Honey didn't immediately follow the other girls. As if she thought she warranted an introduction to my mother. That was never happening.

"Honey, go with the others. I'll see you later."

She bit her lip with a sigh. "All right. See you, Blaire."

When Honey was gone, I walked over to where my mom stood with my stepfather, Hal. Tall and spindly with beady black eyes and a receding hairline. We'd never gotten along. Not that he'd really tried to make my life better after the divorce.

During my freshman year of high school, Dad had moved away to Michigan to be with his boyfriend. I wanted to go with him. The courts thought Mom was a more *suitable* parent. She was a psychiatrist after all with a large following. And my dad was gay and moving out of state with someone half his age. He'd never stood a chance. He still made an effort, writing and sending gifts every holiday. But it wasn't the same.

"Having a good time?" my mother asked.

"Sure." I glanced between them and nodded at my stepfather. "Hal."

"Marie." He looked me up and down in my jean shorts and red crop top. He was one of those modest types. Living with him had been a real joy.

"Well, this is a surprise." Pamela adjusted the purse at her shoulder.

"It is."

"How is your...work?" She hesitated on the word *work*. She'd been thrilled when I got a psychology degree. It was the most enthusiastic I'd seen her about much of anything. She'd wanted me to go on to become a psychiatrist like her. We could have been in business together. She'd honestly thought that was something I wanted after she neglected me my entire childhood. "You're still doing that little blog thing, right?"

A spiteful part of myself wanted to tell her about the speaking engagements, the book, the *Today* show appearance that were all waiting in my inbox. All the things she'd wanted for herself. Things she'd never got. But I knew if I told her, then it would open a door for her to walk back into. And I was very careful not to engage with Pamela about more than I could handle in any one sitting.

"Good. It's going good."

Pamela nodded, glancing at Hal expectantly. I knew that look. She was done and ready to go back to enjoying her evening.

Hal cleared his throat. "Well, Marie, keep up the hard work. We're proud of you."

If only it didn't ring so hollow.

"I'll see you around."

Pamela smiled softly, one reserved for patients and not family. Well, I'd only ever been a patient in her eyes. "Have fun, sweetheart."

Then, they were gone. And I was all alone. Worse than I'd felt in years.

All this success. Everything I'd worked for. And my own mother couldn't seem to carry on a conversation with me.

We were both trained professionals, and we couldn't bridge whatever this was. She was too willfully ignorant to how she'd treated me as a child, choosing to guilt me into getting over everything rather than feeling any form of repentance. And I just...couldn't deal with her.

I swallowed down the resentment. Nothing I could do with it today.

I headed toward one of the last vendors in the line. They had funnel cakes, and a good dose of sugar felt like the way to fix this.

I almost reached the winding line when a group of girls stepped into my path. They were of the college variety—impossibly thin with middle parts and matching outfits.

"Hey, you're Blaire, right?" the first girl asked. They were all blonde, tanned, toned, and nearly indistinguishable.

"Uh, yeah, I am," I said with a smile.

I'd had a few people recognize me around town, but it didn't happen very often.

"You were in that video," a second girl said.

"With the lead singer of Cosmere."

"We're Campbell Soup girls," the first one said vibrantly.

I blinked at that name. I'd heard it before, but I didn't really get it. They were, like, his groupies? I wasn't sure.

"That's nice."

"So, are y'all dating?" the second asked, pressing closer.

I tried to take another step away, but we'd drawn a crowd somehow. I'd not been paying attention, but more people had filled in around me. They'd heard *Cosmere*, *Campbell*, and *dating*, and suddenly, everyone wanted to know. I'd never felt like this in Lubbock.

The closest was that time I'd been in a mosh pit at Austin City Limits. I didn't have a way to get out, and my claustrophobia kicked in so fast. I'd hardly been able to breathe or think or do anything. If it hadn't been for one nice guy who had noticed my symptoms and gotten me out of there, I had no idea what I would have done.

"Uh, I don't really want to comment on Campbell," I said, my voice wavering.

Another group pushed in closer to the first. "Oh my God, it's the 'I See the Real You' girl."

"Because he hasn't said that he's dating anyone," another girl said, anger in her voice.

One girl grabbed my arm as I tried to draw away from them. "Wait, is he here?"

"N-no," I stammered out.

"Are you going to see him?"

There were questions everywhere. I was very alone in a sea of people that I didn't know. I couldn't breathe. I was going to have a panic attack. No amount of proper meditation from Pamela's reserves had ever fixed the claustrophobia. The only thing that had ever helped was surrounding myself with friends who I could use as a buffer.

But my friends were gone. I'd sent them away so I could deal with my mother. Now, I was alone. There was a girl touching. People asking questions. Everyone closing in. Someone was recording. Oh fuck, I couldn't have a breakdown. I couldn't be seen like this. I needed to find a calm way out, or this would show up all over social media. I could see the headlines now—"Crazed Internet Star Flees Fans, Sobbing."

It didn't matter if it was real. It didn't matter how I felt. Perception was all that mattered.

"Excuse me," I forced out. "I need some space."

Then, heedless of the people swarming in around me, I pushed my way out of the crowd. Only when I was away from the mob and past the last row of vendors did I take off at a sprint. My fight-or-flight kicked in, and all I did was run. Run as fast and as far as I could from the point of fear.

And I could *run*. Even though I was small, I was fast. Which was how, a few minutes later, I had no clue where I was, and the sun was setting.

I tried calling Piper, and she didn't answer.

"Fuck," I said, kicking a nearby rock.

Next, I rang Jennifer and then Annie and even Sutton Wright, who was probably too busy with her kids to pick up her phone but it was worth a shot. I should have tried Honey. She was always waiting for my call. But I wanted to be reassured, and while I loved my assistant, she was not reassuring.

"Fuck, fuck." I stared at my phone and then dipped my head back. "Fuck," I said one more time.

Then, I dialed Campbell's number.

It rang twice before he answered. "Hello?"

"Hey," I said, my voice shaky.

"Are you okay?"

"I was kind of...mobbed at the festival by people who were Campbell Soup girls, and I ran away."

"What?" Campbell sounded suddenly furious. "You met Campbell Soup girls, and they attacked you?"

"Not exactly. Crowded me in and asked a lot of questions. One girl grabbed me. They were asking if we were dating."

He paused, as if putting the pieces together. "And you're claustrophobic."

I swallowed back the tears threatening to escape. "Yeah. It was...not ideal."

"Where are you?"

"I don't know. Somewhere in the park. Why?"

"I'm coming to get you."

13

BLAIRE

*F*ifteen minutes later, Campbell's Range Rover pulled up in front of me. My friends still hadn't called me back. Though I'd relented and texted Honey to let her know that I was leaving. She'd sent back a series of frantic texts that escalated so much that after I told her I was okay, I muted my phone.

He parked and hopped out of the car. He was in black sweats and an old Panic! at the Disco T-shirt. His hair was mussed, and he hadn't even changed into something more *rockstar*. He must have come here straight from home.

"Hey, how are you feeling?" he asked.

His face was a mask of such unending concern that I burst into tears. I didn't even realize that I'd been holding it all in until that moment.

"Blaire, Blaire, Blaire," he said, reaching for me.

I fell into his arms without a thought. I needed the hug. I wasn't sure that anyone in that crowd had meant me harm, but living through it had been scary. Even if I wasn't claustrophobic, I wouldn't want to be surrounded by a bunch of people grilling me. And now that the adrenaline had worn off, tears followed.

"You're okay. You're safe now."

"Thanks for picking me up," I said, pulling back from him to swipe at my eyes.

"Of course. Let's get you out of here."

He opened the passenger door, and I climbed inside. Then, he ran around to the driver's side and peeled out of the parking lot, going the opposite direction of the rest of the traffic.

"I didn't mean to cry."

He gripped the steering wheel with such ferocity that I thought he might rip it off the car and throw it like the Hulk. His jaw was clenched, but when his gaze landed on me, he released the tension. "You were scared. You should feel okay about crying if you need to."

"I know. It just feels stupid."

"Trust me, it's not. This is my fault."

I blinked at him. "What?"

"I should have considered how this video would impact your life. But I was selfish and decided if you asked, then I'd do it. I should have stopped this."

"Is that why you looked pissed? Because you didn't want to do the video?"

"No, of course not," he said, turning north. "This isn't the first time that something like this has happened. Ninety-nine out of a hundred times, I can go out in public and interact with fans, and nothing happens. It's wonderful. Just living a sort of normal life. People recognize me, maybe ask for a picture, but otherwise leave me alone. But that one time," he growled. He clenched the steering wheel again. "That one time is when it fucks up the other ninety-nine times."

"So, this has happened before?"

He nodded. "I was mobbed in a park in Atlanta once. It started out as a normal interaction, but then the people wouldn't leave me alone. My shirt was torn. Someone stole one of my shoes. I had bruises on my arms from girls literally trying to climb me." He shuddered. "It only takes one time for me to need security and for me to think long and hard about where I want to be."

"That's why you wouldn't come watch the fireworks with us."

"Yeah. It sounds stupid, but I'm more careful now. I didn't think it would happen to you."

"Me either."

"I'm sorry for putting you through that."

"I still don't think it's your fault. You can't blame yourself for what your fans do."

"Can't I?"

"Okay, you can, but you shouldn't. I'm not blaming you."

He shot me a smile that made my knees weak. "Thanks for letting me help at least."

"I appreciate it." We'd turned off the highway. "Where are we going anyway?"

His look turned sheepish. "I didn't want you to miss the fireworks. I was planning to watch them from the rooftop of my building. I thought you could join me."

"Oh," I whispered.

"I could take you home though, if you prefer."

"No," I said slowly. "No, that would be nice."

I didn't know if it was going to be nice or if it was going to be a disaster. But Campbell had come to my rescue. He blamed himself for it. We had history and all our old complications, but I did want to see the fireworks.

Campbell didn't disagree with me, and then suddenly,

we pulled into a parking spot behind the historic Pioneer building in downtown Lubbock. It had been constructed in the early 1900s, originally as Hotel Lubbock. After changing hands over many years, it was now primarily luxury condos in the top eleven floors and home to the fine-dining restaurant West Table as well as its subsidiaries Coffee Shop and Brewery LBK. I'd never been upstairs, but I'd certainly eaten at all the restaurants.

"You're renting a condo?"

He shook his head. "Nah, there weren't any available. The third floor is the Pioneer Pocket Hotel. I'm doing extended stay in their Legacy Suite. It's more condo than hotel, so it fits my needs."

"Why didn't you just get a house or something?"

He hopped out of the car and came around to my side. "I didn't know how long I was staying. Then, I liked having hotel accommodations and coffee only an elevator ride away. I'd been on tour too long to start cooking for myself again." He glanced at me. "Plus, they offered security if I stayed longer."

"Ah," I said, realizing that safety was always at the fore-front of his mind. After what I had gone through, I could see why. "Smart."

"It's really not always like that," he told me, sliding a key into the elevator. "Just precautions."

"I get it now."

The elevator dinged on the top floor, and then Campbell directed me to a short flight of stairs that led to the roof. It wasn't anything fancy, mostly industrial, and someone had brought fold-out chairs up here. But we had an uninter-rupted view of the skyline.

"It's beautiful," I said, leaning against the railing and

looking toward the park. "This might be a better view than inside Mackenzie Park."

My phone buzzed in my pocket. I glanced down to see that Piper was finally returning my call. I held up a finger to Campbell and then answered. "Hey."

"Are you okay? Honey told me you were mobbed!"

"I'm fine. Campbell came to pick me up."

"Oh, really?" Piper asked, drawing out the word. "*Mira*, I have no room to talk—"

"No, you don't," I said, interrupting her and glancing over my shoulder. "I was in a panic. No one else was answering."

"So, you're staying with him?"

"I'm going to watch the fireworks from the roof of his hotel."

"And you want to be there?"

"I'll be fine."

Piper huffed. "That is not the same thing."

"I want to be here."

"Okay. Have so much fun," she said with all the insinuation in her voice. "Hollin says hi and to have fun, too."

"Tell him to shove it," I said with a laugh, and then we said our good-byes. Campbell was looking out and away from me so as not to eavesdrop. "Hollin says hi."

Campbell groaned. "Great. I'll never hear the end of it."

"Same." I came to stand at his side. "Thank you for picking me up."

His eyes dropped down to mine. "I'm just glad you want to be here."

My cheeks heated at that. He *had* been listening. And despite myself, I did want to be here.

"Yeah," I muttered.

"Why weren't you with your friends at the festival anyway?"

I glanced down. "Uh, I ran into my mother."

"Pamela." He crinkled his nose. "That must have been pleasant. If it was anything like high school."

"Exactly the same, honestly."

I remembered the first time Campbell had met my mother. It had been an accident really. No one from high school knew about us. I hadn't exactly wanted Pamela to know either. She was supposed to be gone for the weekend with Hal on one of their adult vacations. Theoretically, I was old enough to not need a babysitter for the weekend, and as long as I didn't throw a party, she didn't care what I did. One, I would never throw a party since I didn't have friends. And as far as she knew, I'd never had a boyfriend either.

Well, as soon as they left, I let Campbell in through the back door since the front door had a camera on it that Hal watched, and we spent the entire weekend having sex all over the house. It was one of our better weekends.

Then, halfway through their big Fredericksburg wine tour, Hal had gotten sick. They'd driven the six hours home to find me and Campbell watching *Titanic* in the living room. If anything, I was lucky that I was wearing clothes. Campbell was shirtless in sweats and had just gotten up to refill the popcorn bowl when the front door opened.

My eyes widened to saucers as Pamela and Hal sailed in. Campbell was smart enough to get his shirt from the bedroom before coming out with the popcorn, as if everything was all right.

Mother had looked at Campbell with a flat stare and said, "Young man, I believe it's time for you to go home."

And he did. He *yes, ma'am*-ed his way out of my house so fast.

Pamela claimed it was normal teenage rebellion, but I hadn't broken any rules. She put me on birth control the next week even though I'd lied and sworn we weren't sleeping together. Then, she amended her rules—no parties and no boys.

I'd broken the second rule more times than I could count.

"Sorry to hear that."

I shrugged. "I don't talk to her much...or at all. She's, well, you know. How are things with your dad?"

"Better, I guess," Campbell finally said. "We've been working on coexisting."

"That's good."

"I was in therapy for a few years and tried to get all this anger straightened out. I don't know if I succeeded, but I know that everything that happened wasn't Dad's fault. Blaming him for the fights that led to Mom's death only made things worse, but it was easier to blame him than grieve."

"I get that," I said. "I think I blamed Pamela for Dad leaving, too. It wasn't the same, but it hurt so much to have him go. When we're already so tired from the fighting, the wounds hurt so much worse."

His head tilted to the side. As if I'd said something profound. When I'd really been speaking to myself. And all the pain I'd gone through with my family. It was one of the reasons Campbell and I had connected so intensely. We understood each other's pain.

"I've never written about my mom," he said softly. "That just...it made me think about a song for her."

I almost laughed. "More songs?"

"I swear I haven't been able to write music in years." He

tucked a lock of hair behind my ear. "What are you doing to me?"

I froze at the ease of the contact. "I'm not doing anything."

"Yes, you are."

And the words wrapped around me, tight and constricting. Binding me. As if I were a witch of old, tying him in knots like this. But I was just a girl.

"Campbell," I whispered as he took another step closer.

His hand pushed up into my hair, tilting my face up to his. I was pliant and weak in his arms. The place I most wanted to be and desperately feared.

A firework cracked in the distance, illuminating the midnight-black sky beyond. But neither of us turned to look at it. I was too lost in the deep blues of his eyes and the wonder within them. The *want* within them.

Then, he dropped his lips down onto mine, just a soft, questioning kiss. One full of uncertainty. He didn't know if I wanted this, if I'd allow it. And he was testing the waters. His lips tasted like heaven. Like ambrosia nectar from the gods. Like everything I'd wanted in all of my years in one exact place.

When I didn't pull back, he gripped me tighter, dragging my body against his. And then he covered my mouth firmly. It was a knowing kiss. One full of years of desire. It exploded through me, and suddenly, I was kissing him back.

I couldn't get enough. I wanted all of him in that moment. Every single drop of Campbell Abbey. I wanted him the way I'd wanted him in high school when there was only an empty house and sex all weekend. I wanted no consequences and no choices and just the here and now.

But that hadn't been reality then. There were consequences and choices. The *here and now* was a lie. A perfect lie that I'd told myself so that I could have the man I loved.

I couldn't lie to myself now.

I broke away, stumbling backward from Campbell.

We were both panting with exertion from utter need. His pupils were blasted out, and he looked ready to pounce on me. If he did, if I let him, we'd go downstairs, and we'd fuck all night in his hotel room like the idiotic children we'd once been.

And I couldn't be that stupid again.

"I can't," I gasped.

"Blaire, wait..."

But I didn't let him finish. I fled, and I didn't look back.

PART III

ROOFTOP NIGHTS

14

CAMPBELL

I wanted to rush after her.

I wanted to apologize for kissing her. I hadn't intended to do it at all. In fact, I promised myself that I'd give her as much space as she needed. Then, as she stood there on the rooftop, everything flooded back. She gave me a song about my mom, and in a matter of seconds, with her dark hair flying from the rooftop wind, I knew that another was brewing about a girl on a rooftop at night. And I hadn't been able to stop myself from kissing her.

So, I couldn't regret it.

Even if I had royally fucked it all up.

"Stop looking so glum," Hollin said, dropping another drink in front of me.

It was Thursday night and the band had arrived that morning. They promised to drive out to the winery for a drink and to discuss our next move. I figured I should give them as much room as they needed since I was the one who had dragged them out to West Texas for this shit.

"Sorry," I muttered, taking a sip of my bourbon.

"Yeah, why *are* you so down?" Julian asked. He slid into

the seat next to me, carrying a glass of their award-winning wine.

"Is this about Blaire?" Hollin asked intuitively.

I grimaced. "Might have fucked that one up."

Julian shot me a sympathetic look. "Yeah, well, if you have trouble with women, then I think the rest of us are fucked."

Hollin snorted. "Isn't Jen moving in with you this weekend?"

"She is," he said with a secret smile.

I rolled my eyes at the lot of them. "I have just as much bad luck with women as the rest of the world."

"Maybe more," Hollin said. "You have to deal with being a celebrity on top of it all."

"Did you really date Nini Verona?" Julian asked.

I blew out a breath. "Why does everyone always ask me that?"

"Because she's smoking hot," Hollin said. "Objectively."

"We're friends, but no, we never dated."

Hollin leaned forward on the bar and arched an eyebrow. "But Blaire?"

Julian looked at me expectantly. "We've all noticed."

"Yeah. All right," I said with a sigh.

"You finally going to tell us what happened with y'all in the past?"

I gave him a wary look. "Does Piper know?"

"No, we've both been wondering for months."

"I guess we weren't as subtle as I thought."

Julian laughed and clapped me on the back. "It's hard not to notice when neither of you says a word to the other, and Blaire stiffens every time you walk into a room."

I winced at that. Fuck. I'd noticed her reaction, but I hated that everyone else had, too.

"Yeah, so we met in high school right after Mom died." I looked up at Hollin meaningfully. He knew exactly who I'd been at that time. Reckless, headstrong, and hurting. "The high school was big, so I didn't know everyone, and Blaire didn't want to be noticed. But once we were in each other's orbit, everything else just disappeared. It ended when I left for LA. She never forgave me for leaving her like that."

"Ouch," Julian said.

"But that was so long ago," Hollin said. "Maybe she's gotten over it."

"Yeah. Well, I kissed her on the Fourth of July, and then she ran away."

Hollin blew out a harsh breath. "Well, fuck."

"Or not," Julian muttered.

"Yeah, so don't tell your girlfriends because no one else knows about our past."

"But why?" Julian asked. "No one in the high school knew?"

I met my cousin's eyes. He was seeing it all as a rational person would, eight years in the future. Nothing about it had felt rational at the time. "We were young and stupid. It felt like the only place I could be myself after all that terrible shit with Mom went down. Then, I didn't tell anyone because I wanted to respect her privacy."

"Privacy?" Hollin asked. "Because of your fame? Kind of fucked that one up with that video, huh?"

"No. Because 'I See the Real You' is about Blaire."

Julian's jaw dropped. Hollin's face had a dawning recognition. As if everything in the last eighteen months suddenly made sense.

"Fuck," I muttered. A weight had just been lifted off my shoulders. "I haven't told anyone that before."

"Well, no wonder she hates you," Hollin said. "That was

the most popular song in the world for an entire year, and it's still huge."

"And it explains the way she looked at you in that video," Julian said.

"What do you mean?"

"Well, she looked like she was in love with you."

Hollin nodded. I glanced between them in confusion. I'd seen sadness in her gaze. She'd actually cried afterward. I'd thought I'd fucked it all up. That maybe I'd pushed her too hard on the Fourth.

"Seriously, dude?" Hollin asked with a laugh. "All that fame, and you're no better at figuring out when someone is into you?"

I was used to people being obsessed and throwing themselves at me. Maybe I wasn't good at nuance when it came to women. I hadn't messaged Blaire all week, giving her the space she so clearly wanted. But...had I been wrong?

"I should probably talk to her."

Hollin laughed. "Yeah, probably."

"Just come to our soccer game this weekend," Julian said.

"Good idea."

I nodded. Right. The soccer team. Blaire loved the game. Hollin and Julian both played on the team, too. I hadn't gone to see them, but maybe it was the perfect opportunity. A way to fix this.

That was the moment that the barn doors burst open, and in walked the rest of Cosmere. I shot my brother and cousin a look that said this conversation was over. Hopefully, they were smart enough not to bring it up in front of anyone else.

I hopped off my barstool and strode toward them. "You made it!"

Santi threw his arms around me. "Brother!"

I laughed as he picked me up and spun me around. Santi was Cosmere's drummer. He was always talking and smiling and flirting with everything that walked. He was six feet tall with light-brown skin from his Colombian heritage and short black curls.

He set me on my feet, and our bass player, Viv, was standing there next. She tipped her head to the side, spilling recently dyed bubblegum-pink hair across her face. She flipped me off. "Thanks for abandoning us, shithead."

I chuckled and pulled her reluctantly into a hug. "I missed you, too, Viv."

She rolled her eyes at me. "Kris is less than pleased."

"Give her my apologies. I didn't choose this," I told her.

Viv laughed as she brushed past me toward the bar. "When you say, *Jump*, the record label says, *How high?*"

Our lead guitar, Yorke, nodded at me once. "Yep."

"Good to see you, brother."

We slapped hands. He didn't smile, but he wasn't really one for smiling or talking. He was our quiet, taciturn member. He usually went along with whatever crazy thing Santi suggested. They'd been friends since they met at a local LA talent competition as kids. Yorke had his own devoted group of fans. They called themselves the Peppermint Patties. I figured it wasn't any worse than Campbell Soup girls. We had both been reduced to food.

They'd met Michael shortly after that. Michael currently looked like he'd rather be anywhere other than Lubbock, Texas.

"Hey, Michael."

He gritted his teeth. "This sucks, Campbell. Virginia and Maisie are still in LA, and I *just* got back. Maisie's birthday is in a couple weeks. I promised I'd be there."

"We already said that you could fly back for the birthday," Santi reminded me.

Michael shot him a look of fury. "It's not the same and you know it."

"Fuck, man, I'm sorry. Bobby said that y'all were fine with coming out here."

"Bobby didn't ask," he ground out. "Bobby ordered."

I hadn't considered that Bobby would lie to me. Of course, he'd just been mollifying me. Shit.

"We'll get this all worked out quick," I insisted. "I already have three or four really good songs."

"Ten more to go." He pushed past me to the bar and sank into a seat next to Viv, who immediately tried to cheer him up.

Michael had always been like that. I wasn't sure anything could actually satisfy him. He was the quintessential *money can't buy happiness*. Because he had millions now, and he was just as grumpy as he'd ever been.

Once Santi, Yorke, and Michael had been brought on by the label, they'd added Viv as a bassist. Santi was singing vocals and playing drums. And they were getting nowhere. I'd seen them perform at a club I was bartending at in a shit part of Hollywood.

I remembered it like it was yesterday. The band was good. Santi's sound was so crisp and clear. It was almost too perfect really. He needed something gruffer to go with it.

"Hey, I'm going to take my break," I said, throwing down the rag as my manager yelled at me not to leave. The club was packed. Bartenders weren't supposed to take breaks in the middle of the rush. Oh well.

I headed backstage, nodding at the bouncer. The band was standing there. They called themselves Scandal

Campaign. It was an absurd name. I had no idea who had come up with it, but it didn't fit their sound at all.

"Hey," I said, working up the nerve to approach them.

Viv turned to face me. She sank into her hip, and her look was pure sex appeal. "Can we help you?"

"I liked your music," I told her. I nodded at Santi. "You slay on the drums."

"Thanks, man," Santi said, puffing up.

"But I think you need new songs."

Michael scoffed at me. "What the fuck do you know?"

Santi just cackled. "Oh, we have a music critic, do we?"

"No. Just a musician. I write my own lyrics." I felt ridiculous, saying those words out loud.

They all looked at me as if I was just as insane.

"Ballsy fucker. What you play, hombre?" Santi asked.

"Guitar."

He nodded at Yorke. "He thinks he's that good. We should hear this, eh?"

Yorke shrugged, unimpressed, and passed me his guitar.

I started to sweat. I'd been all confidence when I made the decision to come back here. I had no idea what had possessed me. I'd heard hundreds of shit bands come through here. Except this one was different. They weren't shitty. They knew what they were doing. They were just missing something. I hadn't actually meant to tell them that I was what they were missing, but then the guitar was shoved in my hands, and everything disappeared.

I strummed the opening to "I See the Real You" and let loose.

I got through the first chorus when Bobby Rogers stepped out of the shadows and changed my life.

"I See the Real You" was my big break in every sense of the word. I'd never suspected that I'd join this band, this family. Especially not after years of busting ass in LA, trying to "make it" like everyone else there.

People asked me all the time if I was going to go solo, but I'd tried to be solo for years in LA. The only way I'd ever found my way into the music industry was with this band. They were as much my family as Hollin and Julian were. I couldn't imagine ever doing this without them.

"We'll get it worked out," I assured them as I went back to the bar.

"Of course we will," Viv said, reaching out and pinching my cheek. "Because I told Bobby I'd stay until the end of July, and if we didn't have it by then, we'd figure it out in LA."

"Seems fair."

Back to this deadline.

A month.

A month to figure out an album.

A month to make Blaire fall for me.

Again.

15

BLAIRE

"*I* can't believe you're moving out tomorrow," Piper said with a sigh as she drove us to the soccer game.

Jennifer couldn't hide her grin. "I know. But I'll still see you all the time."

"But I won't come home to you in a marathon editing binge."

"That is true," I agreed. "And you're taking the cats."

I was still sad to see Avocado and Bacon go. I definitely wouldn't get to see them as much as Jennifer.

"They deserve to be with Tortilla," Jennifer said of the little white kitten that Julian had gotten her last year that had transformed into a large white cat.

"Your cat names are ridiculous," Piper said.

"I know. That's why I like them."

"We'll miss you," I told her.

"I just want all the tea about you and Campbell," Jennifer said, leaning forward against the center console.

"There is no tea," I said.

Piper rolled her eyes. "Yeah, right. You went to his place

on the Fourth. Something happened. You've been more cagey than normal."

Jennifer poked my shoulder. "Spill."

"Well, he kissed me."

The girls squealed, and I burst into laughter, covering my ears.

"You kissed!" Piper gasped. "How have you kept this from us for so long?"

"That is an excellent question," Jennifer agreed.

"I freaked out and left after it happened."

"Why?" Piper asked.

"It's Campbell Abbey!" Jennifer said. "Come on."

"That's exactly why."

And then I sighed and decided it was beyond time. I should have told them when they first started asking about Campbell. I'd held it so tight to myself for years that it was terrifying to tell someone.

"We dated in high school."

Piper reached across the Jeep and took my hand. "You can tell us."

I nodded and swallowed down the lump in my throat. I could barely talk about it. Let alone let myself relive it.

"It was a vivid few months. As if I were finally living in Technicolor after living my entire life in black-and-white. I don't think I've ever loved someone so much, and I'll never feel like that again." I clenched Piper's hand tighter. "Living with such abandon that I let myself fall that hard."

"What happened?" Jennifer whispered.

"He left," Piper said as if she'd already heard the story.

"Yes. He went to LA, and I stayed here."

"You didn't try long-distance?"

I laughed hoarsely. "At eighteen, when I was about to go

to college and he was a thousand miles away? No. He didn't want to, and it wouldn't have worked anyway."

"Are you going to try again now that he's back?" Piper asked.

I shrugged. "Is he back?"

Jennifer chewed on her bottom lip but didn't say anything. Piper didn't either. Because none of us knew. He was here for a limited time to figure out his album, but then what? I couldn't imagine him ever moving back to Lubbock permanently. And I could hardly see myself leaving Lubbock.

Even if I wanted something with Campbell, I couldn't get past that point. He'd left me once at the hardest time of my life. It wouldn't be enough to have a little fling while he was in town even if I wanted it. And I still didn't know if I did.

When it came to Campbell Abbey, my heart couldn't handle it.

Piper parked, and I grabbed my soccer bag from the back. We trekked across the pavement to the fields beyond. I could see that half the team was already warming up. And to my surprise, as we got closer, I noticed Campbell sitting in the stands. My heart thumped at that sight. I had no idea why he was here now. Not to mention, with the entire band.

Piper and Jennifer did a double take at that.

"Oh my God," Jennifer whispered, like the fangirl she was. "The band is here."

"No Michael though," Piper said.

She was right. No Michael. Interesting. Had he not flown in with the rest of the band?

I could have jumped up there to ask. Campbell's eyes met mine, and he smiled down at me. But I jerked my head away from him and hurried past to the fields. *Smooth, Blaire.*

"Hey, Blaire!" Honey cried as I got closer.

She was standing next to the other forward and our newest member, Eve.

"Blaire," Eve said. Eve was gorgeous with black hair and green eyes and a big chest, currently covered by The Tacos soccer uniform.

"Hey, y'all."

I narrowed my eyes at Honey's outfit. She was wearing black biker shorts and a floral crop top that looked familiar. In fact, it looked like the shirt that had come in last week for me from a sustainable energy designer that I supported.

"Is that my shirt?"

Honey glanced down at herself and laughed. "Oh my God, is it?"

"Yeah, I think it is."

"My bad, Blaire. I must have snagged it on accident. You don't mind, do you?" Her eyes were wide with concern.

I dropped my soccer bag and shook my head. "No, it's fine. Just bring it back tomorrow."

"Sure," she said easily.

Eve glanced between us as Jen and Piper caught up with us.

"Hey, Eve," Piper said with a smile.

Eve was a big reason that Piper's winery had been saved. She always seemed hesitant around us girls, as if she expected us to hate her. That was probably because of her reputation as being a man stealer, but I'd known her a few months, and she didn't seem remotely interested in going after anyone's boyfriend. It seemed like some bullshit label that she'd internalized. We didn't deal with any of that slut shaming here.

"Hi, Piper." She nodded at Jen. "I heard you were moving out."

Jennifer brightened. "Yes, tomorrow!"

"Lucky. I was just evicted."

We all blinked at her.

"What?" Piper gasped.

"I was staying at a Sinclair Realty property," she said, as if that made all the difference.

And considering she had been in a brief relationship with Mr. Sinclair, it was all starting to make sense. They'd ended their fling, and he'd gotten rid of her in every way that he could.

"That's terrible. I'm sorry. We have an extra room this weekend if you want to move in."

Eve's jaw dropped. "What?"

"Yeah. You should take Jen's spot," Piper agreed.

"You can't be serious."

"And why not?" Piper asked.

"I...I don't play well with others," she said in air quotes. "How could you want me to live with you after what you know about me?"

Piper put her hands on her hips. "You saved my winery. You never put the moves on Hollin, and he used to put the moves on everyone."

"Yeah, but..."

"I don't think there is a *but*," I said encouragingly. "If you have a better option, then go for it, but we'd love to have you."

Eve flushed. She considered it a moment and then nodded her head. "Yeah. Yeah, I'd like that. Thank you."

"Sweet. I'll get all the lease information for you. Should be easy. When do you want to move in?"

"This weekend, if I can."

"Done," Piper said.

I left them to work out the details. After pulling on my

cleats and shin guards, I jogged out onto the field. Nora waved me over, and we ran a few drills to get warmed up.

"What's Campbell doing here?" I asked her.

She arched an eyebrow at me. "You tell me."

"Oh boy, you too?"

"Hey, I like you, and I like having my brother back home. I can't complain."

Then, her eyes drifted to the sidelines, and she cursed.

"What?"

I followed her gaze and found August and Tamara striding toward the field.

"Fuck," I muttered. "What are they doing here?"

When Nora had been dating August, he'd been on our team. We'd replaced him with Eve after the fallout of Nora finding him making out with her best friend. Thankfully, Tamara had quit her job at Wright Vineyard. So, Nora hadn't had to deal with her since that had all gone down.

"I have no idea."

We jogged over to the sidelines, but August wasn't heading that way. He was walking toward the other team. That was when we both realized he was wearing the avocado green of the opposing team.

"He switched teams?" I asked in shock.

Hollin came to stand next to us. "I'll kill him."

"Hollin," Nora said, her voice soft.

But her brother wasn't listening. "Hey, August!"

August turned at the sound of his name and then paled. He gulped and left his new team behind. "Hey," he said with more confidence than he had to be feeling. He glanced from Hollin to Nora. "Hey, Nora."

"Don't fucking talk to her. You're on the other team?"

"I didn't know we were going to play you," he told them.

"Marni asked if I'd sub because they lost a forward. She didn't tell me it was you guys."

"I think you should fucking leave."

"Hollin," I snapped, stepping between him and the fight that was about to happen.

"Hey, Blaire," August said with a steady gaze.

"Can you at least tell Tamara to go?" I asked.

His gaze shifted to Nora again, who looked ready to collapse in on herself. They'd been together for three years. And now, this shit.

He ran a hand back through his hair. "Yeah. Yeah, I can do that." He looked to Nora again. "Nor, I'm sorry."

"Don't," she gasped.

"Please."

"Stop it," I said, pushing him backward. "Go back to where you belong."

"I can't do this," Nora said. There were tears in her eyes as the words spilled from her mouth. "It's not fair."

Then, she grabbed her soccer bag and stormed from the fields.

"Fuck," Hollin said.

The ref blew the whistle to let us all know the game was about to start. Campbell had already jumped up and was rushing after his sister. I grabbed Hollin's shirt to keep him from going after her, too.

"Campbell has it handled. You have to play," I told him.

Hollin looked away from his sister and pointed at August. "You'll pay for that."

Then, he jerked out of my grasp and stalked to his spot on the field.

"I didn't know," August repeated.

"And you think that makes it okay?"

"No," he said with a sigh.

He looked so sad and pathetic. As if he realized he'd made one huge mistake in losing Nora, but he had no idea how to dig himself out of the hole.

I shook my head and took a small amount of pity on him. "Stay away from Hollin on the field. He won't need an excuse."

"Don't I know it," he said, touching his nose where Hollin had broken it. "Thanks, Blaire."

"No, we're not friends here. I just don't want to see you die." I looked him up and down. "You deserve all of this and more."

16

CAMPBELL

"Nora," I called as I rushed off the bleachers and after my sister.

She was way past me, and I cursed myself for wearing black jeans in this Texas heat. I was heaving as I reached her. I was not cut out for running. A three-hour set under stage lights? Sure. Running? No.

"Nora, wait. Jesus, I can't run like you."

She slowed and swiped at the tears in her eyes. "God, you're out of shape."

"I'm really, really in shape for a musician."

She rolled her eyes. "Whatever. You can barely run."

"I lift weights," I offered.

"You look pathetic."

"God, I love having siblings," I said as I caught my breath. "Running sucks."

"I'm surprised you're even here."

"Can't want to see my baby sister play?"

"No. You're here for Blaire."

"Yeah, okay. That's true." I slung an arm over her shoulders as we continued to her car. "But I can be worried for you. Should I go knock August on his ass?"

"No," she said, her voice going small.

"He fucking deserves it. What is he even doing here? I thought you replaced him on the team."

"We did. The captain of the other team invited him to sub. He said he didn't know they were playing The Tacos."

"So, why are you running? Tell him to get the fuck out. This is your team. He can't run you off."

"I can't do it, Campbell," she said, leaning back against her car. "I just can't do it. I can't pretend that I'm okay anymore. I had to move out of my apartment with Tamara. I lost my boyfriend and my best friend. I'm living with a stranger. I like Weston. Don't get me wrong. He's cool."

"He is cool."

"But it's just...awful." She started crying again then. "It's awful. I hurt all the time. I want him back. It's been almost two months, and I still feel like I can't fucking breathe when I think about it. Is it ever going to get better?"

I thought about Blaire back out there on the field and how my presence still hurt her like this. It had gotten better, but it was never exactly good. I was working on better. I believed Nora could have better.

I drew my sister into my arms and held her tight. "It will get better."

"When?" she gasped through her tears. "My chest feels like it's been ripped open and my heart is flopping around inside. And every time I see him, it's worse, not better."

"I know. I'm sorry, shrimp."

She cried against my shirt for a few minutes, only pulling back when a car parked across from us. Weston stepped out of the Subaru. Nora tried to wipe her tears, but her eyes were bloodshot. She looked a wreck. But when Weston looked at her, something switched on.

I liked Weston Wright. In fact, I'd already call him a friend. We clicked out of the studio, but *in* the studio, it was as if we'd always been making music together. He had incredible musicality and was a genius on the keys. But that didn't mean that I wanted him to look at my little sister like that. Not when the last thing she needed was a complicated roommate situation.

"Wright," I said with a raised eyebrow.

"Hey, is everything all right?" he asked, walking toward us with his hands in his pockets.

"Yeah," Nora said with a sniffle. "It's okay. What are you doing here?"

"I wanted to see you play. Julian gave me the soccer schedule. You talk about how much you like it, so I thought I'd show. I know shit about soccer."

"That's...that's nice of you," she admitted.

"Real nice."

He caught my tone of voice and nodded once. "Are you not playing?"

She swallowed and glanced over at me. "Maybe I should still play."

"If you're up for it."

"You came just for me?" Nora asked West in a soft voice.

He rocked back on his heels. "Yeah, I like to support my roommate."

Her smile brightened slightly on the edges. And as much as I did not like where this was heading, I couldn't deny that he'd gotten the result that I'd wanted.

"Okay," she said. "Go on ahead. Give me a minute."

"You sure?"

She nodded.

I kissed the top of her head and then headed back to the fields with Weston. "So...you're into my sister?"

Weston held his hands up. "I'm just being a good room-mate. What happened?"

"August and Tamara showed."

"Fuck."

"Yeah. So, you can see why I'm concerned about her getting hurt again."

West nodded. "I hear you."

I wasn't sure that I believed him. But I didn't need to stick my nose where it didn't belong. Nora was too hurt to start a new relationship anyway. She'd figure it all out.

It ended up being a good thing that we went ahead of Nora. Because on the way, we ran into a very disgruntled Tamara. She crossed her arms over her chest and stomped past us. Clearly, someone had told her she had to go home. From what I knew of her, I was shocked that she'd listened. Which meant it had to have been August.

We waited until she was well out of the way before continuing. The last thing I wanted was for Nora to run into her. It was enough that Tamara had stolen her boyfriend. She didn't deserve to deal with the bitch beyond that horror.

"Hey, West!" Santi said, scooting over to make room for him on the bleachers.

West blinked at him. That was just Santi though. He was always the most enthusiastic and inviting member of our group. I didn't know anyone else who would have actually handed me a guitar that night I'd called them out for having bad lyrics. Even if Santi had been making fun of me.

"Thanks, man," West said and took the offered seat.

We'd gone into the studio to get used to the equipment. Michael had been irritable the entire time we were there. LBK Studios was far from what we were used to in LA.

Maybe we'd all gotten a little used to the better equipment, but we weren't recording here. We were figuring out the new songs and finding our sound. Michael had outright refused to come out with us today. Which he wasn't obligated, but I could feel the weight of his refusal on everyone's shoulders.

Viv pulled her phone up. "Everyone, smile." She stuck her tongue out as we drew in closer. "Kris says hi."

"Tell her I said hi," I told her. Viv's girlfriend, Kris, was a riot. She'd joined us for the West Coast portion of our tour. "Better yet, tell her to fly out."

"She's busy," Viv said. "She gets it. It's part of the job."

"At least the music is good," Yorke said with an arched eyebrow.

Viv laughed and kissed his cheek. "That's true, big boy."

There was that. Despite their frustration with coming out here to figure out the album, the songs *were* good. They'd all loved "Invisible Girl," and I'd played the intro to "Rooftop Nights" and the song I'd started writing about my mom, tentatively titled "Alone." I'd even been able to pull in lyrics from the notebook finally. Now that I had inspiration, I could take Bobby's advice and create something out of the nothingness that had been there only a few weeks ago.

We all watched the game. We got some looks, and a few people asked for a picture, but generally, we were left alone. It was like I'd told Blaire—ninety-nine times out of a hundred.

"Your brother is *going* for that striker," Santi said, leaning forward. "He's sure making it interesting."

That striker was August, who was doing an okay job of avoiding Hollin. But not a good enough job. Seeing Nora's tears made me give zero fucks about what happened here.

But even I hissed in shock at a particularly brutal slide

tackle halfway through the second half. The ref blew the whistle, a red card sliding out of her pocket.

Hollin tried to argue, but, well, it had definitely been an illegal slide tackle, and August was still on the ground. Annie smacked him on the side of the head and yelled in his face, something about how they needed him for finals. Hollin stomped off the field, but I couldn't keep the smirk off my face. We met each other's eyes, and he laughed.

I held my fist out, and he bumped me. "Nice one."

He snorted. "Could have been worse."

"The first few were at least clean."

Santi leaned across me, holding out his own fist. "I heard what he did to your sister. Worth it."

Hollin hit his fist, looking like a fucking hero. "Yeah, man."

Viv blew her bubblegum bangs out of her face. "Men."

Despite playing a man down, The Tacos still cleaned house. Blaire was particularly unstoppable. Girl goals counted for two in this league, and between her and Eve, the other team hardly stood a chance. Even with Nora playing as if in a daze.

The team invited us to celebratory pizza after the game, and I drove the band to Capital Pizza, just off the Texas Tech University campus. Blaire hadn't quite looked in my direction when we were invited, and I took that as a good sign. She was still going to be there. She wasn't going to ditch to avoid me. Maybe we were salvageable after all.

Nora had gone home though. After dealing with August and playing throughout the game, she hadn't wanted to celebrate, and I could hardly blame her.

Annie commandeered the long table at the back of the pizza joint. With the band, we were an even larger group than normal. Blaire sat at one end of the table, and I sank into the seat across from her. She looked up at me with surprise.

"Hey," I said with a smile.

She glanced down at the menu. "Hey."

"The band wanted to meet you."

"Really?" Her eyes were wide as they took their seats next to me. "I did kind of meet them backstage."

"That's right," Santi said. "I *knew* I remembered you."

She smiled. "You probably meet a thousand girls on tour."

"Yeah, but you were the only girl that made Campbell stand up in protest when I put my arm around you."

I glared at Santi. Of course that was what he fucking remembered. "That isn't what happened."

"That's how I remember it," Blaire piped up. She arched an eyebrow at me in challenge.

Okay, maybe that was how it had gone down. And worse, she'd shot me that same imperious look as she was giving me now. One that said, *What the fuck are you going to do about it?* A few months ago, when I'd seen her at the show, the answer had been, *Nothing*. That wasn't the answer anymore.

"Well, I felt justified," I said with a shrug.

Her mouth popped open for a second before she covered it quickly. "And why is that?"

"Yeah," Santi said, elbowing me in the ribs. "Why are you justified?"

Viv snorted, nudging Blaire's elbow. "Because she's fucking gorg." She winked at Blaire. "Hey, babe. I'm Viv."

"Nice to meet you."

Eve sank into the seat next to Viv. "You're Viv Underwood."

Viv's eyed Eve appreciatively. She'd tugged her jersey off, and she was just in a sports bra, which did little to cover her chest. I had to force myself to look somewhere else, but Viv was clearly having difficulty.

"Sure am. Who are you, beautiful?"

"Eve." They shook hands in the small space. Eve's eyes turned to the rest of the band. "Santi, Yorke, and Campbell. You're missing one."

"Michael doesn't like soccer," Santi purred.

Viv shot him a look that said, *Come on. Give me this one!*

Santi just looked back at her and mouthed one word —*Kris.*

Viv huffed.

"His loss," Eve said.

"So, are you a Cosmere fan, baby?" Santi asked with a wink.

Eve shrugged. "Not really."

Blaire snorted. "Classic."

"No offense," Eve said. "I like heavier stuff."

"None taken," Yorke said.

"Then, how do you know us all?" Viv asked.

Eve shrugged. "I had a roommate who was a big fan."

Just then, Blaire's assistant, Honey, plopped down into the seat at the head of the table. She had clearly gotten her fangirl under control and just said, "Hey, y'all."

Santi nodded toward Yorke, who shrugged. I knew what that meant. Yorke's preferences ran toward short blondes. Honey fit the bill. Well, at least my bandmates were making the best of a bad situation.

"So, why did you want to meet me?" Blaire asked after introductions were made.

Santi leaned forward with a grin. "We want you to make more videos."

17

BLAIRE

"*A*bsolutely not," Campbell bellowed before I could get a word in edgewise.

I gaped at him along with half of the table. Clearly, this had not been run by him before Santi just blurted it out. And Campbell's vehemence was so strong that I had no idea what to say. He didn't want me to do any more videos? He hadn't been against it when he was tricked into doing the first one.

"What the fuck, bro?" Santi asked.

"We're keeping Blaire out of this."

Viv rolled her eyes. "Why don't we ask the lady what she prefers? She has a brain, Campbell Soup. I think she can make up her own mind."

"Who told you to do more videos? Was it Bobby?" Campbell demanded right over Viv's comments.

"Yes," Yorke said, perfectly monosyllabic.

"Look, Bobby suggested that while we're here, we use it as publicity," Santi reasoned. "The girl already has an audience that is expecting you."

"That girl has a name," I finally got out. "It's Blaire. And I'm sitting right fucking here."

"My apologies," Santi said with a half-bow in her direction. From Santi, it wasn't even mocking. He was utterly sincere about it. "Our manager, Bobby Rogers..."

"I met him," I said.

"Well, he thinks you'd be a valid resource to use. You're already here. He doesn't have to send a team."

"Because I declined a fucking team," Campbell grumbled under his breath.

"Campbell refuses to get on social, but he'll do videos for you," Santi finished. "If you want to do them, we'd be up for it."

"The first video caused her enough problems. I told Bobby not to involve her in any of this."

"Well, you don't get to make all the decisions for the entire band," Viv piped up.

"No, but—"

"Or for me," Blaire added, crossing her arms over her chest.

"Blaire," I said reasonably, "think about what happened on the Fourth of July. I don't want you to be more involved with this if it's going to put you in danger."

"What *did* happen?" Viv asked curiously.

"She was attacked by a group of Campbell Soup girls."

"You said yourself, that almost never happens. And I wasn't expecting it. I would be more cautious now."

His face crumpled as he realized that I was arguing with him about this. Because he hadn't considered that this would be one of the coolest things I'd ever done in my entire career. Sure, I mostly focused on wellness on *Blaire Blush*, but making videos was part of my job. I could do so much good.

"You want to do this?" Campbell finally asked.

"I want to consider it before you throw it out without asking my opinion."

He nodded slowly and then slumped back into his chair. "All right."

"Can we eat now?" Yorke asked, gesturing to the pies that had just been placed on the table. Someone must have ordered a bunch of pizzas for the entire table while we were all arguing.

Eve grabbed the first piece with a muffled, "Y'all are dramatic."

The rest of the table cracked up, and the spell was broken. Campbell still brooded through most of dinner, but the band had no such qualms. And by the end, everyone was enamored with Santi and Viv's banter and even Yorke's deep voice and impenetrable eyes.

I waved Annie and Jen off as they headed toward their respective boyfriend's car.

Piper held up the key to the Jeep. "I'll get it running. You going to be long?"

I glanced back at Campbell, who waited outside while Viv smoked with Eve. Santi stood beside them like a hopeful puppy. I needed to talk to Campbell. That much had been certain before he flipped his shit over the videos. I needed to talk to him even more now.

"Yeah, I hope not."

"Good luck."

"Thanks."

Campbell glanced up from where he was standing just far enough away from the smoke to not inhale it outright. His eyes found mine, and I met his stare straight on. He said something to his friends and then strode over to where I was standing.

"Hey," he said, running a hand back through his hair. "Sorry about..." He trailed off and gestured around him. "I don't know. Everything."

"Look, I think we just need to talk. I've been running away long enough, but it sort of looks like you're here to stay for a bit, and I'm...somehow in your life again."

"I don't mind that," he admitted with a small smile.

I gulped at the way that smile sent butterflies flipping around my stomach. He liked having me here. God, that shouldn't have made me turn into a simpering idiot. "I don't...mind that either."

His eyebrows shot up his forehead. "Really? Because you kind of ran away on Sunday."

"I did," I said, toeing the gravel at my feet. "Sunday was overwhelming."

"I'm not sorry I kissed you."

I laughed. "I'm well aware."

He took another step closer to me. I swallowed and tilted my head up to look into that gorgeous face. The person who had turned my world upside down and shattered it in the next breath.

"But I don't want to be the reason you run ever again."

My knees wobbled at those words. "I don't think you can promise that."

"I'm not the same person I was eight years ago."

Tears pricked my eyes, and I glanced down. "Me either."

Losing him had made me careful. It had made me hesitant. It had made me think before I leaped. I didn't know how not to be that person. Especially with his beautiful face looking down at me so earnestly.

"Why don't we just...try to start over?" I offered.

He accepted it for the olive branch it was. "I'd like that."

Then, he sighed softly. "Look, you don't have to do those videos just because my manager asked."

"Have you considered that I might want to?"

"No," he admitted.

"You seem adamantly against it."

"I'm not. I'm just..." He bit the inside of his cheek, shifting from foot to foot and fidgeting, as he always had. That nervous energy crackled through him. Nowadays, he channeled it onto the stage, but before, it had come out like this. "I want to protect you. When you called me, crying, I freaked the fuck out. It reminded me so much of when the police called the night my mom died."

"Campbell," I whispered.

"It's not the same. I know it isn't. But the instant it happened, I knew that I'd do anything to keep you safe. And the deeper you get involved with me, the more you post videos, the more you let LA weasel in here, into your Lubbock sanctuary, the less I can do about it."

Despite myself, I put my hand on his arm. He jumped at the touch. "You don't have to protect me. What happened Sunday was a surprise. I didn't know that sort of thing could happen. I'll be more careful now. I won't be alone."

"Fuck, I hate that you have to think like that now."

"It might never even happen again," I told him. "And I don't think I should decide everything based on a what-if. Sunday was a lot, but I *want* to do this, Campbell. I've already gotten several offers for things like being on the *Today* show and a speaking tour for *Blaire Blush*."

His eyes lit up with pride. "Really? Blaire, that's incredible."

I flushed, true to my namesake. "I actually wanted to ask about how to navigate it. I need help and thought you might know someone."

"Oh yeah? Like a publicist? I know someone great. She's New York–based now, but before she moved, we hung out a lot in LA. She's great. Let me give you her contact. Just tell her I sent you."

He sent me a text, and my phone dinged. A name and number came up on my phone—Anna English, English & Bhardwaj PR.

"She goes by English," Campbell told me.

"Well, that was...easier than I'd thought." I shoved my phone away with a promise to message English tomorrow.

He shrugged. "I have contacts. I just want to make sure this is what you want. I remember when all you wanted was to disappear."

"I got rid of that girl when you left," I whispered. "After everything happened, I decided that I didn't want to disappear ever again."

As if he couldn't stop himself from touching me, he brushed my hair behind my ear. "Then, go take over the world. I can't wait to watch it happen."

And he was so sincere that it took everything in me to step out of his embrace instead of crushing my lips to his.

18

BLAIRE

*a*nna English was a total hard-ass, and I immediately liked her. As soon as I'd texted her, name-dropping Campbell, she'd scheduled a call. At first to verify I was who I'd said I was and then to go through everything that was already on my plate. We worked out the details for a standard contract, and I signed with her before the day was out. I went through my emails and sent her everything that looked even remotely interesting. Things that I didn't know what to do with, but she apparently ate this stuff for breakfast.

"I've got you covered, Blaire. I'm glad Campbell gave you my number. Tell him hi for me, will you?"

"Sure."

"And if you're in New York or LA anytime, then let me know, so we can meet," she said, all business.

"I'll definitely do that. Thanks, English."

"My pleasure."

English was a hundred percent on board with me recording *everything* that happened with the band when they were in Lubbock. She said she was going to reach out to her LA contacts to see about a possible documentary with Netflix using Blaire's footage of the band as they create their new album. I had no idea how likely that was, but she seemed like the kind of person who didn't take no for an answer.

I was still dazed from the speed of everything when I showed up to LBK Studios the next day. I hauled in my serious video equipment. I did most of my social media stuff on my phone for ease of use, but I had better cameras and high-end recorders that I used for *Blaire Blush* workshops.

I clanked in through the double glass doors, holding a tripod and carrying a backpack full of equipment. If someone had told me when I was getting my psych degree that I'd need to learn how to run my own business, record and manage most of my own videos, and do all of my own marketing, I would have laughed at them. And yet here I was.

"Hey, Blaire. You need any help with that?" Weston asked. He jumped up and offered me a hand.

"Thanks."

"No problem. Campbell said you were coming to record, but I thought he meant on your phone."

"I always have to go one extra step, don't I?"

Weston grinned. "Nora says that's why you're so successful at what you do."

"Ah, well, that's nice of Nora."

I glanced up at him as he carried my equipment to the table by the studio entrance. I'd been worried for Nora ever since August had ripped out her heart and fed it through a shredder. She'd seemed a wreck on the soccer field. But having a cute roommate who quoted her to other people certainly couldn't hurt anything.

"I'm going to leave this here. Why don't you come in and hear what they're working on?"

I nodded and slipped into the studio. The band was set up at their various instruments, messing around with the sound on a song I'd never heard before. It was more upbeat than "Invisible Girl" but just as catchy. It reminded me of a fun summer hit that people would dance to in clubs or sing at the top of their lungs while driving with the top down.

"Oh, wow," I whispered. "What's this one?"

Weston looked down at the sheet of paper in front of him. "It's called 'Rooftop Nights.' "

I flushed all over at that. That could not be a coincidence. Campbell and I had kissed on a rooftop, and now, he was singing about it for the entire world to hear. I'd thought it was bad to have *one* song about me. So far, both songs on the album were about me.

A new feeling awakened in my stomach at that thought. It wasn't revulsion. It wasn't the usual fear and anxiety that someone would find out about me. It was...excitement?

Because whatever was happening here with Campbell felt new and shiny while also nostalgic and comfortable. He'd hurt me in the worst possible way. I'd had no idea that I'd be able to feel like this again. Or maybe I'd kept my distance from him because I knew that if I even dared to talk to him again, I'd never be able to walk away. Campbell and I had an inexplicable draw. The minute he'd actually seen me, everything had drifted away, and I'd known I'd never be alone again.

It had started in the unlikeliest of places.

Sonic.

I still rolled my eyes, thinking about it. I'd gotten the job at my mom's insistence that I learned a hard day's work. I'd been at Sonic a year, delivering orders on roller skates, and I already knew that I never wanted to work in fast food again if I could help it.

Every Friday night after the big game, we'd get high school students in droves. I skipped all the games because the tips at work were just too good to pass up. Which was how I knew that every Friday, Campbell Abbey showed up in his girlfriend's shiny BMW convertible. Jill Patton was high school royalty. Her dad owned all the major car dealerships in West Texas. She had a different car every month of the year. It was obscene.

And somehow, she was dating Campbell.

He'd always been cool even though he never gave a fuck what anyone else thought. Maybe it was because he didn't care.

Jill was dressed in her cheerleading uniform, and he had on his usual outfit of faded jeans and a fitted black shirt. Chuck Taylors on his feet and his hair spiked up. All of their friends took over the spattering of tables in the middle of Sonic, and to my dismay, every Friday, I delivered their food. It sucked because Jill Patton didn't tip. Apparently, her dad hadn't taught her manners.

With a sigh, I hoisted the tray onto my shoulder and skated toward their table. I handed out the food and drinks that had been ordered.

"Chocolate shake," I said, dropping off the drink in front of Jill. "And a banana split."

"That's me," Campbell said.

I passed it to him, barely meeting his eyes.

"Excuse me," Jill said, annoyed.

I glanced at her. "Can I help you?"

"What is this garbage?"

"A chocolate shake."

"It's gross," she said and thrust the open drink at me to see.

It looked fine to me. I had no idea what she was talking about, but the customer came first. "I can make you another one if you'd like."

Then, to my abject horror, she flung the shake at me. I gasped, reeling backward on my skates, as the chocolate exploded all over my uniform. Only years of skating kept me on my feet instead of sailing backward on my ass to add to my humiliation.

And it was humiliating.

Everyone laughed. I didn't look up to meet anyone's eyes, but I could hear their laughter at my benefit. Only Campbell didn't join them.

"Jill," he admonished, jumping up to grab a few napkins. "Come on."

She just set her shake down, as if she'd done nothing wrong, and said, "Get it right the first time."

I was shaking with rage. There was fire in my eyes. I wanted to rip her limb from limb. But I couldn't. I couldn't do anything.

I turned and fled. I hadn't accepted the napkins from Campbell. I hadn't done anything. I just needed to escape this horrible circumstance. I was still supposed to work for another hour, and I couldn't do it. I didn't have a spare uniform on me, and this one was unsalvageable.

I almost made it inside, where I could cry and scream obscenities in peace, when I felt a tug on my arm. "Hey."

I whipped around on my skates. My eyes were red with unshed tears. My hands trembling. "Can I help you?" I forced out.

"No," he said slowly. "No. I just wanted to apologize.

That should never have happened. I can't believe she did that."

"Okay." Because it seemed right up her alley. I didn't know what he saw in her. How could he not see she was vile?

"Can I help in any way?" He offered up a fistful of napkins.

"No." And my voice was forceful and mean. It was savage. It could have cut glass with the ferocity.

For a second, as we stood there in a Sonic parking lot, something shifted. I suddenly wasn't invisible anymore. Campbell Abbey looked at me with all my fury and saw me. He saw the real me that I hid behind a dark brown bob and bangs. That I hid from everyone.

"You're...Blaire, right?"

I gawped at him. How the hell did he know my name? "Yes?" It came out as more of a question.

"We had Spanish together last year, right?"

"Yes," I whispered. He'd slept through half the class and never once looked my way.

"I remember you."

And everything tipped over at those words. They shouldn't have meant anything at all. This was Campbell Abbey. He was dating the most popular, bitchiest girl in school. He shouldn't have remembered who I was. He shouldn't have been looking at me right now, covered in chocolate shake, humiliated and close to tears, with...interest. I definitely shouldn't have been looking back.

But it all changed then.

He and Jill broke up that night.

Campbell started coming to Sonic every afternoon for a whole different reason. And at first, we hid what was happening because of the wrath of Jill Patton. Not even

Campbell wanted on her bad side. I sure didn't. But then it became so private, so intimate, that sharing it with anyone else felt like giving up a piece of it. And I wanted all of him to myself.

Apparently, I still did.

Campbell finished his song and burst out of the recording room. "Hey, you made it."

"I did," I whispered with a smile. "It's later than I thought it would be. I was on the phone with English all morning. She said to tell you hi."

"Oh, great. That all worked out?"

I nodded. "Signed with her yesterday, and we worked out all the things she's going to handle today. She mentioned talking to LA contacts about a possible documentary or biopic of Cosmere using my footage. Obviously, I'd want your consent before going that route."

Campbell looked thoughtful. "I hadn't considered that."

"She thought the angle could be a making of your new album. Lots of artists have been doing them for Netflix recently."

"I'll talk to the band. I'm down if you are," Campbell said.

I smiled and nodded. "There's nothing certain, but if I'm taking footage anyway..."

"Exactly." He turned to Weston. "Could you talk Michael through the keys section on 'Invisible Girl' again? He keeps missing something, and I'm not sure what it is."

Weston grimaced. "Uh, sure."

Then, he disappeared with a backward glance that said, *Save me.*

"Trouble?" I asked as I pulled equipment out of my bag and set up to record some test shots.

"Nah. Michael is just pissed we're here. He doesn't want

to take direction. Once we're back in LA, recording, he'll be fine."

"And how long does that take?" I asked, hoping I kept the discomfort out of my voice.

"If we can get all the kinks out here, probably a couple months."

"Really?" I asked. "That fast?"

"Yeah. Bands used to record a whole album in a night. They just record all day and night, and ta-da, it's done."

"But you don't work that way?" The camera was on his face as he spoke to me about his process.

"I mean, I do. I could sit down today and lay out three or four songs. But to get them right, we have to spend the time on them. I don't want to rush this."

I smiled up at him. At the certainty about him. All that nervous energy he always had evaporated when he talked about music. As if when he had a guitar in his hands, he channeled it all into something epic.

"So, after this set, we break for lunch." I looked up at him over my camera. He ran his hand back through his hair. "If you want to get lunch with me."

"With you or the band?"

He grinned. "Me?"

"Maybe the band."

"All right. Fair."

He shot me one more grin before heading back into the studio. He slung his guitar over his head and talked through the rest of the song with them. Now that Michael was caught up, Weston returned to his perch.

I watched, mesmerized, as they worked through this new song. It was going to be a huge hit. I could already tell. Might even be the one that they opened the album with. And it all started because of me.

19

CAMPBELL

*M*usic spoke to my soul.

It sounded cliché, but it was the goddamn truth. We were making magic in this studio. Even as disgruntled as Michael appeared, he couldn't resist the allure of the new sounds we were producing. Something that Bobby Rogers was going to be salivating for as soon as he heard "Rooftop Nights."

It was that big top 40 hit we hadn't had last album. The one that you just had to tap your foot to and bob your head and dance and rave and lose yourself in. I was already losing myself to it.

And it was all about Blaire. About fireworks in the night sky and kissing under the starlight and dancing the night away. It wasn't what had happened. The girl didn't run in my version, but it was a hundred and ten percent the beautiful siren seated in the booth, watching me. Having her here made it all the better, too. Like I was singing my feelings without having to tell her exactly what was between us. Without asking any of those questions. It was how we'd always worked together.

I wanted more, more, more.

One kiss was never going to be enough.

We played for another hour before Santi finally called it quits. "That's it, man. I need sustenance to survive, bro."

The rest of the band filed out after him, but despite the long hours in the studio, we were all aglow. As if the music filled them up just as much as it fueled me.

"So, where to?" Santi asked, slinging an arm around Blaire's shoulders.

I crossed my arms in silent protest. Santi gave me a shit-eating look. He knew precisely how I felt about Blaire at this point. If the music didn't say it, her being here and how I'd been acting clearly did. I'd dated briefly in the years since we'd been in Cosmere, but nothing was ever like Blaire. If I was reacting to anything at all, he counted it as a win.

"Uh, we're close to Dirk's. It's a fried chicken place," Blaire suggested.

"Done," Viv said. She smacked Santi on the back of the head, and they all headed out the door.

"You coming, too, West?" I asked.

He shook his head. "You go on ahead. I'm going to work on this."

"Want us to bring you something back?" Blaire offered.

"I'm good."

He waved us off, and we followed the band out. Blaire directed us to the restaurant. We grabbed a large round table at the front and put in our order. Cartoon artwork covered every available inch of brick wall space. I'd never seen anything like it.

"This place is cool."

"It's named for the former mayor and Lubbock-area cartoonist," Blaire explained. "This is all his original artwork."

"I dig it," Yorke said with a nod.

Viv looked over Santi's shoulder after his phone pinged. Her eyes widened. "I'm so jealous."

Santi grinned wider, and I only had to guess at what she saw on his screen. Santi was infamous for asking for nudes from women. And neither Santi nor Viv had shut up about Eve since they'd met her. Viv wouldn't do anything unless Kris was here, which meant Santi had won out this time.

"You should be," Santi agreed.

"About what?" Blaire asked.

I huffed. "Don't bother."

"Eve," Santi said dreamily.

Blaire looked between them in surprise. "What about my new roommate?"

"She moved in with you? I didn't know that," I said.

"Yeah, Jennifer moved in with Julian, and Eve took her spot the same afternoon. She'd been evicted because the owner was an assholes."

"Fuck," I muttered.

"Well, she's gorgeous," Viv said with a pout.

Blaire laughed. "Don't you have a girlfriend?"

"She'd be so down if she were here."

"Your loss," Santi said, pointing his thumb at himself, "my gain."

Good for Santi. He was king of *make the best of a bad situation*, and if he was hooking up with Eve, then he'd help keep the rest of the band happy, too. I hoped Eve could handle it. It sounded like she'd been through hell. I didn't want anyone to get hurt.

"You're being careful?" I asked Santi.

He arched an eyebrow. "I don't need the condom lecture."

Blaire took a big gulp of her water at that statement and said nothing.

"With her heart."

Santi held his hands up. "She was the one who said she just wanted a good time. I didn't even have to say anything."

"That sounds like Eve," Blaire admitted.

I was glad because I hadn't been careful with the heart of the girl back home. I'd let her get hurt. If I could save one more person from what I'd done to Blaire, then I would.

Michael abruptly stood and held up his phone. "I have a call."

Then, he left the restaurant. We all watched him answer a call outside.

"Wifey," Viv said with an arched eyebrow.

"Problem," Yorke corrected.

"It'll be fine. Virginia understands." I hoped.

By the skeptical looks on the rest of the band members' faces, I wasn't sure they were any more confident than I was. At least this was par for the course as far as Michael was concerned. He was always curmudgeonly. The only time I'd seen him happy was one section of the tour when Virginia and Maisie had shown up for a few stops.

The rest of lunch went off without a hitch. Michael returned, looking happier after speaking with his wife. We discussed the new songs and what Blaire had planned for videos while we worked.

"A documentary?" Viv asked, looking thoughtful.

"Of sorts," Blaire confirmed. "Like a *behind the scenes of the making of the album* sort of thing."

"Bobby would say yes," Santi pointed out.

"Bobby isn't here," I said. "Obviously, we'd have to work out compensation, but what do you think?"

"Yes," Yorke said.

Santi nodded. "Dude, I'm game."

Viv agreed.

And Michael just shrugged. "Sure. How is it different than anything else we've done? Now, we'll be filmed in Lubbock instead of all over the world."

He had a point, but Blaire flushed at the comment, and I didn't like that she looked smaller for it.

"It's just an idea," she said. "We'll do video content first, and I'll just be recording while you're working otherwise. We'll see what we get."

They all agreed that was good enough and then headed back to the studio. Blaire hung back with me as I paid the entire bill. She protested. Though no one else had. But I ignored her anyway.

"You didn't have to do that," she told me as we walked out of Dirk's.

"I wanted to."

"Well, thank you." She ruffled her bangs and looked up at me. "I appreciate it."

"No problem."

Her phone beeped, and she glanced at it. She rolled her eyes. "Honey."

"She seems invested."

"She is. I gave her stuff to do, but I think she wanted to come to the studio with me. I told her that y'all needed your privacy."

"She could swing by."

"You're sure?" she asked.

"If you want. I want whatever makes you happy and your life easier."

"Oh," she said, returning her eyes to her phone. "She's just used to having more of my time."

"And now, I'm monopolizing it?" I asked, stopping in

front of the studio.

"I wouldn't say that."

"Can I monopolize it?" I shot her a smile when her head popped back up to look at me in surprise.

"I..."

"Go out with me."

She blinked, her mouth slightly agape.

"And no, I'm not kidding."

I was pushing too much. I knew it and yet couldn't stop myself. She wouldn't even go to lunch with just me. After the rooftop, why would I think she wanted more from me? To *date* me? And yet my mouth didn't seem to care about that at all. I wanted to go out with her. I wanted her in my arms again. I wanted *her*.

She looked down and then back up at my face. She had to see how earnest I was. That I was sincere in all of this. It wasn't the same as we'd been when I last asked.

"Okay," she finally said.

I couldn't stop myself from asking, "Really?"

She laughed softly. "Really."

"I didn't think you'd agree."

"Then, why did you ask?"

"Because I couldn't help myself," I admitted. "When I'm with you, all I want is to be closer to you. It's like I got one single taste, and it will never be enough. I tried to leave you alone. I tried so fucking hard. Now that you're here and you're in my orbit again, I can't just let you go. I can't let you walk away."

She swallowed hard at my words. "Oh."

"I know you don't feel the same. I know that I hurt you too bad to ever have your trust..."

"You don't know that."

It was my turn to blink in surprise. I'd been beating

myself up for everything that had happened in the past. Reminding myself that if she said no, I deserved it. I'd left her. I'd fucked it up. And now, she was giving me...hope.

"Could you trust me again?"

She tucked a strand of hair behind her ear. "I'd like to try before you decide for me."

I laughed at that. Why did I keep assuming things for her? Why did I think that she would only see the worst of me? Because she always had, and I deserved it. Still, if she was willing, then I would take all I could get.

"Saturday?"

She nodded. "It's a date."

20

BLAIRE

I had agreed to a date with Campbell Abbey.

I had *agreed* to a *date* with *Campbell Abbey*.

My insides quivered at the thought as I got dressed Saturday night. Piper sat on my bed, and Eve hung out in the doorway. She was still acting like she expected us to tell her to leave.

"It's going to be fine," Piper said.

Eve tilted her head. "Might I suggest something sluttier?"

I snorted as I stared down at myself. I'd picked a form-fitting knee-length black dress and strappy nude heels. It was a date, but it was still just Campbell. I honestly had no idea what to wear.

"I second that suggestion," Piper said.

"What do you have in mind?"

Eve raised an eyebrow and disappeared. A few minutes later, she had a black leather skirt in hand and a dark green crop top. "I don't know your shoe size, but I have these black leather platforms that would make your ass look awesome."

I glanced at Piper. "What do you think?"

"I think Campbell would fall all over himself to get to you, no matter what you're wearing."

"Hmm," Eve said. "How did I get the drummer?"

We all laughed at that.

"Anyway, so you and Campbell, you dated before?"

I nodded. "Yeah, in high school before he left for LA."

"So, he's already seen you naked."

"Well, yes, but not in eight years." I wasn't as fit as I'd been in high school, but I ate better, so I usually called it a win. I taught girls all over the world not to judge their bodies. But then here I was, about to go on a date, worrying about my figure. Fuck, cultural stereotypes about body image were so insidious. "It doesn't matter."

"You're hot as hell," Eve said. "So, you're right; it doesn't matter. He's going to want to fuck you either way, right?"

"You sure get right to the point."

Eve frowned at that. "I didn't mean…"

"I appreciate it," Piper said. "I like a girl who says what's on her mind."

"Me too. It's just complicated. It's not about sex. The sex is the easy part, right?"

Eve and Piper both nodded emphatically. None of us had problems with that at all. It was the *getting intimate* part, the *forgetting the past* part, the *knowing where the hell this is going* part. Would it be easier if we just had a *fuck buddy* situation for a few weeks until he left? Would my heart ever survive it?

Just then, the doorbell rang.

"Guess you're wearing that," Eve said with a wink.

"Guess I am," I said with a laugh.

"Have so much fun," Piper said, standing and pulling me into a hug.

I grabbed my purse, stuffed my phone inside, and went

to answer the door. When I opened the door, all cognitive thought fled my mind. Campbell Abbey was standing before me in a black suit with a crisp white shirt underneath. I had seen him dressed like this in glossy magazine photos or on TV at award ceremonies. It was hard to avoid since my friends were obsessed with his music and, well, I enjoyed the Grammys...of which, he had a few. Hello, Song of the Year for "I See the Real You."

But I'd never seen him dressed like this *in person*.

Unless you counted Peyton and Isaac's wedding earlier this year, but I'd purposely not looked at him then. I hadn't wanted to see how good he looked.

And honestly, even prom night, he hadn't dressed like this.

I could remember that moment so clearly. As if it were yesterday. Neither of us had wanted to go to prom. I didn't have friends at school to hang out with exactly, and Jill had made overt overtures to get Campbell to ask her to go. When he declined, she took one of his friends in a huff. Campbell hadn't wanted to deal with any of that.

My mom, however, thought it was a rite of passage. She'd bought me the dress and given me the money to purchase tickets. When I'd told Campbell, he'd laughed and said we might as well put on the show.

I got dressed to the nines in a purple mermaid dress that clung to me invitingly. Campbell showed up in black trousers and a button-up. Hal offered him a tie, which he declined with an easy laugh. Pamela took a bunch of pictures of us and told me to have a good time. She stuffed condoms into my purse before I left.

Campbell helped me into his truck, and then we were off. Except we blew past the school on the way out of town. We only stopped when we reached the lake house at

Ransom Canyon that we'd pooled our collective prom-ticket money to rent for the evening.

When I stepped into the one-bedroom, it was nothing special at all, and somehow, it was our sanctuary. He turned on our song—"The Best of Me" by Starting Line—and we danced as if we were at prom. Then, he scooped me up and carried me to the bed. We didn't surface until I had to be home the next morning.

I blinked away the vision of prom and just how he'd swept me off my feet. Because as cherished as that night was in my memories, it didn't hold a candle to Campbell Abbey today.

"Wow," I breathed.

"My sentiments exactly," he said, his eyes crawling over my dress. He held a hand out to me. "Shall we?"

I swallowed. Once I crossed the threshold, there was no turning back. "Yes."

I put my hand in his and let him draw me out of the house. Instead of a beat-up pickup, he now had a shiny Range Rover. He helped me into the passenger seat.

"What were you thinking about?" he asked after he got into the driver's side and pulled out of the driveway.

"Hmm?"

"You looked like you were thinking something specific."

Damn. Sometimes, I forgot that he could read me like that.

"Oh. I was thinking about prom."

He chuckled. "Ah. What a great night."

"Do you ever wish that we'd gone?"

His eyes slid to mine, and he reached across the seat to take my hand. "I wouldn't change a thing about that night."

He was right, of course. I could see how it would have been fun to rub it into perfect Jill Patton's face that we were in love. But in the end, had it mattered? We'd been happier without the drama.

"So, what's the plan?"

"Dinner," he said with a conspiratorial smile.

Two could play at this game. If he could read me that well, I realized, now that I was looking at him, I could do the same.

"Oh dear, what do you have planned?"

His head whipped to me. "Why do you think I have something planned?"

"Because I know you."

A pleased grin came to his face. "That's right. You know me."

"Well?"

"Then, you also know that I'd never spoil the surprise."

I laughed. Also true.

So, I leaned back against the cool leather interior of the SUV and let The Civil Wars coming through the radio lull me. We arrived ten minutes later to the front of the Campbell's hotel.

I looked at him. "West Table?"

"Of sorts."

"If I'd known, then I could have just driven over here."

He came around to the other side to help me out. "Yes, but then I wouldn't have gotten to pick you up."

I couldn't fault his logic even if it was ridiculous. So, I put my hand in his and let him walk me to the front of the building. We stepped inside, and I turned right in the lobby to head toward West Table, but Campbell kept my hand in his.

"This way."

He directed me toward the set of elevators. I shot him a suspicious look, but his face was a mask. I had no idea what

I was walking into, and he was giving nothing away. I stepped onto the elevator with him, which whisked us straight to the top floor.

"After you."

I stepped out before him, and then we took the stairs up to the rooftop. After, I'd run out on him on the Fourth of July, I hadn't thought he'd bring me back up here. Yet here we were, and he didn't seem concerned at all. I guess we were past that.

When I stepped outside onto the dingy rooftop, where I'd been only a few weeks ago, my jaw dropped. The entire place had transformed. A red carpet had been rolled out from the entrance of the stairs all the way to a table set with a fancy white tablecloth, candlelight, and real china near the edge of the rooftop. A bucket of champagne was set next to it. Strings of Edison bulbs illuminated the roof. Soft instrumental music played from hidden speakers.

I choked in shock at the display. "Campbell, what did you do?"

He laughed. "I might have pulled some strings."

"This is...beautiful."

"Anything for you."

I stepped up to the table and admired what he'd done for me. It was stunning. I needed to document it. So, I took a minute to take pictures of the table and do a quick video of the walk down the red carpet. Campbell and I weren't in any of the pictures, but it was too pretty not to have photographic proof forever.

I tucked my phone away and sat down across from Campbell. He popped open the champagne, pouring each of us a glass like a pro. I sometimes forgot that he'd bartended before he got his big break with Cosmere.

A waiter appeared a moment later with menus, and after

we ordered our food, he left us all alone again. I sipped from my champagne and looked out across the city of Lubbock beyond.

"I can't believe you did all of this."

He grinned. "I'm glad you like it."

"Is it like this in LA?"

"Like...what?" he asked cautiously.

"Always fabulous and fancy."

"Oh," he said, looking off in the distance. "No, it's not. It shines kind of like gold-plated jewelry. It's beautiful on the outside, but once worn, it flakes off to reveal the dull interior."

"That sounds sad."

He took a sip of his drink and set it down. "I don't mean to make it sound sad. It's great. Honestly, so many people love it. It's its own microcosm of society, all in one place. You can't really understand LA without having b lived it. Is it weird to love and despise something at the same time?"

I shrugged. "I feel the same way about Lubbock. It's too small for my tastes, but it's home, and all my friends are here. I love being here, and I hate being here at the same time. I think we all feel that way about places."

"True. I'm always defending Lubbock to other people."

"I get that. Lubbock is kind of like what I assume a sibling is like," I said with a shrug. "You can make fun of them, but when someone else does, then you get pissed."

Campbell burst out laughing. "Wow. Yeah, that's exactly what Lubbock is like. I have never thought of it that way, and now, I will never think of it any other way."

"Glad I could help. But really, I think we're never perfectly happy where we are. The grass is always greener."

"True. Plus, LA gave me my break. It gave me everything I could ask of it. But sometimes, it feels like it's eating me."

"So, don't live there."

He shot me a look. "You make it sound so easy. Everything is in LA." He frowned. "Well, not everything."

My cheeks burned at that. I was not in LA. I was right here in front of him.

The food came a few moments later to keep me from feeling any more embarrassed. I picked at my butterfish as he dug into his still-bloody steak.

"Tell me about your work. Not the social stuff, but what you're doing with *Blaire Blush*. I read some of your articles."

"You did?" I asked with wide eyes.

It was his turn to blush a little. "A lot of them actually. I've been following you for a while."

"I didn't realize that." I cleared my throat. "Then, you already probably know."

"I like to hear you talk about it. When work comes up, your eyes light up."

God, how could he see that so easily when everyone else thought my work was just a big joke? Like I'd stumbled into some influencer position that wasn't really earned. Like it was just something to pass the time until I got a real job.

"Well, *Blaire Blush* started out as kind of an advice column. People, mostly young girls, would send in letters, and I'd answer them, using my psychology degree and the wellness certificates that I'd earned along the way, to help them. Sort of like unlicensed therapy. Usually, I'd direct them *to* therapy."

"You certainly got enough of that growing up that it must have come natural."

I nodded. "Well, my mom was not on board. She wanted me to stop doing it. She said I had no qualifications to help these people. They needed to see a professional. Then, I think she got jealous that my following bloomed practically overnight. It seemed I could help with everyone else's problems but my own."

He frowned at that. We both knew exactly what I was talking about. I could tell a million girls to get over their ex, and yet here I was, sitting with mine. Unable to let go or move on entirely from the man who had broken me.

"I still maintain the blog and do weekly advice columns. I hold *Blaire Blush* virtual workshops, where we go through my process to a better well-being. I also work with a few sustainable designers. A lot want to work with me and send me free samples and such, but I'm pretty picky about who I want to work with. I want the environmental impact to matter."

"So, you're basically a badass," Campbell concluded.

I chuckled and shrugged. "Sure. But I'm not an international superstar."

"Hey, don't do that. We don't have to judge our success on the same line. What Cosmere has doesn't diminish what you have with *Blaire Blush*."

"Look at me, not even taking my own advice," I said with a laugh. "You're right. We've both done exceptionally well. I'm proud of what I've accomplished. And even though I suppose I didn't want 'I See the Real You' to be your breakout, I'm glad all your dreams came true."

"Not all of them," he said. His voice was soft, and I almost didn't hear him whisper, "Not yet."

21

BLAIRE

*a*fter dinner, when Campbell invited me downstairs to hear the new song he was working on, I only hesitated for a moment. I wasn't stupid. I knew where this was heading. I knew the consequences of where it was heading as well. And still...I said yes.

The hotel he was staying in was more like a condo. It was a two-bedroom with a full kitchen and living room. Much fancier than any hotel I'd ever stayed in.

"This is nice," I told him, setting my purse on the coffee table.

"Yeah, I thought it'd be easier than renting a house or something since I wasn't sure how long I'd be in town, and now, I like the ease of it." He shrugged out of his suit coat and threw it across the back of a chair. Then, he set to rolling up the sleeves of his white button-up.

I tried not to salivate as inch after bare inch was revealed of his forearms. The way he immediately looked more relaxed out of the suit. I almost wanted to tell him he could change, but I also wanted to keep him in this outfit as long as I could.

"It helps that one of the bedrooms can be used as a music room."

He gestured to the open bedroom door. I peeked inside and found loose sheets of paper all over the bed with a few electric guitars on stands and lying on the pillows.

"So, this is where the magic happens."

He laughed and reached for the acoustic guitar. "Not really. It's more like a graveyard for discarded lyrics."

I picked up one of the pieces of paper and read the lyrics on them. "This doesn't seem bad."

He took it out of my hand, balled it up, and chucked it at the already-full rubbish bin. "Trash."

"Dramatic."

"You can't be a musician and not be a little dramatic," he said as he tuned the guitar. "I can't even believe that you just read that. I'll have to make it up to you with this song."

I followed him back out to the living room, where he perched on the armrest. I took a seat at his side and stared up at him, realizing just how similar this was to our viral video. There was a reason it had taken off after all. It felt entirely natural.

"I like the other songs you've been working on."

He plucked the strings. "Yeah, I think they're coming along. The band really picked up 'Alone' and ran with it."

"I love that one." It was about his mom and how he'd felt after her car crash. I couldn't even imagine singing that over and over again as he did.

"Viv singing the harmony on 'After You' is really bringing that one together."

"Do you have more ideas?"

"I have this one," he told me. His eyes shifted to mine and back down. "I haven't even shown the band yet. It's not quite right, but the chorus..." He chewed on his bottom lip thoughtfully. "The chorus is right."

Then, he strummed his guitar and began to sing. It wasn't a bop, like the other songs. It didn't make me want to get up on my feet and twirl and dance and sing at the top of my lungs. This was like sinking into a down comforter—soft and fluffy and all-encompassing.

His voice started off slow and almost mournful before growing more powerful as he approached that first chorus. His silky-smooth voice turned gruff as the words were ripped from his lungs, as powerful and emotional as if he were reliving the very experience that had created this song.

> *"Tell me this isn't the end.*
> *That I don't have to go on,*
> *Because I can't live with myself*
> *Knowing that you're better off without me*
>
> *The one that got away.*
> *The one that got away.*
> *The one...that got away.*
>
> *There you are*
> *With that cherry-painted smile*
> *And all-knowing eyes.*
> *Everything falls to a standstill,*
> *Because you're the one...*
>
> *The one that got away.*
> *The one that got away.*
> *The one...that got away. (away, away, away)"*

The words rolled over me in a torrent. Everything we'd

been and everything we could be, all wrapped up in one song. The others were about me, but this one reminded me so much of how I'd felt the first time I heard "I See the Real You." They weren't the same song by any stretch of the imagination, but they were both *mine*.

Campbell repeated the chorus a second time, skipping another verse and bringing it to a bridge before going through the chorus again. Finally, the soft strum of the song died off, and he opened his eyes to meet mine.

He cleared his throat slightly. "So...it's a work in progress."

I didn't respond because words couldn't accurately describe what I was feeling. So, I got to my feet, ignoring his look of trepidation, and pressed my lips to his.

His hands came to my sides as a smile shot to his face. "I guess you liked it?"

I pulled back just enough to look at him. "I loved it."

"Even without a second verse?"

"Campbell, shut up."

We weren't here to discuss the merit of the lyrics. It was only about how precisely it'd made me feel. Like I was young and in love all over again.

He removed the guitar from around his neck, placing it against the wall, and then he pulled me back against him. "Yes, ma'am."

When our lips touched, everything went absolutely silent in my mind. He'd kissed me on the Fourth, and it had been miraculous, and yet somehow, it paled to this. I hadn't been ready then. I hadn't been anything but tentative and unsure and terrified that he'd hurt me again. I was none of those things now.

I didn't know what our future held. One glance at this beautiful hotel room told me that Lubbock wasn't forever for him. He could leave at any time and take my big heart with him. But if I didn't try, I'd regret it forever.

So, when he kissed me, I kissed him back, and I let the entire world go with it.

"Blaire," he groaned, pulling me into his lap as he settled onto the couch. "God, I've fucking missed you."

"Mmm."

"The way you taste." He kissed down my neck. "The way you smell." His hands tightened on my dress. "The way you feel."

He picked me up and effortlessly dropped me back on the couch. His body covered mine.

"Every single thing about you," he breathed in my ear.

"Oh God."

My legs came up on either side of his narrow hips. They tightened on him, holding him in place against me.

"Every single thing?"

He brushed my bangs out of my eyes, so he could look down into them. "Every single thing."

I leaned forward to capture his lips. It felt like a spiral, like diving into a never-ending kiss, drawing me deeper and deeper down. And I didn't want to stop. I wanted all of this. I wanted all of him.

The kiss morphed in the span of a breath. Suddenly, we were moving with an urgency that bordered on magnetic. As if we couldn't even hope to pull ourselves apart.

With all the weeks of wanting and the months of orbiting each other and the years that had separated us, it all came down to here, in this place. His body pressed to mine. Our lips sealed like a promise.

But there were no real promises here.

None truly.

Just pent-up want and flushed desire and a hazy glow of

need. Something inexplicable and somehow entirely basic. After all this time, falling into each other's arms felt as easy as breathing. As easy as drowning.

He thickened in his trousers as he shifted forward. The layers of material did nothing to hide what was happening to us. The scents of arousal in the air, the wetness building in the black thong I'd put on, knowing where this night might end, and his cock hard against me.

I moaned, tugging on his shirt and trying to get closer.

And it was in this moment, as his hands sought purchase on my bare skin and his lips trailed down my throat and everything superheated to an inferno inside me, that I discovered all my anger had been misdirected. It had just been a wall I put up between us. Because if I'd given just an inch, I'd have ended up right here. Where I always wanted to be.

Hating Campbell was much easier than wanting him. So much easier than loving him.

He, the breaker of hearts, sunderer of kingdoms, and destroyer of worlds.

Because that inch I'd given had led precisely here. My heart cracked, just a small fissure, just a line that opened to a chasm. And it let him in.

I had no hope of escaping it now that he was in my life again.

"Blaire," he whispered my name like a prayer. As if he worshipped at the throne of my unending power. As if he, too, were trapped in this moment that put me equally back in his heart.

"Yes," was the only word I could utter.

I'd only wanted one thing more than Campbell Abbey. And that thing was impossible. And he no longer was.

He kissed his way down my front. My breasts were

trapped by the black material of my dress, but he nipped at my nipples through the fabric. I forced my hips upward in delight and desire. It was his turn to groan at the feel of me against his cock.

But Campbell had never been a selfish lover. Even in high school, when he'd been my first, he'd wanted to be sure that I enjoyed it as much or more than he did. He was never, ever like the other boys who offered so little and took so much. Only in the end, of course.

He moved lower, trailing kisses across my stomach, and then lower. He drew my knee up and added a kiss to it. Then, he slid to his knees on the floor and began to ravage every inch of my milky-white skin, leading up, up, up. I quivered under his practiced tongue as he met the edge of my panties.

"Please," I begged, not caring the slightest about what I sounded like.

He made a noise of approval at that word. Then, he hooked his finger into the side of my panties and pulled it aside. The first touch of him against my core drew another moan from my lips. He pushed my legs farther apart, letting them fall open. Then, he slid his thumb up and down across the folds of my pussy. Every part of me quivered. My body was so starved for his attention that I could barely hold on.

"This?" he asked as he pushed one finger inside of me.

"Oh God, yes."

"More?"

He slid in another finger, curling inward and then dragging slowly back out.

"More," I pleaded. I couldn't be satisfied with just his fingers. I needed all of him.

He wrenched my underwear over my hips and discarded them carelessly to the side before diving back in, licking and sucking my clit. My hands fisted into the couch as I came apart at his ministrations. And I couldn't be quiet even if I wanted to. There was no hope for me as he circled my clit with his tongue and worked his fingers in and out of me. There was only hanging on for dear life and praying that I came out on the other side.

My breathing grew heavy. I was panting on the couch. As my body built into a crescendo, I held on tighter, knowing what was coming.

"Fuck," I gasped when I finally tipped over the edge. My body shuddered and contracted around his fingers. My vision dipped and blurred. And after it all came down, I curled in on myself with a soft groan of pleasure.

He kissed my hip and sat back on his heels with a satisfied grin. "I like watching you come."

I flushed. Even after all that.

With a short laugh at my embarrassment, he hoisted me up and threw me over his shoulder.

I gasped, scrambling for purchase while I dangled over his back. "What are you doing?"

"Carrying you."

"Oh my God, I can walk."

He slapped my ass playfully. "Not if I can help it."

"Awfully cocky," I said as we stepped into his bedroom.

He flipped me forward, letting my back fall onto the bed. "I just watched you come on my fingers." He went to work on his shirt, opening button after button. He wrenched it out of his pants and ripped open the black belt at his waist. "I think I have a right to be a little cocky."

I leaned back on my elbows and watched the show reveal the six-pack that I distinctly did not remember from high school. And the V-line that dipped down into his pants.

I salivated as he popped the button on his pants and let them hang open for my imagination to go wild.

He crooked a finger at me, and I moved toward him, drawn like a moth to a flame. His finger came under my chin and tipped it upward. "Now, imagine what it's going to be like on my cock."

I licked my lips. Oh, I could imagine. I remembered what it had been like eight years ago, and Campbell was more muscular, more confident than he'd been then. We'd learned together. Now, we were older and wiser, and we had all the time we wanted to enjoy it. He might be cocky, but I'd bet he had reason to be.

He pressed one more kiss to my mouth before lifting me back onto my feet and turning me away from him. He tugged the zipper slowly down my back until it reached the base of my spine. Then, he pushed the sleeves over my shoulders. The dress was tight, but with little resistance, it fell to a heap on the ground.

"That's better," he said as I spun around.

He withdrew his cock from his boxers and stroked it once, twice, three times. I looked on the whole time, salivating at how little he cared that I was watching him touch himself. He wanted me to see exactly what I'd done to him. How he could barely contain himself in my presence.

I stepped forward and took him in my hand. He inhaled sharply at my first touch.

"Fuck," I murmured.

"Yes," he said through his teeth. His eyes were closed. "Fuck, baby. Fuck."

I felt so powerful. This international superstar was barely able to stand before me, helpless for wanting me. It was sometimes difficult to pull apart the layers of Campbell because when he fell to his feet, he was just the boy I'd loved, but as he'd unabashedly stroked his cock, he'd turned into the rockstar. And I found that I liked both versions. I *wanted* both.

He grinned at me. "I need you."

I nodded. "Yes."

He reached into a desk drawer and retrieved a condom. There was the tear of foil, and then he sheathed himself.

He pressed a kiss to my nose and then my mouth. "Going to come for me again?"

"If you're lucky."

"I have you, don't I?"

There was no arguing with that. At this moment, I was unequivocally his.

Then, he took complete control. He rotated me, bending me forward at the waist. As his fingers explored my core, slicking through my wetness, anticipation tore through me. He stroked in and out of me a few times before aligning the tip of his cock with my opening.

He slid in roughly, meeting no resistance, and I gasped at the pure bliss of him.

He must have been barely holding himself back because as soon as he was inside of me, he unleashed. He was fierce and unrelenting. I could barely keep up with him pounding inside of me. I reached back for his hand, and he laced his fingers with mine, using the other hand to grasp my hip and leverage himself deeper into me.

Everything mounted as desire turned to a hazy, disoriented need. I built up to an insurmountable cliff, and all I had to do was hit that peak and fall over the edge. Campbell held me there as he worked himself to the same point.

I squeezed his hand. The increased tempo of my moans urging him on.

"Don't stop," I gasped.

"Fuck," he said.

Then, I dropped, plummeting into the great nowhere. And he followed me. We cried out together. Passion and pleasure releasing all at once. Until there was nothing left. Until I was utterly spent.

Campbell slumped forward over my body. "Fuck," he gasped. Then pressed a kiss to my shoulder.

As he withdrew, I shuddered all over at the loss of him in every tender and sensitive bit of my body. He tossed the condom as I curled into a ball on the bed. Then, he crawled in after me, cradling me against him.

"You're perfection," he whispered into my shoulder.

I rolled over to look at him. With my hand on his cheek, I stole another kiss. "Don't go."

He drew me in closer. "I'm right here."

And I wanted nothing more than to believe him.

PART IV

TIGHTROPE

22

CAMPBELL

*B*laire was still in my arms the next morning. I'd had her several times before we passed out, utterly exhausted sometime in the early hours. And yet I woke up, starving for her.

"Babe?" I murmured against her bare skin.

I kissed her shoulders, shifting lower to press a kiss to her side, stomach, waist.

"Mmm," she muttered incoherently. She reached for me in her sleep, and I kissed her again.

"Babe?"

Lower. Still lower.

She groaned but said nothing.

I hooked one of her legs over my shoulder as I settled myself between her legs. My body ached for her in a way I hadn't remembered was possible. When I thought about me and Blaire in high school, I'd always assumed it was just the rush of hormones that made everything so intense. No one had known about us, and we had been insatiable.

And now, here I was, all this time later, and I still couldn't get enough of her.

If I had it my way, she'd be in my bed every night. No panties ever again. Just like she was now as I buried my head between her legs. I licked gently at her clit and spread her lips with my fingers. I stroked at her opening to find that she was already wet for me.

Had she been dreaming about us? Or was she still wet from everything that had happened last night? Either way, I liked it and wanted it for always.

"Babe," I muttered again as I worked her clit with my tongue.

Her eyes slowly fluttered open, and I met her gaze as I slid two fingers inside of her. She came fully awake then as I stroked her body.

"Oh. Ohhh," she gasped. "I thought I was still dreaming."

"What were you dreaming about?"

"You." Her mouth opened on a moan as I fingered her again and again. "You were inside me."

"We can remedy that," I told her.

I licked her one more time before grabbing another condom and sliding it over my already-aching and heavy cock. I'd woken up hard. Clearly, I'd been dreaming the same dreams.

I scooped her up into my arms as I fit our bodies together like a puzzle. She arched into me as I slid deep into her.

"Campbell," she groaned.

I kissed her. "I like the taste of you on my lips in the morning."

She shuddered, a blush coming to her cheeks. "You're dirty."

"I don't hear any complaints."

"And you won't hear any."

I had her cradled against me. Our bodies moved to a perfect tempo, as if following the buildup of a song. Our fucking was the only music I needed right now.

"Fuck, that's the best sound," I said as the slapping of our bodies together created a wet smack.

"Oh God, I'm going to come."

She tightened her arms around me. We could barely move with how tangled we were together. And still, somehow, even though the movements were smaller, they became more intense, more powerful. I was right on the cusp as well.

And as she came all over my cock, I lost it, too. I came fast and hard, buried deep inside of her. My body went boneless, and I collapsed forward over her.

"Well," she murmured, kissing my temple, "that was quite a wake-up."

I grinned at her lazily. "Good morning."

"Better than my dreams."

I sprawled out across the bed and sighed. "Definitely." I glanced over at her. "You hungry? I could pop downstairs and get coffee and bagels."

"Coffee," she said with an excited smile. "Yes, please. Iced coffee preferably."

"Excellent. Feel free to use the shower or whatever you need."

I kissed her one more time, pulled on jeans and a T-shirt, and then padded downstairs. I ordered drinks and pastries at Coffee and talked to the barista for a few minutes. The employees had been starstruck the first couple weeks I was in here, but by now, they all knew me, and I was just a person to them. I preferred it that way.

Despite not ever posting to social media, I did *have* it on my phone. So, I scrolled my feed for a few minutes before I stopped on a video Blaire had posted last night. When the hell had she found the time?

It was of her walking toward the dinner I'd set up. Red carpet, fancy lights, rooftop view, and all. It had over a million views. She'd posted a videos of the band that had gotten a couple million views. Nothing like our "I See the Real You" challenge video. Probably because I hadn't shown up in any of the other ones.

There was plenty of speculation about us. Some people thought we were dating. Some thought we were just friends. Most people thought the whole thing was a publicity stunt. As much as I wanted to scream from the rooftops that she was all mine, I saw the wisdom in letting it ride on social media. The press would have a field day if we confirmed anything. And sometimes, it was easier to just say nothing than to let them in a fraction of an inch more than they were before.

Against my better judgment, I clicked on the comments for the video. Many of them were her followers congratulating her, but even more were people wondering who exactly had set this up. And at the very top, with twenty-eight thousand likes, was Nate King with a comment that said, *Secrets, secrets*.

Well, if that wasn't a fucking pot-stirrer comment.

Blaire had still been posting videos she had of her and Nate. She posted two, sometimes three times a day. So, it wasn't surprising that she'd used the content she already had. But now, people thought that Nate had done this for her. Not only that, but a large portion also apparently thought he was proposing.

A spot of jealousy opened in my stomach at those comments. See, this was why I didn't read any of this shit.

Nate wasn't proposing. They weren't even dating. Blaire

was upstairs in *my* bed. Why did I care what a bunch of people thought of it?

I picked up our coffee and headed back upstairs, trying to shake that feeling. If I hadn't read the stupid comments, I'd still be in that blissed-out place. Not with my head all fucked up.

"Blaire?" I called as I walked into the room.

The shower abruptly cut off, and she came out in nothing but a white towel. My jaw dropped as I caught sight of her shapely legs and the tops of her breasts. Her hair was wet and dripped as she towel-dried.

"Hey," she said.

"Fuck the coffee," I said, dropping the coffee and pastries as I grabbed her and threw her back on the bed again.

She giggled but didn't protest as we went at it again. Fuck, I would never, ever tire of her. Only after we were both panting and spent did I finally release her.

"Coffee is going to be cold," I breathed against her skin.

"Mine was already cold. You're the only one suffering here."

"Oh, yeah, I'm really suffering."

She laughed. "I can see that."

She kissed me again and then came to her feet, stepping into panties and one of my T-shirts. She took a sip of her coffee and peeked into the brown paper bag full of pastries and bagels.

We went back into the living room and ate.

"When did you have time to upload that video last night?"

She blinked at me. "What video?"

"Of the dinner."

She looked at me, confused. "I didn't upload it."

"Uh...it has a million views."

In a second, she snatched up her phone and was staring at it in shock. "I mean, I'd planned to upload it in a few days but probably to my Stories. That way, it wouldn't be the same day that it happened."

"Then, what happened?"

She shook her head and then sighed. "Oh fuck, I didn't even think. I added it to the shared account I have with Honey for content. She usually handles when and what goes up unless it's something I say specifically. Clearly, I did not say anything yesterday because I was busy." She bit her lip. "Is it bad?"

"Well, apparently, half of the internet thinks Nate is proposing."

"What?" she asked with a giggle. "Why would they think that?"

"Probably because he commented."

She scrolled. "Oh, I see it. He's ridiculous. That comment could mean anything. And anyway, I see *your* name nearly as much as his."

"So, your followers don't know you broke up?" I asked, trying for calm and levity, but by the look on her face, I hadn't managed it.

She was smirking at me. She put her phone down and climbed into my lap, straddling me with her powerful thighs. "Campbell Abbey, are you jealous?"

"Why would I be? You're in my bed."

"That I am," she agreed with a teasing smile.

"And I am the first person to be like *fuck the press, fuck social media, fuck followers wanting to be in my business.* Whatever you want to share is up to you."

"But..."

"But I don't like seeing his name on your posts like that."

"Nate and I are just friends. We were never emotionally

invested. It was always more business than it was anything else. We ended on good terms. In fact, he's supposed to be in town this week to record some more videos."

"Even after the breakup?"

"It was more a mutual understanding that it was going to be strictly business from now on. He was cool with it. I swear."

I had doubts that a guy like that took to losing someone like Blaire that easily. But maybe she was right. I was still friends with some of my LA exes. They had always been temporary things, and ending the sexual side of things hadn't affected the friendships.

"You could meet him," she offered.

"I'm sure he'd fucking love that."

She shrugged. "Who cares?"

I chuckled at her nonchalance. I wasn't threatened by Nate King, but a part of me knew LA was beckoning in a few weeks, and Nate was here. I didn't want to think about the future, but it suddenly felt like I had no future without her.

"Fine. But you're mine."

She pressed her mouth to mine. "No question."

23

BLAIRE

I had been shoved into a time machine.

Eight years ago, every waking moment had belonged to Campbell Abbey.

And now, eight years later, my entire existence belonged to him again.

I stayed at his place every night. We ate all our meals together. We texted all day when I wasn't at the studio with him. My friends smirked behind their hands, but not a one of them complained that I had been spending all my time with him. How could they when our time was entirely limited?

This was the first break I'd had in days and mostly because I'd promised to do these videos with Nate. No matter what I was feeling about Campbell, I couldn't let my work suffer. I still had to be on top of things. And I hadn't seen Honey in almost a week. She messaged me constantly about work stuff, but I'd been working from Campbell's hotel room or the recording studio rather than at home.

I met her at my place when I went home to get ready to record videos with Nate.

"Okay," Honey said, staring down at her iPad when I finished blowing out my long hair, "this is the list I have for videos with Nate. We have ten planned for the next couple hours. Plus, the additional behind-the-scenes footage that I'll take care of."

"Sounds good, Honey."

I applied a full face of makeup, knowing what my skin would look like otherwise under the glaring lights. For most of my live videos and such, I just wore mascara and maybe some concealer. I liked to be as natural as possible for my viewers to normalize acceptance of skin texture and the like. But these videos were different.

"You've been busy the last couple days."

"Yep."

"Are you and Campbell..." Honey trailed off.

I couldn't hide my grin. "I'm not ready to talk about it."

Honey arched an eyebrow. "Not ready to talk about it or you're going to move to LA here soon and leave me behind?"

I laughed. "Definitely not the latter."

"You sure? You two seem serious."

"I don't know what's going to happen. Kind of just living in the moment." I puckered my lips, making a red kissy face at the mirror. "Okay, I'm set."

Honey and I piled into my Lexus and drove to downtown Lubbock. We were surprisingly close to Campbell's building. I'd spent an hour in his place learning one of the dances we were doing today. Most of the other videos were trends, where we mostly lip-synced songs I'd already known or comedians that I'd listened to on repeat so I knew my part. It wasn't that hard. It was mostly just forcing myself to record them. That was why it was nice to have recording days with Nate. There was no backing out.

"Blaire!" he said, scooping me up and twirling me around in a circle when he saw me.

I laughed and stepped out of his embrace. "Hello, apparent fiancé."

He chuckled and winked. "What can I say? I move very fast. So fast in fact that I made a beautiful rooftop dinner for us without even being present."

"Shut up." I smacked his arm.

"We are so using this footage," Honey said.

I hadn't even realized that she had her phone up. "Oh my God, did you capture our hug?"

"Yessss. We should absolutely set this to music. Your fans will eat it up."

Nate arched an eyebrow at me. "And how would the new beau feel about that?"

"Don't be an ass, King."

He winked at me again. "Just seeing if I still have a chance."

"You're ridiculous." I snorted and strode away from him to watch the footage on Honey's phone.

When Honey played it back in slow motion, it looked like one of those old movies where the soldier came back from war. She was right that we should post this. But Nate wasn't wrong that Campbell probably wouldn't like it. He'd been cool about Nate showing up again after our talk about it just being business. And Campbell was supposed to be here at the end of filming to meet him. Maybe that would help.

"All right," I said, "let's get started."

A few hours later, we had the ten planned videos and who even knew how many additional videos we'd managed to get. When Nate and I got together, ideas just spilled from a fount. Whatever we started with, we almost always doubled because we couldn't stop from coming up with more and more. There was a reason we'd both increased our audience since working together.

Not that anything had done for my audience what one video with Campbell did. I'd never seen numbers like that. And I'd never see them again. Well, not unless we went *very* public with our relationship. Something neither of us was keen on doing. Not to something this new and special. I wasn't even ready for my assistant to be in the know. I couldn't imagine the rest of the world.

"That was a great day," Nate said.

"It really was. I feel so accomplished."

He leaned back against his yellow Jeep Wrangler Rubicon that he'd driven up from Midland. "So, are you going to tell me what's up?"

I shrugged. "Sorry about the video. Honey posted it without my knowledge, and then I didn't know that everyone would think you were proposing."

"Yeah, I don't care about that." He laughed and pushed up the sleeves of his white button-up. "It was kind of fun."

"Shit stirrer."

He pinched my arm playfully. "So, I'm guessing that was Campbell?"

I bit my lip and nodded.

"Are you two an item? How did that even happen?"

"Would you believe me if I said that I got mobbed?"

His eyes rounded. "What?"

"Yeah, on the Fourth of July, right after the 'I See the Real You' challenge video."

"That video fucking blew up. But seriously, mobbed? Are you okay?"

I nodded. "I'm kind of claustrophobic. So, some of it was just that. I got away and ran, but all my friends were at the fireworks already, and no one was answering. So, I called Campbell."

"Ah," he said with a knowing smirk.

"So, it kind of happened like that."

"Well, lately, I've had some crazy-ass shit happen to me, too." He raised his eyebrows. "Involving you, actually."

"What? What do you mean?"

"I don't know. There was this girl who kept messaging me. I thought she was hitting on me at first, but then I think she was snooping for information on you. She wanted me to confirm whether or not we were dating." He shrugged. "It was bizarre. I wonder if it was like how you got mobbed."

"Yeah. Campbell Soup girls."

Nate blinked. "Excuse me?"

"Uh...that's what Campbell's fans are called."

"That's a terrible name."

"Tell me about it."

We both burst into laughter. It was nice and comfortable. I'd been a little worried that there would be some lingering...*thing* here with me and Nate. But it just wasn't there. We looked *great* on camera. We were entirely authentic because we enjoyed each other's company. But there wasn't anything else there.

"So, what now?" he asked. "When's he leaving?"

"I'm not sure. He has to go back to LA in, like, two weeks."

Nate crossed his arms over his chest. "And you're going to, what? Go with him?"

"I haven't gotten that far."

He sighed. "Can I say that I'm worried about you without you getting mad or thinking I'm coming on to you?"

"You don't have to worry about me."

"Just be careful, B." He shot me a mournful look. "He's a rockstar, you know?"

"I can handle myself."

"Yeah, but you've only known him for a few weeks. This, here in Lubbock, isn't real."

I flinched at those words. Because everything felt damn real to me. I knew he was going back to LA, but it didn't feel like it had last time.

"We actually went to high school together."

"So, you have experience with him leaving."

"I guess I do," I admitted. "But it's not the same."

He looked skeptical. "I don't want to push this, but he lives in LA. He's going to be on tour. You know what that's like?"

"Yes."

Because I remembered exactly the one night I'd ended up backstage at a Cosmere concert. There had been girls on top of girls, all scrambling for Campbell's inebriated attention.

"I don't want you to get hurt, is all. I'm looking out for you."

"This is different," I told him.

"I hope it is, for your sake."

Nate and I were close, and I could see where he would think the worst. That Campbell was just using me while he was in town. The way that Santi was using Eve. Her eyes were wide open that their relationship would end the minute he returned to LA. My eyes were not like that. I didn't want to lose Campbell a second time. But no one, let alone Nate, knew that we'd even had a relationship before.

"Look, keep this to yourself, but we were together in high school," I told him.

He arched an eyebrow. "It's been a long time since high school."

I shook my head. "No, Nate. Like 'I See the Real You' was written for me."

His eyes widened as he realized what that meant. "Well, no wonder that video looked so good."

"Yeah," I said with a laugh, pushing my hair behind my ear. "We were each other's worlds. It finally feels like the universe has aligned for us again. It's not the same. I promise."

He nodded. "All right. Well, I said my piece anyway. I hope he doesn't fuck it all up."

"Yeah. Me too."

"Blaire," Honey said, making me jump. I'd completely forgotten she was there. "Can I send the videographer home?"

I put my hand to my heart. "Sure. Thanks, Honey."

"Also, Campbell texted." She waved my phone at me. "I didn't look at it."

"Thanks." I took the phone from Honey and checked the message as she headed toward the videographer. "He's on his way."

Nate arched an eyebrow. "I guess that's my cue."

But there was Campbell Abbey, striding down the street in black jeans, a white T-shirt, and Ray-Bans. His hands were shoved into his pockets, and he looked off in the distance.

I didn't run and throw my arms around him like I wanted to. We were in public, and there were *a lot* of cameras around. I didn't need the world to know about us before we were quite ready for them to.

He stopped in front of us, pulling off his shades. "Hey."

I bit my lip. "Hey."

"You must be Nate." Campbell offered him his hand.

Nate glanced at me once and then put his hand in Campbell's. They shook a little longer and more forceful than was strictly necessary.

"I've heard a lot about you."

"Same," Nate said. "Blaire was just saying how you're leaving in two weeks."

I rolled my eyes. "Nate, don't be a dick."

He laughed. "I want to make sure he's going to take care of you."

"Again, I can take care of myself."

"And, yes," Campbell said, "I plan to."

Nate shrugged. "If you say so."

"Y'all should chill," I said with an eye roll.

Campbell smiled then and looked like he was fighting not to kiss me. "All right. All right."

Nate nodded, ruffling my hair. "I'm going to head back home. Let's do this again soon."

"Sure." I fixed my hair. "I'll send you a text."

"Sounds good." He tilted his head at Campbell. "Nice to meet you. Blaire's special, so...take good care of her."

"Will do."

Campbell watched him walk away, and I smacked him on his arm. "What was that?"

"He's into you."

I laughed. "I was just thinking that there was nothing between us at all. Because all I see is you."

"It's hard not to kiss you."

"Really hard," I said, biting my lip.

"Can I steal you?"

"Always."

"Oh, and...I meant to ask you before you left this morning. The Wrights are throwing a birthday party for my aunt Helene. Would you want to...go with me?"

I arched an eyebrow. "Like a date? In public?"

He nodded. "Well, at least public with my family and the Wrights."

That was a big step. So far, we hadn't done a single thing in public. In some way, it wasn't that different from what we'd done as teens. Only we had a lot more time and room for sex.

"I'd like that."

"Good." He took a step forward until he was very nearly in my face. "Now, let's get you back to my bed."

I laughed and nodded. "Yes, please."

24

BLAIRE

*T*he Wrights were Lubbock royalty. There were five Wright siblings—Jensen, Austin, Landon, Morgan, and Sutton—and after their father had died, Jensen had taken over as CEO of Wright Construction. Even though he'd handed over the company to his younger sister Morgan, he still lived like the king he was.

My eyes widened at his enormous house as Campbell parked his Range Rover on the street. I'd been to Jensen's lake house, but nothing had really prepared me for his freaking mansion. It felt surreal sometimes that I was in this Wright orbit. They'd been so closed off for so long, but now that the siblings were all attached and with the appearance of their cousins, their circle had opened.

"Jesus, this place is huge," I said as I stepped out, slinging my *Blaire Blush* bag on my shoulder.

"In LA, this place would be ten million dollars," Campbell said.

"Or more."

He nodded. "Yep."

"What's your place like in LA?"

"Not like this," he said with a laugh, sliding an arm across my shoulders.

I chuckled as we headed toward the front door. I couldn't imagine Campbell having a massive house like this. It would be a lot of space for one person. At least Jensen was married to Emery and had two kids that lived with him. Plus, his son Colton from his first marriage. He lived full-time in New York City but was in Lubbock for holidays.

Campbell knocked on the front door, and before he even finished, it sprang open. Emery stood in the doorway with her three-month-old, Logan, on her hip. "Hey!" she said. "You made it."

"We did," I said, giving her a quick hug and pinching the baby's adorable cheeks.

Emery's eyes drifted up to Campbell's, and she blushed a little. Someone was a Cosmere fan. "Hi, Campbell."

"Emery," he said with a head nod.

She noticed we were joined at the hip, and her smile widened. "I see the rumors are true."

"Rumors?" I asked as we stepped inside.

"That you two are dating," Morgan said, appearing around the corner.

"Who is spreading that rumor?" I asked.

"No one." Morgan sealed her lips and threw away the key. "I mostly guessed."

I glanced at Campbell to see if he was worried by that news. It wasn't that we were hiding it. Well, we were but not from our friends and family. I didn't want to be mobbed again like on the Fourth of July. But I didn't want to hide away in his hotel room forever, as much fun as it'd been.

"You guessed right," Campbell said.

"Are you getting excited for the wedding?" I asked Morgan.

Patrick had proposed last Fourth of July, and Nora was the wedding planner for their upcoming nuptials at Wright Vineyard.

Morgan gulped. "I left Patrick in charge of a lot of it."

"No, you didn't," Emery said with a laugh. "You're delegating by sending him to meetings and then having him call you to get your opinion."

Morgan huffed. "I might be a bit of a control freak. But it's going to be beautiful."

"Hey, y'all," Jensen said, stepping into the entranceway. He took Logan from Emery's arm and then shook Campbell's hand. "Glad you could make it. Help yourself to drinks. The rest of the party is out back at the pool."

"Don't have to tell me twice," Emery said with a teasing glint in her eye as she snaked an arm through mine and carried me away from the guys.

We grabbed drinks from the kitchen and then stepped outside in the July heat. She headed for the pool to check on her daughter, Robin. Austin and Julia were playing with her in the pool, and she kept gurgling excitedly.

My friends had staked out a row of chairs poolside. Annie posed for Jennifer's camera while Sutton watched her son, Jason, cannonball into the pool with their two-year-old, Madison, toddling behind fearlessly, jumping into her husband, David's, arms. Piper and Nora were slathered in sunscreen and tanning oil, evading the kids splashing.

Landon and Heidi were in the pool with their three-year-old, Holden, while the two babies, Hudson and Harrison, were passed out under an umbrella. Emery's sister's kids, Lilyanne and Bethany, were playing in the deep end with Aly. And Jensen's son Colton was egging them on. A bunch of kids I didn't recognize were there, too. They must have all invited friends. New, unfamiliar faces. I loved it.

Though I didn't see the birthday girl or any of the rest of Campbell's family, except Nora. I flopped down on a chair next to her. "Hey, where's your family?"

"Inside," she said. "Being grown-ups."

"Hollin is inside with them, too," Piper said with a devious grin. "So, they can't be that grown-up."

Nora snorted. "So true."

"Campbell stayed inside, too."

Nora arched an eyebrow. "You came with my brother?"

I bit my lip and nodded. "Yeah, I did."

Nora looked between me and Piper. "Am I the last to know?"

"No, no one knows really. We haven't made any public statements about it."

"Why would you? That sounds terrible. You know what his life is like."

"See," Piper said. "You don't have to go public." She added air quotes on the words. "Just enjoy your time while he's here."

I hadn't seen much of Piper since I'd started dating Campbell, but the time we'd had together at the house, I'd confessed all my fears about the relationship. About him leaving and no one knowing we were dating or everyone knowing we were dating and what the future looked like. I didn't worry about any of it when we were together, but it crept in when I was alone. I didn't have answers, and I didn't know if I was ready to ask for them.

"I have been at his place every day this week. I'm enjoying myself."

Nora covered her ears. "Little sister sitting right here." We all laughed at her reaction, but she removed her hands and rolled her eyes. "I don't want to know about my brothers' sex lives, thank you very much. But I do like to see them happy. And you wouldn't remember this, but I was one of the few people who knew you and Campbell were dating in high school."

I blinked at her. "What? No, I don't remember that at all."

"He was a senior, and I was a freshman. Dad made him drive me home after practice sometimes, and we'd swing by Sonic."

My cheeks heated. "Oh!"

I had no recollection of Campbell ever having Nora with him when he had come by Sonic. But she remembered that. My tunnel vision when it came to Campbell was intense.

Piper smacked her arm. "You knew this all along and never told us?"

Nora laughed. "Hey! Clearly, Blaire didn't want anyone to know."

"I appreciate it."

"Yeah, yeah," Piper said with a sigh. "I just hate not knowing things about my best friend."

"Aww, love you, bestie." I squeezed her tight. I turned back to Nora. "And where is your new roommate?"

"West went home for the weekend to see his family."

"West, is it?" Piper drawled.

"Yeah. I guess his friends call him West. No one really calls him Weston."

I smirked at her reddening cheeks. "Does someone have a crush?"

"What?" she gasped. "No way. He's just...my roommate."

Piper and I shot each other a glance. Yeah, right.

"Besides...I'm still upset about August. I saw him again Thursday at Starbucks and had a breakdown. West made us go get ice cream because I was sad."

"That was nice of him," I said.

Piper wrinkled her nose. "Sorry about August. You should forget that loser."

"I know. I'm trying. I just...never dated before August. So, all of this is so out of my depth. He was the one, you know?"

Piper looked like she was going to tell her exactly where she could shove the whole "the one" business, but I quickly cut in, "I get it. First, find happiness and love with yourself, and the rest will be there, waiting when you're ready."

She nodded. "Thanks, Blaire."

That was when the rest of the party came out of the house. They ushered the birthday girl, Helene Wright, into a chair. She laughed at the entire display as we crowded in around her. Then, Jordan and Julian came out of the house, carrying a brightly lit sheet cake between them.

Helene covered her mouth with her hands in delight.

It had been a hard few years for Helene. She'd moved to Lubbock to be back home after her cancer diagnosis. The boys had followed her here, and though she was fully recovered, she was much more fragile than she had been before. I loved that they wanted to do it bigger and better for her each year.

Campbell stepped up to my side, snaking an arm around my waist as he sang "Happy Birthday" perfectly in tune. It was unfair. No one should sing this song this well. He smirked at me, as if reading my mind.

Then, the cake was placed in front of Helene, and Jordan said, "Blow out the candles," at the same time Julian cried, "Make a wish!"

Helene laughed, closed her eyes, and then blew out the candles, all in one long breath. She stood then and kissed both of her sons on their cheeks. Then, Sutton, who worked in a local downtown bakery, squeezed in and began to expertly cut up the cake.

Campbell drew me in a little closer, pressing a kiss to the top of my head. "You're my wish."

My eyes met his, and the entire party fell away. I was here with him, and we'd never had this a day in our life. I hadn't quite realized how much it would mean to me to be here with him.

"You're mine."

"I am," he agreed. He tucked my hand into his. "Come with me. I want you to meet some people."

"Okay," I said, grabbing a piece of the chocolate cake and following him to where his family stood around Helene.

The family relations were interesting in the whole mix. The Wrights were Jordan and Julian's cousins on their father's side, but the Abbeys were their cousins on their mom's side. So, the Abbeys and the Wrights weren't related, but they were tied together through Helene. I thought it was beautiful. Especially considering I'd never had big, family affairs.

My mom was...well, Pamela. She and Hal had always celebrated holidays with me when I lived at home, but after that, it'd just kind of slipped away. And Dad was in Michigan, where most of my cousins were, too. I saw them on occasion, like if someone was getting married. But otherwise, we just lived different lives. I wished I had something special like this. I spent more holidays with Piper's wonderfully large and festive Mexican family than my own.

A woman I'd never seen before skipped right up to Campbell and punched him in the arm. She was average height with two full sleeves and a winning smile. "Is this her? Took you long enough to introduce us."

Campbell laughed. "Blaire, this is my aunt Vail."

"Pleasure is all mine," Vail said, shaking my hand. "Come meet Lori. She's not as effusive as I am."

"You mean, *intrusive*, darling," Lori said. She was beautiful with flowing red hair and a yellow sundress.

She and Vail clearly belonged together.

"I did not," Vail grumbled.

"It's nice to meet you. I'm Lori."

"Blaire," I said, shaking her hand.

"And this is Gregg," Lori said.

Campbell cleared his throat. "My dad."

Gregg Abbey wasn't as tall as either of his sons, but he carried himself in a way that said he could still put them in their place. Even with the cane in his hand. Campbell had told me that he hated carrying it around, but it was necessary with his knee problems. I thought it made him look regal and refined. No one could look at him and think him weak.

"Nice to meet you, sir," I said, offering him my hand.

He shot Campbell a look that I couldn't interpret, but it made Campbell frown. Then, he smiled for me and shook my hand. "Hello, Blaire."

"I am so glad to meet you all."

"We wouldn't miss my sister's birthday," Gregg said.

"And Jensen was nice enough to host," Hollin said, elbowing his dad as he snuck into the conversation.

Gregg rolled his eyes. "He really didn't have to."

"Dad wanted to have the party at his house," Hollin explained.

"I admit that the pool is a nice touch," he said.

"So, you're dating my favorite nephew, huh?" Vail asked.

Hollin gasped. "I'm not dating Blaire."

Vail arched an eyebrow. "I didn't say you were."

Campbell shook his head. "You're going to get yourself in trouble."

"You know I love you all equally," Vail said, holding her

knuckles out to Hollin. As soon as he dabbed her, she added, "But Campbell brings me the good stuff."

Hollin snorted. "Typical."

"Can we not, Vail?" Gregg said, pinching the bridge of his nose. Then, he looked to me and said, "I promise we're not always like this."

"No. We're normally worse," Hollin said. "Nora isn't around."

"She's the little instigator," Vail agreed.

"And who do you think she learns it from?" Lori demanded.

"Hollin," Campbell said at the same time Hollin said, "Campbell."

And they both pointed at each other.

Their dad smiled genuinely at the pair of them. I didn't see any of the animosity there that Campbell had made seem was a constant. He'd said that he'd been working on his relationship with his dad. And it was great to see them like this.

The only problem was every time his dad looked at *me*.

I wasn't sure if Campbell saw it, and I had no intention of pointing it out if he missed it while he was joking around with his brother.

But one thing was clear: his dad was not pleased that I was dating his son.

25

CAMPBELL

"*L*et's top off your drink," I told Blaire, pulling her away from my family.

We could be overwhelming. And though she was far from the kind of person to get overwhelmed—at least not in crowds of people she knew—meeting the family was a big deal. I'd always intended to keep it as short as possible. She knew everyone else here. She should enjoy herself. Not stick around and cater to my family.

"All right." She smiled and waved at my family before heading back inside with me. "They're nice."

"They like you."

She grinned. "Good."

"And I like you," I said, squeezing her hand.

"I sure hope so, considering how much time we've been spending in your bed."

I grinned devilishly. "Well, it doesn't just have to be a bed."

Her eyes twinkled. "Oh?"

"Trust me?"

"Always."

Instead of veering into the kitchen, I drew her away from the party. No one else was inside at this moment, as the kids were all eating too much sugar and playing in the pool. So, we entered the bathroom, closing and locking the door.

She laughed. "What are you doing?"

But I didn't answer with words. I crowded into her space, pushed my hands up into her hair, and crushed our mouths together. She tasted sweet, a mix of the chocolate cake and vanilla buttercream icing. She was every bit as addictive as the sugar.

I walked her backward until her ass hit the countertop. She fisted her hands into my shirt, but she was only wearing her tiny white bikini. I could remove the entire thing off with the pull of two little strings. Just the thought had my cock lengthening in my pants.

"Fuck," I groaned against her lips.

I lifted her up onto the countertop and pushed my way between her open legs. She moaned softly as I rubbed hard against her. I smothered the noise with another hard kiss. I couldn't get enough of her.

I was having her twice a day, every day, and still, I wanted more. I wanted her every second. It wasn't even that she was mostly naked in a bikini. Though that didn't fucking hurt anything. It was that she was *mine*.

My Blaire.

"Campbell," she gasped. "Do you have a condom?"

I panicked as I realized...I didn't have a fucking condom on me. Goddamn it. "Fuck."

She pulled back hard, nearly cracking her head against the mirror. "We can't..."

"I know," I reassured her.

"We can't," she repeated more firmly.

"I can still get you off," I growled at her.

Then, I grasped the strings of her bikini and let the material fall away, revealing her pink pussy. All wet and waiting for me.

I tugged her ass off the counter and turned her away from me, bending her over.

She yelped, "Cold, cold, cold," as her stomach braced against the counter.

Then, I was on my knees behind her. I pressed my mouth against her clit, and she bit back a moan. I spread her ass cheeks wider, so I had better access, and then I went to town. I licked and sucked and circled her clit with my tongue, drawing out each squirm of pleasure. Then, I plunged two fingers deep inside of her. She pushed hard back against me.

"Are you imagining my cock?" I asked, slamming harder inside of her.

"Yes," she gasped.

"Am I going to have to take this pretty pussy hard when I get home tonight, too?"

She whimpered. "Please."

I returned to her clit, speeding up my movements until I felt her entire body shudder with pleasure. She physically bit her hand to keep from crying out. Her legs went all wobbly, and then she dropped onto the ground with a short laugh.

Her eyes darted up to mine and then lower—to the erection in my shorts.

"You can't go out like that," she teased.

"Then, do something about it."

She came to all fours and crawled a foot toward where I now towered over her. "And what would you like me to do about it?"

"Suck it."

Blaire rose to her knees and drew my swim trunks down my legs. My cock jerked up toward her mouth, as if begging her right then and there to do as she had been told. She smiled something devious that made pre-come drip from the tip. Blaire Barker on her knees in front of me was every erotic fantasy on replay in my head.

She wrapped her hand around the base and stroked the shaft up and down. Then, she leaned forward and licked the pre-come from the head. I nearly came all over her face right then and there. Just from the way she'd casually laved my cock, as if she had all the time in the world and we weren't in someone else's bathroom while an entire party of practically every person we knew in the town stood outside.

"I don't know if you remember," she said right before she took the entire head of my cock in her mouth. She drew it out really slow. "But I don't have a gag reflex."

I jerked forward toward her mouth. Holy fucking shit. "Fuck, Blaire."

Then, she took me all the way down. Until her lips were pressed against my body and my cock filled her entire mouth. It took a lot of concentration for me not to come then. I'd been too preoccupied with fucking her and eating out her glorious pussy that I hadn't even realized that she hadn't blown me since high school.

And, man, had I been fucking missing out.

She went to work, as if it were her fucking job to get me off. Bobbing up and down and running her tongue along my cock. I wanted to hold on just to watch her go at it longer, but she was a fucking expert. I had one hand in her hair and one gripping the countertop.

"Yes, baby," I whispered, closing my eyes and just enjoying the ride. "That's it. Just like that."

She made a hum of approval, and something in that hum sent me over the edge.

"Fuck."

Then, I was coming inside of her hot, wet mouth. She held herself in place until I finished, and then she looked up at me and swallowed.

"You are magnificent." Then, I lifted her to her feet and kissed her. Heedless of the sex on both of our lips. She giggled softly and kissed me back.

We hastily cleaned ourselves up. I was half-ready to throw her over my shoulder and go home to find a condom. But I'd promised her a day out in public. So, I owed her that.

She retied her bathing suit strings in a state of happy delirium. "Should you go out first or me?"

"You," I told her, kissing her lips one more time.

But then the handle was turned, followed by a knock on the door.

Blaire blushed furiously. "One minute," she called.

"Well, I guess we'll go out together."

She bit her lip and nodded. I unlocked the door and opened it to find myself face-to-face with my dad. He looked flat and if not unhappy, then at least not pleased. Like a parent about to tell you they were so disappointed in you. Well, fuck, this couldn't be worse timing.

"Campbell, there you are. I've been looking for you."

"Sorry. I..."

Blaire pulled the door open a little wider. Her cheeks were still flushed, and she dipped her chin. "Hello, Mr. Abbey."

My dad looked between me and her. His already-grim expression turned into a full-blown frown. "Hello, Blaire. Do you mind if I have a minute with my son?"

"Of course not," she said.

She snuck one glance at me before pushing past my dad and out of view. I ran a hand back through my hair. What the fuck was this about?

"You didn't have to be rude," I told him.

"I wasn't rude. I was perfectly nice."

"You looked like you were going to yell at her."

"It has nothing to do with her," he assured me without any reassurance at all. My dad sighed. "I don't want to have an argument."

"That's news to me."

I wasn't a kid anymore. I had my own career and my own place and my own life. Then, why did I suddenly feel so small when he looked at me like that?

"What are you doing with Blaire?" my dad finally asked.

"Doing with her? I'm dating her."

"For how long? You're going back to LA soon."

"I know I have to go back, but things are different with Blaire."

"Different." He gestured to the bathroom behind us. "This isn't exactly how you behave on tour and in your myriad of parties in LA? This isn't how you always treat woman? Love bombing them with fancy dinners and lots of sex and attention and then getting bored?"

I glared right back at him. "I am not *love bombing* Blaire. And no, this is absolutely nothing like how it is with anyone else but her."

He shook his head. "You might think that, but have you considered her? That girl is in love with you."

I opened my mouth to contradict him. She couldn't be after this little time. It was absurd. But it wasn't just this little time, was it? It was this and the months we'd spent together in high school. It all blurred together. Wasn't I falling in love with her?

"You're going back to LA. And any girl you leave behind will be a wreck. That isn't fair to her," he said. "I'm not saying this to come down on you. I'm saying this to protect her. What happens to *her* when you leave?"

I wanted to tell him that I wasn't leaving. That I couldn't leave. That I wanted her above all else. But Blaire wouldn't want that. Not when my career was everything to me. Music was my very soul, and she was the muse I'd found to burn through it.

But I knew what would happen when I left.

I knew intimately.

It had been raining the night I climbed through her window to tell her I was leaving. I didn't know why that had stuck with me. But it had.

My Converse were sodden, and when I pulled myself over the ledge, I got dirt on her carpet.

"Ignore it," Blaire said to me.

She wrapped her arms around me despite the fact that I was dripping wet and leaned up to kiss me. I could admit that I was a bastard and kissed her back. I kissed her hard and rough and desperate. Because I knew it might be the last time she ever kissed me. Ever gave me the time of day. And I wanted her desperately. I just didn't know how to have everything I'd ever wanted. I had to give something up, and she was what I'd sacrifice to find success.

She tugged on my belt. "Come to bed," she whispered.

"Blaire, I..."

"Shh," she breathed, pulling me forward two steps.

She dropped onto the bed and crawled backward, so I could get a look at her. She was just in a long T-shirt. Her bare legs exposed before me.

I wanted to give in more than anything. I wanted to put it

off another night. Be here with the girl of my dreams and damn the consequences. But she deserved better than that.

"I can't tonight," I forced out.

She sat up and crossed her legs, drawing her shirt over them, suddenly self-conscious. "Why not?"

"I have to tell you something."

She didn't move. Barely breathed. "What?"

I took a big enough breath for the both of us.

"I'm leaving."

"Leaving," she said flatly.

"I'm moving to LA."

She swallowed. "When?"

"After graduation."

"That's in two weeks."

"I know. I talked to my aunt who lives in LA. My mom's sister," I clarified even though I didn't need to, but I was rambling because I hated this. "And she said I can stay with her while I look for a job out there."

"You're going to go out to LA without a job?"

I kicked at nothing on the carpet. "I want to play music. If I don't go now, then I'll never go."

She said nothing, and when I looked back up at her, tears were in her eyes. She looked away from me, but she was furious, as if she was angry that she couldn't keep the tears in.

"Blaire..."

"What about us?" she choked out, as if she already knew the answer.

"You know I love you."

"Then, what. About. Us?" she bit out.

"I don't know."

"You don't know."

"I love you, Blaire. I want us to be together, but long-distance when I'm in LA and you're here at Tech?"

She jumped to her feet and took my hands. Tears were streaming down her face now. "Then, I'll go with you."

"What?" I asked, aghast. "No! You can't go with me. You have to stay here. You're going to become a psychologist. You're going to fix all the things that your mom screwed up. You're going to do beautiful, amazing things."

"I can do them in LA," she said even though she had to know that wasn't true.

"Blaire," I said, pushing her hair back from her face and swiping at the tears on her cheeks. "I'm leaving. You're staying."

"I don't accept this."

And to my deepest regret and horror, I hardened. I had to leave. I had to fight for my music. I refused for her to give up on her dreams for my own. "You have to accept it. We're over."

Then, I crawled back through her window, sank into my truck, and cried all the tears I couldn't show her.

"I know what happens when I leave," I told my dad. "And I'm never going to put her through that."

"For her sake...I hope you're right."

26

BLAIRE

"How'd it go with your dad?" I asked later that day when we finally left the party.

Campbell grimaced. "Not great."

"I don't think he likes me."

"What? Why would you say that?"

"Intuition."

He shook his head as he drove us back to his place. "No, not at all. That all has to do with me. Not you." He grasped my hand in his. "There is absolutely nothing that anyone could dislike about you."

"Well, he saw me coming out of a bathroom with his son. I bet he could guess what we were doing."

"He did. But he's more worried for you than anything."

My eyes widened. "What? Why?"

"He thinks I'm love bombing you."

I nodded slowly. "Actually, that makes perfect sense."

Campbell blinked at me. "What?"

I dealt with a lot of girls with *Blaire Blush* who got love bombed by their boyfriends or latest Tinder find. Love bombing was a complex, manipulative tactic that was usually a form of psychological abuse. It was when a person showed excessive amounts of attention and affection in a way to make the receipt more dependent on them.

His father may not know that he'd helped me gain millions of new followers and was stealing all my time, but he was meeting me after assuming we'd only been together for a matter of weeks. It was perfectly reasonable to have that fear. Especially since Campbell was a celebrity and I was just a small-town girl. But that didn't account for our past and the fact that we had a much deeper connection than what might appear on the surface.

"He doesn't know the truth about us. So, he came to his own conclusions. Maybe you just need to have a real conversation with him about us. That way, we can all be on the same page."

A smile tugged at his lips. "There's therapist Blaire to the rescue."

I laughed. "I promise that I am so much worse at diagnosing my own problems than everyone else's."

"Fine. I will talk to him," he said with a sigh. "Again. It's going to suck. He thinks the worst of me."

"He loves you," I assured him.

"Yeah, yeah."

It wasn't until we got back to his place and he was drawing me inside that I realized he had been waiting to say anything more.

"He actually was worried about what will happen after I leave again."

I tucked a lock of hair behind my ear. "I also was wondering that."

"Come with me," he said, taking my hand.

My eyes widened. "What?"

"Not forever. But for a week...or two even. Last time I left for LA without you, it was traumatic, to say the least. I don't want to leave you behind. So, come be with me there while I iron out what we're doing for the album. We can decide the rest as we go."

I opened my mouth to tell him all the reasons that I couldn't leave Lubbock, but was that true? I could leave Lubbock. For a week or two. I didn't have a traditional job. There was no college holding me back, as there had been last time. And hadn't I been the one begging him to let me go to LA with him when he left in high school? Why had I been brave enough then and not now?

"Okay," I finally said.

"Really?"

I nodded. "I need to run things by Honey for production and move some meetings around. But yes. Yes, I'll go to LA with you."

Campbell pulled me tight against him and kissed me as if he'd never imagined I'd say yes to this.

"Will we be...a couple in LA?"

"If you want. I think we should get English in the same room with my music publicist, Barbara, and see what they think about it all."

I nodded. That sounded like a lot.

"But we don't have to decide anything before we get there. There's already been a few press pieces about you recording the band. So, it won't be strange for you to travel with us."

I breathed a sigh of relief. "Okay. Good. I'm excited."

"Me too."

But if I was going to LA with the potential that my relationship might be public with Campbell, then I needed to tell one more person before that. The last person I wanted to talk to.

My mom.

Pamela had been working at the same doctor's office for almost her entire career. I'd called ahead to speak with her secretary, Lacey, about fitting me in. There was no other way to see her during business hours, and I wasn't willing to go home to have this conversation. I knew too well what it would be like there.

"Blaire," Lacey said with a smile when I walked in. "It's good to see you, sweetie. It's been a while."

It had been at least a year since I'd been at the office. It would have been longer if I could have helped it.

"Good to see you, Lacey."

"She's ready. If you want to head inside."

I nodded and pushed into my mother's office. It looked like a generic therapist's office with seats and a lounge for people to talk to her, and she had a desk, plus actual filing for her records. The business had gone digital, but she still swore by paper and handed it all off to Lacey to type up later.

"Hi," I said as I walked inside.

My mom looked up in surprise. "Marie, I didn't know you were going to be here. I have a client."

"I'm the client," I told her.

Pamela blinked at that. "Oh? You've come for a session."

"No," I said quickly. "Just to talk."

"Ah, couldn't we have done that out of business hours?"

We could have, but I refused to go home. Plus, there, I'd have had to deal with Hal, too.

"I thought this would be better."

"All right," she said, folding up the records she had been

working on and lacing her fingers together in front of her. "What can I help you with?"

I swallowed and took a seat. "I don't have a problem. I just wanted to tell you something."

"Oh?"

"I didn't want you to hear about it from someone else. I thought it would be best from me."

"Sit up straight, Marie. Tell me what this is about."

I straightened automatically. It felt like a grape was lodged in my throat. I needed to choke it down, so I could breathe these words to my mother. On a good day, I didn't like talking to my mom, and this was hardly going to be good in her book.

"I started dating Campbell again." I cleared my throat. "Campbell Abbey."

Whatever she'd thought I was going to tell her, that was not it. Her eyes widened marginally. Then, she clenched her hands tighter together and set her jaw.

"I see," she said slowly. "Since when?"

"Since the Fourth of July. Sort of," I tacked on at the end. It was when it'd all started at least.

"Well, on a scale from one to ten, how confident are you in this decision?" She kept steady eye contact for a moment before turning the page on her notebook, as if she was going to take notes.

I ground my teeth together. Of course, she was going to treat this like a patient problem and not reality. I was her daughter, but my problems...my entire life was just a colossal test run for her career. She was so in her own head that she'd never seen what this did to me.

"Mom!" I snapped. "Don't treat me like one of your patients. I'm your kid."

"I know, Marie." She slapped her hand down on her

notepad. "The easiest way to assess situations is to use my methods. I don't want to elicit an emotional response about this. I want to be practical."

"Screw practical. Can you even *be* emotional?"

Pamela stared back at me, stunned. "Of course I am emotional. Why would you ask me something like that?"

"Because you don't *have* emotions."

"Just because I am not ruled by them does not mean that I do not have them. You should know that very well, Marie. You play by the same rules."

I glared back at her. I hated that she was right. I hid so much of what I was feeling from others. My friends still didn't know everything that had happened with Campbell, and I'd only told them the bare minimum when I finally confessed to it. Hell, Campbell only knew the half of it. It was a defense mechanism, and I'd learned it from my mom.

"Fine," I said, getting to my feet. "On a scale from one to ten, I feel a ten about my relationship with Campbell. Thanks for asking, Pam."

"Marie, I—"

"Blaire! It's *Blaire*. Why can't you call me by the name I prefer?"

She met me stare for stare and steepled her fingers in front of her. "All right, Blaire. The definition of insanity is repeating the same action and expecting different results."

I balked at my mother. That was *not* what I'd expected from her. "It's not the same as it was in high school. He asked me to come to LA with him this time. For a week or two when he has to go back."

"I see. And you believe that changes what happened last time?"

"No. It's just different."

"Need I remind you, the last time he left you alone and

refused to handle his responsibilities, I was the one who was there for you when you were eighteen and pregnant."

I winced and closed my eyes around that word.

Pregnant.

I didn't even think that word in my mind anymore if I could help it. The memory hurt far too much.

It shouldn't have been possible for me to get pregnant anyway. Mom had put me on birth control after finding us that one weekend. We always used condoms. But then, one time, we were out. Neither of us knew how it'd happened. We were in the middle of nowhere. I'd been taking my pills. And we'd decided, *Fuck it. We'll be fine.* He'd pull out.

My mind reeled back to that day when I'd held the tiny test in my hand and seen the two pink lines. I'd never cried so hard in my life. And I'd thought that Campbell telling me he was leaving was the worst thing that had ever happened to me. Now, here I was, with this.

I called him until he answered. It took a dozen calls before he finally picked up and said, "Blaire, we can't talk."

"Campbell, I need to see you."

He sighed. "It won't make it any easier."

We had four days until graduation. I had been shamelessly calling and texting him since he'd ended it. I didn't know what else to do. He had been my life, and now, I was just supposed to go on without him? Without even talking to him every minute of every day like I had for months? It was impossible.

But today was not about that.

"I don't care," I said, my voice wobbly. "I need to see you now. I'm sneaking out. Meet me at the park."

"Blaire," he said on a long-suffering sigh. "I can't. This is going to be harder."

"Campbell Abbey, you meet me at the fucking park in a half hour."

Then, I hung up on him. I figured that would get the message across that it was important. And as I pulled up to the park, I saw that I had been right. His truck was already parked there. I got out of my beat-up Civic and walked to where he was seated on the swings.

"Hey."

He tipped his head at me. He looked at me as if I were a goddess that he had forgotten existed, and now, he was bathing in my light. "Blaire."

I held my hand up. "I know you don't want to make this harder. And I tried, all right? I tried so hard to stay away, but I'm not good at living without you."

He hung his head. The swing creaked as he moved. "I know. Me either."

"But I had to see you tonight."

Then, I pulled the test out of my pocket, and I held it out to him. He looked at it as if it were a hand grenade.

"What is that?"

"You know what it is, Campbell."

He jumped off the swing and took the test in his hand. He looked down at the two pink lines. Then, he shook his head. "No."

"I know."

He glared down at it and shoved it back into my hand. "No, Blaire. No."

"Look, I didn't think this would happen. It had to have been that time we didn't use a condom."

"No, no, no," he repeated like a mantra. "What do you want me to say? I'm leaving for LA in four days!"

I shrank back from his anger. I hadn't known what to expect. I hadn't exactly been *happy* to see the news. That I was going to be a teen mom. A fucking statistic in my mother's book. I'd cried. I'd sobbed. But this was visceral.

"I know, Campbell. Jesus Christ."

"I'm not staying," he shouted.

I reeled back. "You're...you're going to go anyway?"

A part of me had thought of this new world, where Campbell stayed and we had a small family. Where everything was different and hard but also wonderful because we had each other. It was the only way I'd been able to get past the news. To think that he would make it all better by being an incredible father.

"Did you do this so that I'd stay?" he asked, gesturing to the pregnancy test.

Tears came to my eyes. "Do what?" I glanced down at the test. "You think it isn't real?"

"I don't know, Blaire. Fuck. You said you'd do anything to make me stay."

"I said I'd leave for you," I yelled back. "Why would I fucking fake this? What could I possibly gain? You'd hate me forever, and I'd deserve it. Instead, you're being a total asshole."

He shook his head and paced away from me. The news was sinking into him now. It was real to him, as it had been real to me since I had taken this test this morning. But he was still shaking his head. I knew then that the carefully optimistic fantasy I'd had in my head was never going to be a reality.

Campbell wasn't going to stay for me. He wasn't going to stay for the baby inside of me. He wasn't going to stay for anything.

And he hadn't.

He'd gone.

I'd stayed.

"It's not the same," I finally got out to my mother. "It won't be the same as last time."

She gave me a perfectly blank therapist look and held up her pen. "Tell me more about that."

Which I knew, as well as she did, meant, *You're lying to yourself.*

27

CAMPBELL

*W*e were a week away from returning to LA and only had about half an album. I had been working on new songs, but none of them were ready. At least we had a solid six with "The One That Got Away" as a strong seventh spot. It still wasn't finished. I'd finally agreed to let the band hear the chorus and bridge I'd sung to Blaire. They'd all been pissed at me for not playing it for them earlier. But seven songs wasn't an album. So, we were going to have to return home with a lot more work to do than I'd planned.

And Blaire had been...out of it the last couple days.

"You sure you're okay?"

She glanced up at me from where she was seated with her laptop open. She was waiting for Honey to show up to the studio. She was going to work from here today while she recorded a few new videos and set up her calendar for when she was in LA with me. "Yeah. I'm fine. You can stop asking."

But something wasn't quite right. She was still in my bed every night, but I could tell that something was bothering her.

I dropped into the seat next to her. "You know you can tell me anything."

She nodded. Then, with a heavy sigh, she took my hand. "I went and talked to my mom about us. She just upset me."

"What did she say?" I asked, already getting defensive for her.

"Nothing that matters."

"Blaire..."

"She just...she was there for me when I was..." She bit her lip and said the word neither of us had spoken, "Pregnant."

"Oh."

"She's not a great mom, but she was in that one instance. And you were..."

"Gone."

I kissed her fingers and mournfully looked up at her. "If I could change how it all happened, you know that I would. I'd go back in time and not be an utter jackass that night."

"I know," she whispered. "She just pushes all of my buttons."

"Yeah, I get that. My dad is the same way."

She nodded. "So, I'm in my own feels about it. Don't worry about it. It'll pass." She drew me in for a kiss. "And you need to stop beating yourself up about the album."

"I'm not beating myself up. I just thought I'd have all the songs ready."

"You have seven songs. A month ago, you had zero. I think it's okay to give yourself at least another month for the rest of the songs to come to you."

She was right, of course. But I'd always worked in manic fits, and a part of me was worried that I'd already lost mine. It sounded ridiculous because that wasn't how it worked every time. That didn't mean my brain would listen when I told it that I'd figure it all out.

"All right. Sure. We still need to get 'Tightrope' just right anyway."

"You'll get it." She turned back to her laptop. That far, distant look in her eyes again. Fuck. I hated that. "When is everyone else showing up?"

I glanced down at my phone. "Should be any minute. West is getting everything set up."

And as if summoned, the rest of the band strode into the studio. Viv with a pointed yawn. Santi practically skipped in, clapping me on the back and offering a chipper, "Good morning." Yorke said not a word, and Michael was on his phone.

"Tell Virginia I said hi," I called to him.

He flipped me off and kept walking.

I chuckled. Viv smacked a kiss on my cheek.

"You ready to go, bro?" Santi asked. He bounced from foot to foot.

"Yeah. You look *real* ready to go," I said sarcastically.

"I love this place." He beamed.

"You mean, you love getting laid every night."

"Don't you?"

Blaire rolled her eyes. "You and Eve are really hitting it off, huh?"

"What? Eve? Oh no, we decided we would be better off as friends. I've been meeting with this girl Alejandra. She works at a local winery."

"What? Really?" Blaire gasped. "Ale has a boyfriend."

"*Had* a boyfriend," Santi corrected. "They broke up. She's my dream girl."

"I can't believe that happened," she said. "I thought you really liked Eve."

"I do." He winked at her. "We had a good time. But that doesn't mean it's forever. Honestly, she hooked me up with Alejandra."

Blaire glanced up at me in confusion as Santi headed for the studio. "Wow. Eve never told us."

"She's a new roommate though, right?"

"Yeah, she is. I don't know her as well as Piper or Jennifer, obviously, but she seemed to be into him."

"Eve seems like someone who can handle herself."

"You're right. But I'm totally asking her about it when I get home."

The bell tinkled overhead, and Honey entered. "Hey, y'all. What did I miss?"

My eyebrows shot up my forehead at the transformed Honey. Her once-honey-blonde locks were now a deep, dark brown. Nearly as dark as Blaire's pitch-black hair with the same fringe bangs. She'd always had kind of short hair, but she must have gotten extensions or something because it was nearly down to her back. It was a little disconcerting. She was practically a dead ringer for Blaire.

"Whoa, new look," Blaire said, jumping to her feet.

She giggled and did a little wiggle. "You like?"

Blaire nodded, running her fingers through the extensions. "It's so cute. Who did them?"

"A friend recommended this place downtown. I just wanted something completely different. You know, after my catastrophe with my last boyfriend."

"It's definitely different," I muttered.

Blaire shot me a look that said, *Be nice*. I drew her into me again and kissed her hard on the lips.

"I'm going to get to work. Let me know if you need anything. Lunch?"

"Of course."

"See you, Honey," I said, waving at her as I left them behind.

"Bye, Campbell," she said with a wistful tone to her voice.

I cringed and hurried back into the studio. Everyone was set up, getting ready to focus on "Tightrope" again. And I had the sound of Honey's voice in my head. That was utterly discordant with the song I was about to sing about how falling in love was like walking a tightrope. You had to let trust take you out on it and push forward with confidence, or one wrong step, and everything could fall apart.

I suddenly had a bad feeling about Honey. Was she trying to look like Blaire because of me? She was a Cosmere fan. She'd been desperate to meet us that first night. Now, I was dating Blaire, and suddenly, she was trying to look like her. That didn't sit right with me, but maybe it was just all the problems I'd had with fans in the past getting to my head. I didn't know where to begin to tell Blaire without sounding irrational.

"Campbell, you ready?" Viv asked. "We're all set."

"Uh, yeah. Let's do it."

I closed my eyes and let the opening chords of "Tightrope" roll over me. It was finally coming together. Santi had suggested pulling Viv in on backup vocals for this one, so it had a female voice on the call and response. And it added this perfect blend that I'd never known I was missing. It was what we'd all been missing. And after spending the next couple hours hammering it all out, I felt like it was finally in a place to show people.

"That's a wrap," West called through the speakers. He shot me a thumbs-up.

He was right. That was the one.

"Fuck yes," Santi roared. He jumped to his feet. "I have a crazy idea."

Yorke sighed. "Surprise, surprise."

Viv cackled. "You said it, Yorke."

"Why don't we come back?"

We all stared at him blankly.

"Come back?" I finally asked.

"Yeah. We're all going to LA in a week to show the studio what we got and where the album is heading. They're going to want to keep us in town and finish out the album. We don't want to get in there and record all six finished songs before we have the rest of them finished. It'd ruin our whole roll."

He was right. If we didn't do the entire album in one stretch, we would lose so much momentum. Things were done in an order, and we weren't ready to get in there and record officially yet. There were still kinks to figure out. Not to mention, a few more songs.

"So, why don't we go home, do all our meetings, show how kick-ass we are, and then have them send us back *here*?"

A pin could have dropped as everyone assessed his words.

I didn't want to say anything. My vote was an obvious yes. Blaire was here. But I never in a million years would have suggested that everyone come back. In fact, I hadn't suggested they all come here in the first place. So, I wouldn't hold any sway on this vote.

Viv shrugged. "I talked to Kris last night actually. She was promoted, and she'll be entirely virtual. She had been talking about coming out this week. I bet she'd come with us if I asked."

"Excellent," Santi said. He was twirling his drumstick over and over and over again.

"Sure," Yorke said with a shrug.

Santi looked to me. "I know you're in, bro."

"I am." But my gaze turned finally to Michael. We all looked at him. "Michael?"

He was staring at us all as if he'd never met us before. It wasn't surprise on his face. It was actual rage and disbelief and betrayal. Like we'd kicked his puppy or something.

"Are you all out of your fucking minds?" he asked, low and vicious.

"Course not," Santi said cheerfully. "We just came up with this idea—"

"Oh, you just came up with it." He laughed, but it had no humor in it. "Don't bullshit me. You've all been talking about this behind my back, haven't you?"

"This is the first I'm hearing of it," I told him.

He rolled his eyes at me as pushed away from the keyboard and stood. "You all knew that I wouldn't want to come back. So, you worked it out together to ambush me. What am I supposed to say to this? You know I don't want to be here."

"It's not an ambush," Viv said. "Honestly, none of us have talked about this before. And we're *asking* you right now."

"Sure, Viv."

"I am *not* lying," she said.

"Even if you're not, you're all ganging up on me. How did you think this would go? I'm not fucking coming back. We've spent enough time in this place. Campbell can write his songs in LA, like a normal person."

"It was just an idea," Santi began.

"No, let him say what he wants to say," Viv snapped back.

"Guys," I said, standing and trying to mediate the volcano that was about to erupt.

"Don't come to my defense," Michael roared at me. "This is all your fucking fault."

"I didn't ask you to come out here. I had no idea that Bobby hadn't asked you if you wanted to come. Don't put all of this on me."

"Who else should I put it on? You weren't coming back to LA. We needed to start working on the new album. What the fuck did you think was going to happen? Cause and effect, man."

"You could have told him no."

"Contrary to popular belief," Michael snarled, "no one gives a shit what the rest of us do. Everyone only fucking care about you."

I staggered back a step at that. "That is not even remotely true."

"Campbell is right," Yorke said.

Viv nodded, and Santi looked aghast that he would even suggest it. I was a part of the team. Yes, I was the lead singer, and I wrote the lyrics, and I was the face of the band. But I was *not* the only one who mattered. If I were, then I would have told Michael to just fall in line. We were standing here, asking him what he thought, and his response was to attack me.

"I see how it is," Michael said. He was visibly shaking at this point. "You're just taking his side. Well, fuck you. Fuck this band. Fuck this fucking city. I'm tired of being treated like shit. I *quit*."

Then, he wrenched the door open and stomped out.

28

BLAIRE

"*I*t's only going to be a week or two," I told Honey for what felt like the fiftieth time.

I really didn't have the energy for this conversation. Honey was the best assistant I'd had. Her independent and headstrong energy were what had endeared her to me. I did not have the time or mental capacity for her to be clingy.

"I know. I know."

"You have nothing to worry about. It's going to be great."

I was too drained from that interaction with my mother for it to be anything else. And then I'd actually said that word...that *word* out loud to Campbell. We'd hedged around it this last month. It had happened. It was our past. His huge error. The thing I'd sworn I'd never forgive him for. And now, here we were.

There was nothing else to discuss really. It was not going to be the same as it had been the first time. No matter what my therapist mother thought about the definition of *insanity*.

"Blaire?" Honey said, snapping her fingers in my face.

I jerked backward. "What?"

"Did you hear anything I said?"

"Sorry, no. I haven't been sleeping great." I shot her a wan smile. "Just excited about the upcoming trip, I guess."

She frowned. "You're not feeling well? Are you sure you should be going?"

"Yeah, I'm fine. No worries."

"Okayyy," Honey said in disbelief. "You'll be able to record in LA and get all the stuff with the band. We'll have so much new content to work with. It'll be good for the business. I'll just miss having you around. It'll be boring without you."

"It's not that long," I said *again*. Then changed the subject. "So, let's run through what we need to do this week before I head out."

She nodded and flipped to a different document when the studio door crashed open. We both whipped around as Michael stormed out of the recording studio. We gaped at him, but he said not one word to us. Just barreled through the front door and was gone.

I jumped to my feet and dashed into the back. "What happened? Is Michael all right?"

Campbell had his hands balled into fists. Viv had her hand over her mouth. Santi's jaw was dropped. Only Yorke looked the same, but that was probably because he always appeared somber.

"Are you all right?"

Campbell sank into the seat and tugged his guitar over his head. "Michael just quit."

"What?" I gasped.

Viv nodded when I glanced up at her. "He just lost it."

"It was my fault," Santi said. He blew out harshly and then threw his drumsticks at the wall. "Fuck."

"It's not your fault," Campbell said automatically. "You

had no idea he would blow up like that by asking a simple question."

"We knew he was unhappy," Viv said.

Yorke nodded. "Yep."

"But not enough to *quit the band*," I insisted.

Campbell nodded at me. "Yeah, I never thought he'd be mad enough for that. He's just...Michael."

"He is always unhappy," Viv agreed. "He's always been that way. I had no idea he was at a tipping point."

"Me either," Santi said with a sigh. He ran a hand back through his hair. "What the fuck are we going to do?"

"I don't know," Campbell said.

"Someone should talk to him," I said.

"I can," Campbell insisted.

Viv walked over and put a hand on his shoulder. "I love you, Campbell, but no. He won't see reason with you about this. I'll go and talk to him once he's had a minute to calm down."

"What do we do in the meantime?" Santi asked. "What if it's for real? We're out a keys player. We only have half an album. Fuck."

"It'll be fine," Campbell insisted. He looked like he was going to put his fist through the wall. "Why doesn't everyone go get some lunch? Then, we can meet here later to discuss what we're going to do."

Everyone nodded and slowly filed out of the room. Honey wavered in the doorway with wide eyes, but I shooed her out.

"Hey you," I said, wrapping my arms around his waist.

He pulled me tight against him and kissed my hair. "Blaire, Blaire, Blaire, what have I done?"

"You can't blame yourself for someone else's decision."

"I'd been so wrapped up in us that I didn't see it."

"Hey," I said, tugging his head down to look at me. "You are not responsible for everyone's feelings. He should have said something before this. He let it fester. It sounds like this will all just blow over, and you will be back to normal."

"I hope so. I have no fucking clue what to do otherwise."

"You'll figure it out."

"Yeah." He and rubbed his eyes. "This is so fucked."

"We should go get some lunch."

"I want to, but I need to call Bobby. I need to figure some shit out."

I nodded. "All right. I'll go and grab you something and bring it back."

"That would be great." A smile cracked the surface. "Thanks, Blaire."

I kissed him again and then left him to the dreaded phone call. I couldn't imagine Bobby Rogers was going to enjoy hearing about what had happened.

Weston stood at the door as I exited.

"Uh, how's he doing?"

I tilted my head away from the door, and he followed me out of earshot. "He's blaming himself."

West stuffed his hands into the pockets of his dark jeans. "I've had the pleasure of working with Michael the last month. And let me tell you, that guy does *not* know how good he has it."

"They never figure it out until it's too late."

He shrugged. "I guess. I feel like I won the fucking lottery, just being in the same room as Campbell. Let alone the entire band."

"Yeah, but he was there before Campbell. He's hurting because he's away from his family and lashing out."

"True. I still think he's angling for *the grass is greener*." He looked far away, as if remembering all the tours he'd been on, playing backup and dealing with the shit from performers. "It's not. It's really, really not."

"I hope he comes back."

West nodded. "Me too."

"Want to come grab some lunch? I'm bringing it back for Campbell."

"Sure."

"Hey, Honey, we're going to head to Market Street. Want to come?"

She flipped her newly dyed hair, which I was still *not* used to. Like, could she have gotten any closer to my signature look?

"You don't have to do that. I can go." She reached for her keys. "I'll pick something up for everyone."

"I think Campbell needs a minute," I admitted, glancing back at the studio.

"Okay. Then, sure."

We left Campbell alone to deal with Bobby Rogers and the fallout of Michael's actions. When we returned, the rest of the band had just pulled back up at the studio.

"Did you get ahold of Michael?" I asked Viv as I carried Campbell's sandwich inside.

She looked grim. "Uh, yeah. He booked the first flight out of town."

"Oh God."

"Yeah. He hung up on me after I tried to convince him to stay. And he wouldn't answer either Santi or Yorke."

"Damn."

We stepped inside and found Campbell on the floor of the studio, staring up at the ceiling. Santi flopped right down next to him, and Viv kicked him lightly.

"Yo," she said.

He looked up at them with a resigned expression. "Hey."

"We tried to talk to Michael, but he's leaving Lubbock on the first flight west."

"Great," Campbell said.

Campbell had been on such a high since returning to Lubbock that I'd forgotten how utterly far he could crash when things weren't great. I'd seen him like this in high school after his mom's death and subsequently every time he tried to write music and it didn't work out. I didn't like seeing him like this right now.

"What did Bobby say?" I asked.

"He said he'll talk to Michael. That I need to give him this week to let it blow over. When we get back to LA, we can reach out again. He thinks Michael will change his mind."

"I think so, too," Santi said confidently.

Viv cringed. "Yeah, but let's be realistic. What if he doesn't come back?"

Campbell sat up on his elbows and shrugged. "I don't know."

"We can't replace him," Santi said.

"We might have to," Viv said.

Yorke nodded. "Yep."

"I don't want to talk about that," Campbell said. "Michael isn't gone for good. He could still come back."

"We need a contingency plan," Viv argued.

"Why?"

"Because this is our livelihood. We can't just assume Michael is going to let this blow over. And even if he does, the band might never be the same. We've seen this happen with other bands. It won't be peachy keen after this."

Campbell wrapped his arms around his knees and looked up at his band. The biggest band in the world right now, collapsing all around him. He looked so lost.

West cleared his throat and took a step forward. "Not to interrupt, but I think it's a little less black-and-white than this."

The entire band turned to stare at him then, as if they had forgotten he was even in the room. He flushed at the attention.

"I've probably seen more bands fall apart than all of you combined. It was kind of an occupational hazard with what I did in Seattle. A lot of times, the band just continued with one less member, and they'd have someone play backup for the lost member. Honestly, I did that all over the world for the last couple years." He ran a hand back through his hair, as if to hide that he was shaking, even mentioning it. "I stopped to come to Lubbock with my...brothers. But I already know all of Michael's parts. In fact, I wrote most of the keys for this album. I can play backup until you figure all of this out."

Campbell's stare was solid and heavy. I, for one, knew that it must have been hard for Weston to even offer that, knowing that being *in* the band meant an entirely different life for himself. But it was brave, and it was the right thing to do.

"Seriously, man?" Santi asked, jumping off the floor and throwing his arms around West.

West laughed. "Yeah, I mean, I can if you want me to."

Viv arched an eyebrow at Campbell. "It's an elegant solution until we know more."

"I say yes," Yorke conceded.

Campbell got to his feet and held his hand out to West. "Let's do it."

"Yeah?" West asked.

Campbell nodded. "You'll come to LA with us?"

West looked startled, like he hadn't anticipated that.

"Uh, I mean, I can write the music out for someone else to play there if you prefer."

"No," Campbell said automatically. "We want you."

Viv squeezed his arm. Santi bounced, almost like a little kid. Yorke just nodded.

"Well then, yeah, I can do that."

Viv put her arm around West's waist. "You have no idea what shit you just got into."

West laughed. "I think I know you well enough at this point. I'm happy to help."

Campbell released West's hand and came over to give me a kiss. Already, the despair in his eyes had evaporated. The sparkle returned as everything knit back together. So fast, like turning on a light switch.

"Where's that lunch?"

I laughed and tugged him back out of the studio. Campbell was all back to himself, but I knew LA was going to be very interesting.

PART V

GOLD-PLATED

29

BLAIRE

"You didn't have to drive us," I told Hollin as he lugged my two giant suitcases to his truck.

"I know, but Campbell said he was going to store the Rover and then hire a driver to take y'all." He shot Campbell a look. "Pretentious shit."

"Hey, I was just trying to make it easier on everyone."

"What? You think I don't want to drive the Rover while you're gone?"

Campbell rolled his eyes. "Have at it."

"Well, I appreciate it, Hollin." I bowed under the weight of my backpack, full of recording equipment and all my work stuff.

Campbell reached out for it. "Let me get that."

"Thanks," I said with a smile.

My boho bag fell to the crook of my elbow, and I hitched it back up. I had half a dozen other bags inside of it, my iPad, and a spicy romance novel I'd borrowed from Piper. Still, I was sure that I was forgetting something.

"I didn't bring enough hats," I told Campbell, tugging on the *Blaire Blush* baseball cap on my head.

"Never enough hats." He opened the back door to let me inside.

"Look, don't make fun of me," I said, sticking my tongue out at him as I slid into the back. "I like the hats."

"Then, we'll buy you more in LA." He stole a kiss from me before closing the door and jumping into the passenger seat next to his brother.

"We?" I asked with raised eyebrows.

Campbell turned around, shooting an arched eyebrow right back. "What? You think I'm bringing you to LA, and I'm not planning to spoil you?"

"There was no talk of spoiling."

"What's the point of having all this money if I can't spend it on you?"

"Well, I don't know. But I don't expect you to spend any of it on me."

"I know." He winked at me and turned back to the front.

"All right, kids. We're set," Hollin said as he pulled out of the driveway.

The boys bantered and fought over the radio station—Hollin opting for country and Campbell wanting anything but—until we pulled up to the private airport terminal.

I hopped out of the back, lugging my bag when another car pulled up alongside us. Nora waved from the driver's side. She hopped out onto her characteristic four-inch heels and threw her arms around her brother.

"I'm going to miss you."

He laughed and hugged her tight. "Shrimp, it won't be forever."

"I know. Not as long as last time or the time before that, okay?" She gestured to me. "You have to bring Blaire to Morgan's wedding."

"We will be there for your big Wright wedding at the vineyard."

Nora smiled and nodded. "Good. It's the biggest wedding I've ever done. Even at my internship. Do you know how many friends the Wrights have?"

"I have some idea if that pool party was any indication," I said.

She shook her head. "This is going to make that look like *nothing*."

"But she's going to kill it," Weston said, coming around to the other side with nothing but a duffel bag and a guitar.

"Is that all you have?" I asked in dismay.

He shrugged. "I'm used to packing light. Figure we'll just be in the studio all week anyway."

"I overpacked," I whispered to Campbell.

He cracked up. "Maybe a little."

"Have a great time," Nora said. "And bring West back with you, too. I don't want to have to find another roommate."

West grinned down at her. It was not a *friendly roommate* look in the slightest. It was one that said he was this close to kissing her, if she'd only let him. "I'll be back, Nor. Before you know it."

She swallowed hard and nodded. "Better be."

Hollin grumbled from the trunk about my luggage, breaking the spell. We all hurried back to help him get everything out. Campbell said his good-byes, and then we walked into the private terminal. I handed all my luggage off and then walked through our own TSA check. Then, we were escorted directly onto our own private jet.

"Holy shit," West whispered behind me.

"No kidding."

I'd flown private exactly once, and that was when we'd

taken the Wright plane into Dallas for the Cosmere concert. That had been a plane full of my friends. This was *just* for Cosmere.

"The record label sent it for all of us," Campbell said.

The rest of the band was already on board with drinks in their hands. I dropped my bag and took a proffered glass of champagne. West held his hand up, declining the drink.

We settled into our seats with Campbell at my side. My phone dinged right before takeoff.

Have so much fun and come back soon!

Oh, Honey. She was really going to miss me.

Taking off now! Talk in a few hours.

And then we took off as smoothly as anything I'd ever been on. The flight was full of laughter and, of course, music. Everyone had an instrument with them. Even Santi had drumsticks and banged on anything he could find. I joined in with them at the chorus of "Rooftop Nights," which I knew entirely by heart now.

"Girl, you've got some vocal cords," Viv said, punching me in the arm.

I laughed and shook my head. "No way. I am mediocre at best, but singing is fun."

"She did chorus all four years of high school," Campbell said. "It's a losing battle. She never sings for me."

"I sing," I said defensively. "I just don't want to make my career out of it."

Viv smacked Campbell's foot. "Well, leave the girl alone. She can sing in the shower for all I care. I'm just giving her a compliment."

"*Ay, mami*, I'd listen to you in the shower," Santi said with a wink. Campbell threw a pillow at his face. Santi died laughing. "I did it for the reaction. Your boyfriend is a possessive motherfucker. I hope you know that."

Campbell looked ready to get to his feet, but I put my hand on his chest. "Santi, I think you have your hands full with every other female in Lubbock County."

He sat back and twirled his drumstick. "*Sí*, doesn't feel like a problem to me."

The rest of the band laughed, and the next couple hours disappeared in no time. By the time we landed at LAX, I could tell that Campbell wanted to go straight to Michael's to try to work everything out, but Viv refused.

"We will all go to see him Monday morning before we go into the studio to record. Go home and rest."

Campbell sighed. "Fine. See you Monday." He clapped hands with West. "You sure you want to stay with Santi? I have plenty of room."

"Yeah, I have some friends in the city, and they live near him. It'll be good to see them."

"All right. See you Monday then."

We watched them go and then went to Campbell's driver. He didn't have pushy siblings here in LA to pick him up.

"Are you missing Hollin right now?"

He nodded. "I was just thinking that. I was here all alone for so long that I got used to it. But it feels so much...less without them now. I already got used to them making fun of me all the time again. It's weird how fast you can get used to something."

The drive into Hollywood Hills took about an hour, and my jaw dropped at the enormous homes we passed before pulling to a private gated entrance.

"Campbell," I whispered with wide eyes.

"Yeah?"

"You didn't tell me that you lived in a gated community in Beverly Hills."

He was quiet for a second before asking, "Does it matter?"

"No," I said automatically. "I just don't think of *this* when I think about you."

"And you don't think that is part of the reason this is so easy?" He ran a hand back through his hair. "Cosmere's rise to fame has been amazing, but they've been full of people, specifically women, who are interested in me because I have money and celebrity status. With you, I'm just me. I didn't want this to be what you see when you see me."

"Well, that isn't going to change, but maybe a heads-up would have been nice," I said on a laugh as we were let through the gate and circled ever higher through the hills.

We finally came upon his house, which was admittedly smaller than some of the mansion homes we'd passed on the way but it still had to be a few million dollars. I'd been joking about Jensen's house, and then here he was, with something smaller but easily ten times as pricey. Fuck, I really had *not* considered how much of a celebrity he actually was. I'd seen him perform to a packed stadium and gotten fifty million views on one video with him in it, and still, it hadn't clicked until I saw this house.

I blinked at it as the driver unloaded my luggage to carry inside. Campbell came around to my side of the car, lugging my camera bag on his shoulder.

He laughed at my expression. "It's just a house, Blaire. Let's go inside."

He took my hand and guided me to the front door. I pulled out my phone and did a walking tour of the house to show my friends later. No one was going to believe me otherwise.

The interior was a dream of charcoal, velvet, and polished bronze. Everything was lush and evocative and entirely primal male. There was no way in hell that this had all come together on its own. It looked like a master class in interior design. From the artsy collection of guitars to the set of Grammys just casually displayed next to an antique record player, it screamed musician. As if he lived and breathed his art.

I sent the video to the group chat I had with Piper, Annie, and Jennifer. Then a separate one to Honey. My phone dinged immediately with texts of oohs, aahs, and *oh my God*s!

Honey sent back heart eyes with a quick, *You're never going to want to come home now!*

I laughed, silenced my phone, and pulled away to live in the moment. "Wow, Campbell."

"Yeah. I might have had some help. I wanted it to feel like me, but I had no idea where to start. English recommended the designer. She normally works in New York but came out for my house."

"It's incredible."

"Thanks. I'm pleased. English is coming in tomorrow. Have you decided what you want to do?"

I had been thinking a lot about what I wanted. We could continue to keep our relationship a secret. But I was done with that. I was tired of living in the shadows. I didn't want anyone to think that Campbell was on the market still. He was mine. And I knew that it would come with consequences for the world to know that, but I was ready.

I glanced over at him with a coy smile. "I have."

"And?" He arched an eyebrow.

"I'm tired of hiding. We lived our entire last relationship without anyone knowing. I don't want that a second time."

"You know it will be...complicated?"

I nodded. "Yes. Complicated with you is better than simple or easy with anyone else."

He smiled then. A real, uninhibited smile that said I had said exactly the right thing. "Good. I hoped you'd say that."

I stepped up to the full set of glass windows along the back wall and admired the rectangular pool set into the hill just below eye level. But the real beauty was the endless Hollywood Hills on display. It was a treasure.

Campbell wrapped his arms around my waist and pulled me in close. "I dreamed about you being here."

I turned in his embrace and laughed. "No you didn't. You never thought we'd ever talk again."

"That's why it was a dream," he said, bumping his nose gently against mine. "I never thought it would be a reality."

"And now that it is?"

"I don't ever want to wake up."

Then he kissed me, and we both forgot the entire world existed.

30

BLAIRE

*E*nglish showed up at Campbell's house the next morning. She was relatively tall with stick-straight blonde hair and wore a white suit that screamed *powerful woman*.

"You must be Blaire!"

"That's me."

"I'm so happy to finally meet you. I hope you and Campbell don't mind that I brought my fiancé with me. He wanted to see the famed Hills." She whispered behind her hand, "He's so New York."

I laughed. I had also never seen the Hollywood Hills. So, I understood what her fiancé must be feeling. Though I was clearly a Texas girl through and through. "I don't mind. I'm sure Campbell won't either."

"All right." She turned around and yelled, "Court Kensington, get your ass over here."

The passenger door popped open, and one of *the* hottest guys I had ever seen in my entire life stepped out of the car. My eyes rounded, and I had to keep my jaw from dropping. He was nearly six and a half feet tall with striking good looks, piercing blue eyes, and a suit that molded to his body. His stride looked more like a predator come to feast on his prey. And like you would be happy to let him do so. I had friends with money. I was dating a bona fide rockstar. But I'd never seen anything like Court Kensington.

English laughed when she saw my expression. "Oh yeah, he kind of has that effect on people. It's the old, *old* money, I think. They drink the Kool-Aid."

Court straightened his suit and then held his hand out. "Hello, I'm Court. Thank you for allowing me to interrupt your meeting."

I shook his hand and stared practically straight up. He was over a foot taller than me and gorgeous. Like, *good for English*! "No problem. Come on in."

Campbell appeared then in a pair of jeans and an old band shirt. "English! Hey, you made it!" They hugged like old friends, and then Campbell shook Court's hand. "Heard so much about you. Excited for you're finally tying the knot."

Court smiled, and I saw the depths of his affection for English in that one look. "We're looking forward to it. Aren't we, honey?"

English shot him a look. "It's not fair that your brother eloped, and so now, I have to do the giant New York wedding thing. I already had the giant LA wedding. This one should be small. Can't we be like Penn and Natalie?"

"Please don't ever say that again."

English snickered and winked at me.

"Plus, my mother would kill me," he explained to the two of us.

"She's the mayor of New York City," English filled in.

I gaped. "Oh, *that* Kensington."

He grimaced. "Yes, that Kensington."

"Well, I'm sure it's going to be beautiful."

English smiled, and the fight left her. "It really is. Y'all should come!"

Court rolled his eyes. "Don't overwhelm her. She met you one minute ago."

"But seriously, there's going to be, like, hundreds of people. You could definitely come." Campbell and I glanced at each other, and then English laughed. "You know, once we get all of this worked out." She gestured between us. "Speaking of, where should we sit? I am ready with a plan. If I can clean up Court Kensington's mess of a reputation, I can do anything."

Court snorted but didn't argue. It must have been true.

Campbell directed us into the dining room. He had coffee made, and while he poured for Court, English got out a large notebook full of her blocky handwriting.

"Okay. So, let's start with what you want before I get into what I have," she said, snatching the cup out of Court's hand and taking the first sip. He just shook his head at her and then poured another mug. "I know that when we talked last, Blaire, we were working out endorsement deals for your career. But since then, things have...changed." She arched an eyebrow at the pair of us.

"Yes, we're a couple," Campbell said. "Which you probably guessed when you took Blaire on."

"Obviously," she said with a smile. "Half of the world already thinks that you are. The rest are hoping you aren't. What do you want to do about that?"

Campbell threaded his fingers with mine and nodded his head. I swallowed. "I think we're ready to go public."

"Okay. Explain. How public? *Make a TikTok video* public? *Be seen together at a gala* public? *Answer questions from paparazzi* public?"

Campbell laughed at my horrified expression. "What do you think, English?"

"We should do what you're most comfortable with. I would probably schedule everything to happen all at once."

"You already planned for this," I guessed.

She nodded. "I'm the best for a reason. Need to be ready for all contingencies." She flipped the page over. "So, since you're already known online, you'll start with a video. Maybe you kiss on-screen. That sort of thing. That will release exactly a half hour before you appear at this event." She tugged out a card and passed it to Campbell.

I glanced over his shoulder and read about the gala for music education in local schools. The letter was thick solid black card stock with embossed gold lettering. It was fancy.

Campbell groaned. "I'll need a tux?"

"Obviously," English said with a laugh. "We'll send you to the event together. I'll have handpicked reporters there to speak to you with specific questions to ask at the entrance. You'll be prepared with answers from yours truly. And then it's up to you. You can go quiet for a few weeks and just let it kind of die down and blow over. Which is probably your best bet. I see a lot of people go work the media circuit and be seen in clubs and such." She cringed. "It's a lot of wasted energy. Plus, it looks like a PR stunt, which you are not."

"It sounds good. Though I didn't bring anything nice enough for a gala," I said.

English smiled brightly, and Court groaned, "Oh no."

"I guess we'll have to go shopping then, won't we?"

Campbell laughed. "That's a good plan. You think it will blow over?"

"You'll get questions about your relationship for a while, but if you just let people know, make it firm but polite, and then don't talk about it, it will be smooth and steady."

"I didn't realize this much planning went into a relationship announcement."

English beamed. "It doesn't usually, but that's how rookies make mistakes. When you're as famous as Campbell Abbey, it's better to be safe than sorry."

"All right," I said with a shrug. What did I know about Hollywood?

"Now, Campbell, go show Court around. He's fidgeting."

Campbell stood and did as he had been told. "Just as bossy as ever, English."

"Bossy girls get shit done." She waited until they were gone, and then her smile dropped. "Are you sure you want to do this?"

"What? You just had this whole plan."

"And it's a great plan. I made it after all. As long as you're comfortable." She put her hand on mine. "I know you love him." I balked because I hadn't even said those words yet. "He's an amazing guy. I'm lucky to call him my friend. But dating a celebrity is scary. Trust me, I know. I was married to Josh Hutch once upon a time."

I gaped at her. "The movie star?"

She nodded. "Yep. I want to watch out for *you* first. This will come down harder on you than him."

"Do you think it's a bad idea?"

"Telling the truth is never a bad plan. But public outcry will fall on you. People will want to be you. They'll want what you have. They're going to be jealous. And jealous people are mean. You handle social media like a pro, but this is next level. I've lived it, and I know how devastating it can be to see what total strangers say about you on the internet. So, you have to be a hundred percent sure." She shot me a meaningful look. "Are you?"

I gulped. I was totally sure about Campbell. Things were

tricky with our past, but I had never been happier since I'd let him back into my life. I was here in LA. I was sure this was what I wanted. Right?

"You know what? Don't answer," English said. She squeezed my hand. "Think about it. The gala isn't until this weekend. We can plan for it like it's all happening, and if you want to back out and give it some more time, that is A-okay. No one's feelings are going to be hurt if you want to protect yourself."

I swallowed and nodded. "Okay. Thanks, English."

"I'm your publicist. Not Campbell's. I am looking out for you, girl. You are my number one priority."

"Really, thank you."

English smiled, and it reached her eyes again. "Why don't I show you around Rodeo Drive, huh?"

Campbell was jittery the rest of the day. He was ready to get into the studio Monday to talk to Michael, but I forced him to spend the afternoon here with me in the summer sun, lounging poolside. It was relaxing after the conversation with English, where she'd warned me that my entire life was about to change. I hoped that I was making the right decision.

The next morning, I found what Campbell spent his money on.

"Holy shit," I gasped as I stepped into his garage, full of sports cars. "What the fuck, Campbell? You drive a Range Rover at home."

He ran a hand back through his hair but was smirking. "I have a thing for classic sports cars."

"I can see that."

I wasn't a car buff, but even I knew that most of these were worth a pretty penny.

"I didn't buy them all mint. Sometimes, Vail helps me figure out which ones to get. She's been out a few times to work on them with me. It clears my head."

"And you get your hands dirty," I said with a wink. "Hot."

He snorted and pointed one out. "This baby. That's what we'll take. It's a '61 Ferrari California Spider."

"I don't know what that means, but yes."

I ran my hand down the shiny black finish, opened the passenger door, and sank into the leather interior. It was the most beautiful car I'd ever seen, let alone ridden in.

"We'll take the top down on the way home," he told me as he revved the engine.

He brought my hand to his lips and gave me a kiss. Then, he shifted into gear, and we shot out of the garage and down out of Hollywood Hills.

Campbell dropped me off outside of The Beverly Hills Hotel, where Court and English were staying. He kissed me before driving off toward the studio. I met English at the front entrance.

"You ready?" she asked.

"Yep."

We took a cab to Rodeo Drive, and I was mesmerized by all the shiny boutiques. English knew exactly where she wanted to go, as if she was a pro. We tried out outrageously priced gowns half of the morning before we found *the one*.

"Oh my God," she gasped. "That fit is fire."

I laughed. It was stunning. Maybe the most beautiful thing I'd ever worn.

I passed English my phone. "Grab a picture."

She held the phone up and took a bunch of snaps from different angles. "That's the one. I know it is."

I sent it to my group chat and Honey, who had been messaging me about work all morning. I immediately received a wall of responses.

Annie: Yes!

Jennifer: Holy shit, Blaire!

Annie: Yes, yes, yes!!!

Piper: Whoa, that is gorgeous. Where are you wearing something like that?

Annie: Don't ruin this for us, Pipes. Tell us you're buying it!

I glanced down at the tag. My eyes bulged. It was in the mid-four-digit range. For *one* dress. I gulped. Well, that changed things. "It's too much."

"No worries," she said. "Campbell slipped me his card to cover it for you."

"He *what*?"

English laughed. "He said something about spoiling you."

"That sneaky bastard."

"You'll get used to it," English said with another laugh at my outrage. "Court is the same way. I make great money, and still, he wants to pay for all my shit. I've learned to go with it. It's better than the alternative when the guy is an asshole and nickel-and-dimes everything he pays for, as if you owe him after the fact."

"Well, yes, I suppose so."

"So, we'll get it." She gestured to the clerk to ring it up.

I responded to the long string of messages.

It's official. It's mine!

The girls all squealed with delight in my messages, and I just laughed. I wished they were all here, shopping with me. I missed them.

Honey's response came in then.

Wow, Blaire. It's perfect. I've never seen anything like it. You're still coming home, right? Everything is so glamorous out there!

I laughed and shot back a text.

I am definitely still coming home. This is for one event. You'd love it here.

English crossed her arms. "Now, I have one business question."

"Okay." I handed her back my phone and then stepped into the dressing room to remove the gorgeous dress. I still couldn't believe it was going home with me.

"Nate King."

I winced. "Oh."

"Yeah, oh. You know, he's actually the cousin of a friend of mine."

"Is it Gavin?"

"Yes!" English said. "You know Gavin?"

"I knew that Nate went to New York to visit him."

"What a small world," English said. "So, what's up with you two? I noticed he hasn't been on your feed in about two weeks, but he was all over it before that. What happened? All the sordid details, please. It's better for me to know what I'm walking into. Nothing seems confirmed either way on social, which makes it a lot more amorphous."

I sighed and then stepped back out of the dressing room. "Nate and I never dated. He went to my friend's wedding with me, and we hooked up. Nothing official, and then I realized we weren't into each other. We're still friends and business associates. He's met Campbell. He knows what's up."

"I see. Hmm...do you think he'd be willing to make a video, congratulating you on Saturday? That way, it's clear you two aren't together and you haven't been for a while?"

"I could ask him. I don't see why he wouldn't."

"It's going to be sticky either way." She tapped her mouth. "But no worries. I'll figure it out. If you give me his contact, I can reach out to him myself."

"Okay. Sure. You think people will be mad?"

"Campbell Soup girls? Definitely. The rest of the world? Probably not."

"All right."

English signed off on the receipt and thanked the sales-person. The dress would be delivered to Campbell's house later in the week. She linked arms with me as we traipsed out of the designer boutique and then stopped in her tracks at the next location. Her smile curled up on the corners like the Grinch when he had a terrible thought.

"What?" I asked. Then, I saw the lingerie boutique in question—La Perla.

"If we're using Campbell's credit card, we might as well use it for good, right?" English asked.

My grin matched hers. "Oh, definitely."

31

CAMPBELL

"He's not here yet," Viv said before I could even open my mouth.

I deflated. "How did you know I was going to ask?"

She arched an eyebrow and picked at her new neon-purple nail polish. "Because I know you."

"Bobby is waiting for us," Santi said, bounding in my direction.

We hit knuckles.

"And West?"

"I introduced him to Micky, and they started in on technical speak. I lost whatever the thread was and left them to it. I bet they're already in the studio, figuring shit out."

I nodded. Well, that was a relief. Micky worked in the recording booth. He knew his shit. He'd helped record our last two albums. If he and West hit it off, it was going to make our lives a lot easier.

"Good. And Yorke?"

"Can you believe that one of the receptionists is a Peppermint Patty?" Santi asked.

"Yes," Viv and I said together. We glanced at each other and cracked up.

"He's like the fucking Witcher. He basically grunted and said *fuck* through the whole conversation, and she had heart eyes." He opened his eyes wider and fluttered his eyelashes.

Viv smacked him. "Hey, be nice."

I laughed at the whole spectacle. I was glad that we were all still good, even with everything that had happened with Michael. He felt like an essential part of our team. Like we'd lost an appendage. I hoped we wouldn't have to learn to live without him.

Yorke came around the corner with a smirk on his lips. His hands were in his pockets, and he nodded at me. "Sup."

"Heard the receptionist is a Peppermint Patty."

He arched an eyebrow. "Yep."

"You get her number?"

"Yep."

"Cool, bro."

The door opened then, and Bobby Rogers stood there, waiting for us.

"Campbell, you made it!" He shook my hand vigorously. "You ready to get back into the studio?"

I frowned. "Yeah, Bobby, I'm ready. We have, like, half an album, but what about Michael?"

"Michael. Yes, of course. Let's go chat with him."

I glanced at the rest of the band in confusion. Bobby seemed ready for us to get started, but Michael was still the biggest unknown for me. We'd written and released the last two albums with him. I couldn't imagine doing this one without him.

We followed Bobby into a conference room. Michael entered as we were all taking seats at the table. He looked... good. Better than I'd seen him in Lubbock. He'd shaved, and his clothes were neat. But the biggest change was that he was smiling. I didn't realize until then that I hadn't seen him smile in months.

"Hey, Michael," I said, jumping to my feet to shake his hand. "Good to see you, man."

"You too, Campbell."

He hugged Viv and then shook hands with Santi and Yorke. Santi looked like he wanted to pull him in for a hug of his own, but we were on uneven ground here. Santi's normal antics had started the explosion that ended with Michael leaving the band. None of us knew exactly what was going to go down.

Michael took a tentative seat across from me.

"Go on, Michael. Tell them," Bobby said.

We looked from one to the other.

"Tell us what?" I asked.

"I thought a lot about it, and I want out of the band."

"Michael," I said, getting back to my feet.

Santi followed my suit. "Come on, man. It wasn't like that."

Yorke kicked his seat back onto two legs, looking more somber than normal. Viv bit her lip and crossed her arms. She looked like she had been bracing herself for this. As if she'd known it was coming since she'd tried to talk to him before he got on that plane out of Lubbock.

Michael held up his hand. "I know it's a big step. I know you're probably all mad at me for leaving. I don't blame you for any of it. I was mad, and I said things that I regret. You're all still family to me as far as I'm concerned. The last couple years have been incredible. More than I ever thought was possible for me to have. But my journey with Cosmere ends here."

"But *why*?" I demanded. "Because of Lubbock?"

"No. Look, we made the best music in years there. I get why we got out of LA. I just can't keep on with this lifestyle. I can't be away from my Virginia and Maisie like this. I owe them more than that." He shrugged. "We have enough money to live off for life if we needed to. And Bobby...he offered me a role in production if I wanted to stay in LA."

I looked at Bobby, as if seeing him for the first time. He was very calm. He'd already known *exactly* what this conversation was going to be. He'd decided Michael was out and offered him a way to still be in the music industry without being in the band and away from his family. Best of both worlds. And he'd told none of us.

"You knew," I accused anyway.

Bobby shot me a look full of pity. Then, he smiled that viper smile. "Of course I knew, kid. This isn't my first rodeo."

"Then, why did you get us all together like this? I thought we were going to talk to him to get him on the same page. You said we just needed to give him time."

"Campbell," Viv whispered.

But my carefully controlled anger, the anger I'd spent years in therapy getting under wraps, was catapulting to the surface. I didn't want to lose Michael. Not to this.

"Whose side are you on?" I snarled.

"There are no sides, kiddo," Bobby said with that same smile. "There's just the music industry. Michael wants out. You want to stay in. If you wanted out, that'd be a different story. You're the front man. You write the lyrics. Cosmere doesn't exist without you."

Viv looked down at her nails. Santi glanced at Yorke, who was staring fixedly at the table. Michael huffed in irritation at the brush-off. That he could leave and everything would be okay but not if I left.

"No," I said. "There's no Cosmere without the band. There's nothing without Michael either."

"Campbell," Santi said with a sigh, "Michael wants out."

I whirled on Michael. "You *love* this band. You love performing and creating music. Do you really want to give that all up in our prime? So you can sit behind the booth and watch other people do it?"

"I..." He hesitated, as if he hadn't considered that question.

"Cosmere is as much your band as mine. We *want* you to be in it," I insisted. "We flew home to talk to you, to try to bring you back. Not to just roll over to Bobby Rogers, just because he's fine with you going."

"All right, Campbell. He heard you," Bobby said.

"We do want you back," Viv said.

Santi nodded. "We're sorry about what looked like an ambush. It was my stupid mouth. You know how I am."

"Yeah," Michael said with a soft laugh. "I guess I do. I was just so frustrated that I was missing everything with Maisie. I don't want to do that anymore. I don't want to miss anything."

"We get how important they are to you," I said.

Michael shook his head. "No, you don't. You can't understand. None of you are married. None of you have kids. It's just a different world. And fuck, I want to stay in the band. You know I love you, but it feels like it's one or the other."

"We can bring them on tour. We can stay in LA to record," I bargained.

"These things weren't offered until I threatened to *leave*," Michael said. "That's bullshit, Campbell, and you know it."

"It's not Campbell's fault either," Santi said. "We did what was best for the band. We didn't realize you were going to leave because you had to make some sacrifices."

"Sacrifice is *all* I've done for this band," Michael said.

"So, what are you going to do?" Viv snapped. "Leave? Quit? Are you a quitter, Michael?"

He opened his mouth and closed it. "Fuck, Viv. That's how it's going to be?"

"There's a compromise here," I interjected. Because Viv had my temper, too, but it was not the Hulk; it was Black Widow—slower to rise but inevitably swift and merciless.

"If he wants to go, then let him go," Viv shot back. "We have been here for you for *years*. We're your family, too. And you're abandoning us. So, sure, run home to the wife and kid. Leave us behind and in the lurch without you. If that's what you want but remember that you left your family behind."

"That's not what this is," Michael said.

"Isn't it?" Yorke asked. It was the first time he'd spoken, and the fact that he was agreeing with Viv was like Thor bringing down his hammer.

Michael flinched at the words. "I want to stay, but I can't. So, if that means I'm abandoning you, if that's how you see it, then fine. Say what you want. I wanted to reconcile. I'll be around. I'll help with the album even. It's just...it's just over for me."

Then, he stood, turned on his heel, and walked out of the room.

We were silent for a few minutes as Bobby followed him.

Then, I slumped back into my seat, all my anger dissipating in an instant. "Fuck."

Viv nodded. "Yeah."

"What are we going to do?" Santi asked.

Yorke got to his feet. "We're going to get into the studio and record the best album of our career. Fuck him."

Our eyes widened at that. It was the most words I'd ever heard him string together. And it also got us moving.

We trudged out of the conference room and down to the studio. West was in the recording booth, playing the piano for Micky. I recognized it as the melody for "After You," which was heavy on keys. We waited for him to finish before entering.

"Let's try it from the top," I told him.

West arched an eyebrow. "Michael?"

"He's out."

West's face crumpled. "Sorry, man."

I just shrugged. We'd talked to him. He'd chosen. There was nothing more we could do.

"Let's just show them what we have."

32

CAMPBELL

We didn't leave the studio until after nine that night. I rubbed my eyes as I drove the Ferrari back into the Hills. I'd promised Blaire that I'd pick her up and drive with the top down, but it hadn't worked out. Studio days were always *long* days. I just hadn't anticipated it.

I'd sent a car to drive her back up to my house on one of our breaks and told her about the dinner options. I had nothing in my fridge or pantry, thanks to the tour and then months in Lubbock, but some places delivered at least.

She'd assured me that it was fine. But we'd only been in the city for a few days, and already, I was breaking promises. Was this how Michael felt? Was this the reason he'd left us?

It was too heavy for me to think about. My fingers were cramping for the first time in years. The riffs in "Rooftop Nights" were next level. Even though Yorke had insisted that he could take the bulk of the work, I couldn't give it all up. Plus, our harmonies sounded better together than anything either of us could do solo.

I used to relish these nights. My brain fuzzy from hours

in the studio. My voice scratchy and fingers aching. Crawling into bed and passing out, only to do it day after day. It was all I'd wanted.

Now, that had changed. The other thing I wanted was waiting for me inside.

I parked in the garage and came upstairs, dropping my guitar at the entrance. "Blaire?"

"I'm back here," she called from the bedroom.

As I trudged through the living room, I covered a yawn with my hand. "Have a nice time shopping?"

"I did."

Then, I stepped into the bedroom and froze. It was lit with dozens of candles of all different shapes and sizes. The bed was strewn with rose petals. The darkened bachelor pad had turned miraculously into something straight out of a movie. And lying at the center of it all was Blaire Barker in nothing but a forest-green lingerie set that left absolutely nothing to the imagination.

"Fuck."

She ran a hand down her bare side with a mischievous glint in her eye. "Do you like what I got at La Perla?"

"Are you going to like it when I rip it off?"

She grinned. "I thought you'd never ask."

I took three long strides to her side, cupped her face in my hands, and devoured her mouth. She made a soft squeak of acquiescence before our tongues tangled together in a passionate kiss. I drew her bottom lip into my mouth, biting down hard enough for her to gasp.

My hands moved down over her jet-black hair and to the scrap of lace fabric that must have cost her a small fortune at the lingerie store. And I didn't give a shit that she'd spent my money on it. It was the best gift I could have asked for in this moment.

Here, I'd been worrying that she'd be frustrated with my late nights. Meanwhile, she had been planning a surprise for me that I would never, ever forget. Her sprawled on my bed with nothing but a few choice pieces of lace covering her body would be ingrained in my brain for the rest of my life.

I drew my fingers across her sides and under her breasts. Green elastic hugged the sides of her breasts with a petal of green lace obscuring her nipples. I flicked the sensitive skin, plucking it like the strings of my guitar as she groaned.

"Campbell," she gasped.

I tipped her head backward and kissed down the line of her throat. Then lower and lower until I pulled that erect nipple into my mouth. Even through the little fabric, she squirmed and clutched at me.

"Oh!"

I yanked down the other strap, exposing her full breast before diving back in and sucking her nipple. She arched against me as I massaged the other breast. I couldn't get enough of her body. Of the way she moaned at every little touch and tried to get away while also pushing me down harder.

This girl, this woman, was too much. She was everything. Everything I had ever wanted. I had no idea how I'd lived without her.

My lips moved lower, down the flat of her stomach, to her navel. The panties were high-waisted, a strip of material along her waist with a triangle of lace obscuring her sweet pussy. Garter straps dangled off the bottom, attached to pantyhose.

She was a vision.

I dragged a finger down the front of her. I arched an eyebrow. "Someone has been thinking about me."

She smirked. "It was hard to wait."

I stilled at that comment. "Did you get off while you waited for me?"

"Maybe," she whispered. Her eyes glittered with desire.

I tugged aside the lace of her thong and slid two fingers through her. She *was* so wet. Oh fuck. "And what were you thinking about when you got yourself off?"

"You."

I inhaled sharply. "That's what I like to hear. Would you like me to get you off again?"

She nodded. "Fuck me."

"Oh, my girl, you don't have to ask me twice."

I shed my clothes in a frenzy. My cock was already rigid with desire. If it hadn't been before she told me she'd fucked herself, waiting for me, it certainly was now. I ripped a condom open and sheathed myself before dragging her ass toward me off the edge of the bed.

"What are you—"

But I slammed into her before she could finish. She gasped as I bottomed out deep into her pussy. She was so wet from masturbating that she needed no warm-up. Just opened herself up perfectly for me.

"Fuck," she moaned.

I wrapped her legs around me, grabbed her hips, and dragged slow and steady out of her. Her eyes rolled into the back of her head.

I swept my thumb across her bottom lip. "Eyes open, love."

They snapped wide to meet me as I drove home into her again. She shuddered at the feeling, and truthfully, I was barely holding on. I could have come right then and there at the sight of her nearly naked on my bed.

My hands slid up her sides as I pressed our bodies

tighter together. Her eyes were trained on mine as soft pants escaped her lips.

"More," she pleaded with me.

And I gave her everything she could ever want. Everything I'd ever held back. I sealed our bodies together until there was nothing left but a few scraps of lingerie and the beading of sweat on our bodies as I claimed what was mine.

She had always been mine.

She would always be mine.

It was incredible how I had existed without her. One minute, I had been living the dream—or so I'd thought. I'd had my music out to the entire world. I had been hitting bestseller lists and selling out stadiums and winning awards. Somehow, none of that compared to when I held Blaire in my arms.

It was then that I realized what I'd really been feeling all this time.

It wasn't that I'd made a mistake. I'd followed my dreams, and I had the world on a platter. I was at the top of my game. I wouldn't give that up.

But I should have let her come with me. I'd thought I was doing the right thing by breaking up with her and demanding she follow her own path. I didn't want to be responsible for her not going to college. I didn't want to see her lose her way, all for some guy. I'd known then that we meant more to each other, and still, I hadn't let her make her own choice. I had chosen for her.

And that resulted in eight years without her.

That was my regret.

My one regret in this otherwise seemingly perfect life.

I wanted Blaire.

I wanted to come home to this goddess every day of my life.

I'd never felt that with anyone else. And I didn't want to give this girl up again. I couldn't lose her. Not for anything.

"Blaire," I said as I felt everything crest inside of me, "I want this. Us."

She pressed her hand to my face and kissed me. "Yes."

It was the word that broke the dam. I felt her contract all around my cock.

"Fuck," I spat. "God, you're coming hard."

She writhed underneath me, trying to get closer, digging grooves into my back with her nails. A keening emanated from her voice as her orgasm hit her like a ton of bricks. And all it did was trigger my own.

I let out a string of curses as my body went rigid, and I unleashed deep inside of her. She milked me for every single drop as we came together. Everything shook inside of me, and then I collapsed forward.

Kiss after kiss I pressed across her shoulders and chest. "My goddess. My queen. My everything."

She laughed softly at my words. "So, it was good for you?"

I met her wild blue gaze. "Perfect."

"I'm glad you liked the lingerie."

"You are perfect. The lingerie is just a bonus," I said as I kissed her collarbone.

She threaded her fingers through my messy, dark hair. "I want to stay like this forever."

"Me too."

I laid my head against her chest and listened to the rhythm of her heart slow to a steady drumbeat. Then, I hoisted myself off her and discarded the condom. She headed into the bathroom and returned a few minutes later to crash back down on the bed.

"How was the studio?" she asked as she snuggled up against me.

"It was work."

"Sorry about Michael."

I shrugged. "We tried. We'll figure it out. What did you do today other than shop?"

"Work," she said, glancing up at me dreamily. "I edited a ton of videos and talked to Nate."

I arched an eyebrow. "Nate?"

She laughed at my expression. "English thinks he should do a video on Saturday to congratulate us after we announce our relationship. She thinks it'll go a long way toward goodwill."

"Ah," I said. "That English is smart. How did Nate take that?"

"He didn't care. We're just friends."

"Uh-huh," I said, tipping her chin up with my finger and pressing a kiss to her swollen lips.

"Girls and guys can be friends."

"Sure. Just not ones we recently slept with."

She swatted at me with a laugh. "Even those."

I took her hand and kissed each individual finger. "Blaire, you know you're important to me, right?"

"You're important to me, too."

"I know that my job isn't ideal for a relationship. Seeing Michael today showed just how problematic it can be."

"It's new, Campbell. We don't have to decide all of that today."

"I know. But I've realized that I can't live without you."

Her eyes were wide with that statement. "Is that so?"

"I made a mistake, not letting you make a decision. Not being there the way you needed me in the past. I don't want to be that guy this time." I took a deep breath before saying, "I love you."

She gasped softly, as if she hadn't been expecting those words. Truthfully, I hadn't known that I was going to say them. I was in love with her. She was my entire world. And the last thing I wanted was to be separated from her. I just couldn't have her not knowing that.

"I love you, too," she said, pushing to her elbows for another kiss.

"You do? It's not too soon?"

She shook her head. "I can't deny it either."

She snuggled down against me, her breathing going even again. She repeated the words, as if she couldn't quite believe we'd said them, "I love you."

And as she fell asleep in my arms, I repeated them back to her. Three words, one promise. "I love you."

33

BLAIRE

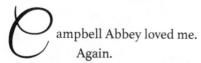ampbell Abbey loved me.

Again.

It felt surreal to even think that we could be here. After everything, we'd made it back to this point. And somehow, it was both easier and harder than before.

Easier because we were older and knew the extent of our feelings. We knew precisely what it would be like to be without the other. How difficult it was. But more difficult for so very many reasons. Not the least of all, his celebrity status and the fact that...while it was amazing to be here, I'd eventually have to return to Lubbock.

My life and friends were there.

Campbell's life was here.

But I believed we could find a compromise. I just didn't know yet what it was.

Even though I was in LA with him now, he was at the studio at all hours of the day. It wouldn't always be like this, of course, but then he'd be on tour and promoting and award season. It would be difficult but not impossible.

At least, I wanted to try before dismissing it entirely.

We had a second chance. I refused to squander it.

But while he was in the studio, rehearsing and structuring the songs that would one day become an album, I still had to run my own business. I'd dropped all the content with Nate on English's suggestion. It pained me to give up a week's worth of videos that we'd scripted, recorded, and paid for. But that was for the best, long-term, considering what I would be walking into at the gala this weekend.

Luckily, Honey had backup content ready to go and I had plenty of footage of the band. Though I also felt like I shouldn't show *too* much of it since English was now consulting with an entertainment lawyer about the docuseries. Which meant more work for me here in Hollywood.

I'd taken to carrying my tripod around with me early in the morning and shooting a bunch of *Blaire Blush* discussions at various famous LA locales. Yesterday, I'd even taken a cab over to Santa Monica Pier and recorded on the actual Ferris wheel.

Today, I was on the Hollywood Walk of Fame in front of Grauman's Chinese Theatre. My phone dinged for the five hundredth time today just as I'd set up my tripod.

I clicked to my text messages and found another one from Honey.

Wish I were there to film this one. I've always wanted to go to Grauman's!

I shot back a quick note.

Next time!

Is Campbell there with you?

Nope! Just me. He's too busy.

Too bad! Well, don't have too much fun without me.

I sent her back a dancing emoji, which was my cue to her that I was getting back to work, and pressed record. I stepped back and performed the dance I'd learned the night before. I was halfway through when a man stopped in front of me.

"Uh, excuse me," I said, gesturing to the tripod.

"Are you Blaire Barker?" He had a camera in his hand and pointed it in my direction.

I gawked at him. How the hell did he know that?

"Uh, yeah?" I stepped forward, shutting off my camera and slinging my bag over my shoulder. It never felt like a good thing when a random stranger knew my name.

"You run *Blaire Blush*?" He was still talking to me through his camera.

"I don't want to have this conversation."

I turned and walked away. My hands were shaking slightly as I made a hasty retreat, passing over Bruce Willis's Hollywood star. The man kept up with me, and suddenly, another man with a camera was jogging across the street toward us.

What the *fuck*?

"Blaire," the man said.

"Leave me alone."

"Is it true that you're in a relationship with Campbell Abbey?"

I gaped at them, which was probably answer enough. I needed to get my facial expressions under control. Now, they had that shocked look on camera forever.

I continued walking away from them. But as I turned the corner, I nearly slammed into a group of tourists.

"Sorry," I gasped.

"It's her!" one of them said, clutching my arm.

"I knew we'd find her nearby. She went live in front of the theater," another said.

I tried to tug away from the person, but she was still holding on to me. "Let me go!"

"You're the person that Campbell decided to date?" a third said in disgust.

"She doesn't look like much."

I had no idea how any of them knew I was dating Campbell or who the hell they were, but my fight-or-flight was kicking in. I was ready to get the hell out of here.

That was the moment I realized that they were all wearing the same jean jacket. And on the chest was a Campbell Soup symbol. These were Campbell Soup girls. They'd *tracked* me down. Let me repeat, what the fuck?

"Let me go," I said, jerking away from the girls. I finally pulled away hard enough that she released me. But this mob of girls looked much more menacing than the set of Campbell Soup girls I'd met in Lubbock.

I turned for another escape, but the paparazzi had caught up to me and were shoving cameras in my face. Flashes went off. The world tilted as my claustrophobia hit fresh and new and disorienting. The internet had speculated that Campbell and I were dating, but I had been more careful about what I was posting. Many people had moved on to thinking that I was just filming the entire band for their new album, which was also true.

But these people *knew*. They had been stalking me and come out to my last known location to harass me. I didn't know their objective, but it couldn't be good.

"This can't be the girl," the first woman said.

"Blaire." One of the cameras was stuffed into my face, and the flash went off.

I blinked, momentarily blinded by the light.

"Is it true that you're the 'I See the Real You' girl?"

My vision dipped, and my stomach went with it. "What?" I whispered, horrified.

That was one of the questions that I'd gone over with English for the gala on Saturday. We figured we might as well admit that I was the girl everyone had already guessed at. She'd thought it would make a good angle for people to be sympathetic to our love story. Or something.

But now that the question was out in the open, being asked by multiple paparazzi with cameras in my face, I went blank. I forgot everything she'd told me. All I could think about was the sad little girl left behind by Campbell. The person I'd shattered into after he set off for LA, like he'd always planned, leaving me alone and pregnant. I'd forgiven him for what he'd done to me. For making me the "I See the Real You" girl after all of that. The constant, ever-present reminder of what I'd lost. But I still had qualms about the world finding out.

It was one thing to be his new flame from home. It was another thing entirely for my entire life to be out there for the world to digest as they saw fit.

And now, I could barely breathe. I had no right answer. No way to get this past my teeth.

This was not our carefully controlled situation. This was chaos incarnate. This was being mobbed *again*. A group of angry Campbell Soup girls and a flood of paps, trying to get the latest gossip, trying to break me. The small-town girl from the middle of nowhere, Texas, who couldn't hack it in LA.

No amount of minor celebrity status could have prepared me for this. Not even the mob feeling on the Fourth of July. That had been *nothing* compared to this.

Everything felt like it was closing in on me. I couldn't move. I couldn't breathe. I was panicking. All that preparation was out the window with this unexpected setback. My phone was buzzing noisily. I was sure that the news must have broken already. That Campbell or English or Honey or any of my friends were checking in on me. And I was just standing here, paralyzed, as questions were fired at me.

No one was going to help me. No one was going to let me out of this. And it wasn't like Lubbock, where I knew the city like the back of my hand. I was on Hollywood Boulevard and had no idea how the fuck to get away from here.

My eyes scanned the area directly around us. I was only five feet tall on a good day, and it was hard to see over the crowd of people. One of the Campbell Soup girls grabbed at me again. That was the moment that I'd had enough.

"I said, let me go," I shrieked at her.

Then, I lowered my shoulder and rammed through the crowd. I needed out, and I needed out any way that I could get out of there. I didn't have to stay and be polite. If they wanted to paint me as unstable because I didn't want to be mobbed in public, then I just couldn't care anymore. I couldn't care when this was unacceptable. I didn't deserve this.

We'd had a plan.

A *plan*.

And it was all falling apart.

My chest hurt, and I managed to hold back my tears by sheer force of will. I was glad that I'd dressed in an athletic kit and tennis shoes because I moved a lot faster than anyone else. I'd always been small and fast. It was to my advantage today.

As soon as I cleared the crowd, which had grown with people stopping to find out what was going on and what celebrity they could see, I took off at a dead sprint. All those hours of soccer practice had sure helped me in this regard. It wasn't until I found a convenience store and stumbled into the restroom, bolting the lock behind me, that I finally was able to catalog how I felt.

Which was terrible.

My body was trembling. The claustrophobic feeling had ebbed, now replaced with shock. Tears finally cascaded freely down my cheeks. I'd lost my tripod somewhere in the melee. Luckily, I'd held on to my phone, which was still vibrating. But I didn't answer.

I just sank onto the toilet seat and let tears rack my body. The danger was gone, but the fear and misery remained. I needed a minute before the rest of the world could be let back in. Before I was going to be okay again.

34

CAMPBELL

"Come on. Come on. Come on," I argued with my phone as I dialed Blaire for what felt like the millionth time.

Still fucking nothing.

I nearly threw it against the wall with irritation.

"Hey, you'll get ahold of her," Viv said. "It will be fine."

Santi nodded. "It's not the end of the world."

"Blaire is strong," West added. He was slumped into a seat nearby, looking solemn.

Only Yorke said nothing.

"She was fucking mobbed the last time we were photographed together. I don't have high hopes for the rest of humanity," I growled.

A half hour ago, Micky had stalled recording when he got a call from Bobby. A minute after that, we were all in front of the computer screen, staring at breaking celebrity news on TMZ about *Campbell Abbey's new girlfriend*. The picture featured was us standing together in Lubbock after she finished shooting with Nate. We weren't even touching, but just the way I looked at her...fuck, it was so obvious that I was in love with her.

That all might have been okay, but the headline read, "At Last, We Meet the 'I See the Real You' Girl." I'd slammed my fist into the wall when I read it. My knuckles were bleeding, which was the only damage done.

But my anger, once ignited, was an inferno. I was snapping at everyone. Getting progressively more irritated and terrified that I couldn't get ahold of Blaire. English had called and was already running interference on the whole thing. It was a disaster. We had a matter of days before we were going to go public, and now, this bullshit.

Controlling the narrative was important. I knew that. And now, we were fucked.

English kept saying it would be fine, but it didn't feel fine. I wouldn't feel fine until Blaire was safely tucked into my arms again. Until then, I was going to fucking freak out.

I dialed the number again, holding the phone to my ear and pacing relentlessly. Finally, the line clicked over.

I gave a relieved sigh. "Blaire?"

"Hey," she said, her voice all shaky and full of tears.

My heart contracted at that sound. "Oh, thank God. Are you okay?"

She was slow to respond. "I...I don't know."

"What happened?"

"The news about our relationship broke."

"I know," I said on a sigh. "I saw the article on TMZ."

"Apparently, I'm the 'I See the Real You' girl now," she said, "and your fans don't like that."

"What did they do?" I asked, low and dangerous. I didn't have much interaction with the Campbell Soup girls, but if they hurt Blaire, I would burn the world down.

"Some paparazzi found me based off the videos in my

Stories, I guess. And the Campbell Soup girls found me the same way. I was kind of bombarded. I ran away, and I'm hiding in a bathroom."

"Fuck." She was hiding in a *bathroom*. "I'm so fucking sorry, Blaire. I should have been there. I should have handled all of this for you."

She swallowed back more tears. "Yeah. I mean, yeah, I don't know."

"Where are you? Can you send me your location? I'll come pick you up."

Santi shook his head in front of me. "Send someone. It'll be worse if you're seen."

"I am picking her up," I spat at him.

"Campbell," West said with a sigh, "think about who you are."

Viv crossed her arms. "He's right."

"I don't want to hear it."

"What's going on?" Blaire asked on the phone.

"Nothing. Santi thinks I should send a car to retrieve you. I was going to drive out there."

"Your car is recognizable," Viv argued.

"She's right," Blaire said after clearly hearing Viv that time. "Just send someone. I'll meet you at the studio."

I hated this. I hated it so fucking much. I couldn't even safely pick up my girlfriend when she was in distress.

"If that's what you want," I told her.

"Please," she whispered. So small. Not at all the fierce, wonderful woman I was in love with.

"It's going to be okay," I said the words for her sake.

"Yeah. I'll send the location."

We said good-bye, and then a second later, I had a location. Viv was already on the phone with a car service. I showed her the address, and she had them send over a car to pick her up.

"Thank you."

Viv touched my shoulder. "I know this feels like terrible, but it's going to be okay. Blaire knew that this was always a possibility when she came out with us."

"I just fucking *hate* it."

"Price of fame," Santi said. "Unfortunately."

"You'll feel a lot better when she's here," West said.

Yorke nodded.

They were right. Yet I wanted someone to channel my anger into. I needed something to make me not want to punch the wall again. I was a caged animal on the prowl. I'd had girlfriends before I got back together with Blaire, but they had all been in the spotlight. They'd all known how to deal with this. We hadn't even bothered hiding it because it didn't matter. None of it had mattered.

This mattered.

She mattered.

And waiting for her to get here in one piece was like slowly dying.

When she appeared a full *hour* later—*fuck you, LA traffic* —she'd composed herself. The tears were gone. Her eyes were only lined in red. She took one look at me, and a half-smile hit her lips. Something cracked in my chest at that look. Fuck, I loved her.

"I lost my tripod," she muttered.

She threw herself into my arms, and I squeezed her tight to me. "Oh, Blaire."

"I had it with me, and when I got to that bathroom, it was gone."

"Don't worry about it. We'll replace it."

"Okay," she said, so soft and pliant.

"Are you okay though?"

She nodded. "All in one piece. My claustrophobia really doesn't like that this keeps happening to me."

"I don't like it either."

"Glad you made it, Blaire," West said with a head nod.

She swallowed and shot him a smile. "Me too. That was a nightmare."

"We've been there," Viv said. "Remember that time in Brazil?"

Santi groaned. "How could I forget? We were chased down the street, and we *had* security."

"Campbell was accosted that one time in a restaurant in Shanghai. I thought the girls were going to strip him naked in the place," Viv reminded us.

"Or when a Peppermint Patty group snuck backstage. Where were we for that?" Santi asked.

Yorke smirked. "Edinburgh."

"That's right! It was nuts."

Blaire nodded. "I see what you're doing. You're trying to make this seem normal."

"No. There's no normal about it, babe," Viv said. "It's why we remember the worst offenders. It's never fun. Crazed fans and paparazzi are part of the life, but it's what we try to avoid as much as we can."

"It's half the reason I liked being back in Lubbock," I admitted. Though I had never said that out loud. People for the most part left me alone there. I could come and go in LA, but I had to live in the Hills, behind a gate. There was a reason Lubbock was more enjoyable.

"And the other half?" Blaire asked.

"All you, love." I kissed her palm. "All you."

That was the minute English stormed into the room. "Jesus fucking Christ, the 10 is a goddamn nightmare today.

It makes the 405 look like a walk in the park." She swished her long blonde hair off her shoulders. "But I am here now, and we will fix this." She took one look at Blaire and frowned. "Campbell filled me in. How are you?"

Blaire shrugged. "Not my best day."

"I imagine not. I've seen some of the footage. You look like a deer in headlights. I think it works for us because you're so endearing on camera. And you're clearly scared. Sympathy points are helpful."

The rest of the band nodded at English as they headed back out to the studio. West frowned like he wanted to say something more, but he just touched Blaire's shoulder and then disappeared.

"How did this even get leaked?" I demanded as Blaire sank into Yorke's abandoned seat.

"I'm still not sure. The source was anonymous to TMZ. But I'd guess it was either someone who saw you in Lubbock, or you were followed out there. I've put pressure in the field to find out, but I'm not hopeful that they'll give away their sources."

"Sounds right," I grumbled. I'd thought we were safe in Lubbock, but again, I had been proven wrong.

"What are we going to do about it?" Blaire asked. "There's no reason to go to the gala now."

"Wait, wait, wait," English said. "I absolutely think you should make it. They control the narrative right now. Let's flip it on them and prove that we don't care what they've done."

"But we do," I said.

She shrugged. "They don't have to see that from you again. We can still respond to select reporters. We can continue to practice what how you're going to respond. You two will look so glamorous and stunning together that no one will even remember what happened today."

Blaire bit her lip. "Do you think that's possible?"

"The internet is forever, but media shifts *so* quickly. If we give them something else to focus on, it will pass. You have nothing to worry about." She paused, glancing over at me and then back. "That is, if you still want to go through with it."

"Do I have a choice?" Blaire demanded.

"Of course you have a choice."

"They already know we're together."

"But we wanted that," I said. "Not this way, but we were tired of hiding."

Blaire sighed. "I mean, yes, but I didn't want this either. And it's scary, having people attack me like that. I don't want it to happen again."

"We'll be more careful," English cut in. "We have a plan. We're running damage control. If you don't want to appear because it leaked, then I understand. We can just post a picture of you two together on your account. Giving the middle finger to the press is also a perfectly acceptable way to handle this."

She met my gaze. "What do you want to do?"

"Whatever makes you the happiest." I pressed a kiss to her lips. "We don't have to go to the gala. We don't have to do anything. I just want you safe and happy."

She breathed out slowly, lingering on my kiss. "Okay. I really want to wear my dress."

I cracked up, and English arched an eyebrow. "You're going to want to see this."

"So, we'll do it?"

A flicker of reluctance flashed across her face before she nodded. I just hoped we were doing the right thing.

35

BLAIRE

"*A*ll right, that's it. You look like a masterpiece," the makeup artist said. "Let's get this girl into a dress." He kissed his fingers. "Perfection."

I laughed. "Thank you."

I chanced a glance in the mirror and gaped at myself. I still looked like myself but somehow *better*. So much more dramatic and defined. My cheeks were plump and rosy. My blue eyes luminescent. My lips wide and fire-engine red. It was better than I ever could have imagined.

I turned away from the mirror and reached for the dress. English was there with a smile, holding it out for me. Finally, I stepped into the jeweled Jimmy Choos she had talked me into.

English zipped me up and then took a step back. "Damn, girl, I can't *wait* to see Campbell's reaction."

I ran my hands down the silky material. "You think he'll like it?"

"If he doesn't fall on his knees in supplication, then return the whole man."

I cackled at her. "You know just what to say."

She dipped into a small curtsy with a wink.

Having English the last couple days had been a lifesaver. I wasn't sure I would have survived without her. Not with the alarming amount of comments, emails, and shocking phone calls. People were *psychopaths*. We'd quickly scrubbed all of my information from the internet and limited all forms of contact.

I'd posted a photo of Campbell and me together, per English's suggestion, and closed commenting on the post. It was confirmation the world had apparently wanted, but I'd signaled that I wasn't interested in anyone's comment on my relationship.

Nate had also posted his video. And though some people had commented hateful things, they were far nicer to Nate than to me. Wasn't internalized misogyny delightful?

"Thanks for all you've done, English."

She grinned at me. "Hey, this is what I live for. There isn't a problem I can't fix. You are going to have a great time tonight. Forget everything else and just enjoy the night."

I nodded. That was the plan. A few questions and then a fun night. Felt worth it.

A knock sounded on the bathroom door. Campbell had rented a room at The Beverly Hills Hotel for the evening. Both for us to get ready and to have a room nearby to crash in after the event. I hadn't been looking forward to driving forty-five minutes back up to his place after a night out.

"Ready in there?" Court called.

English arched an eyebrow. "Are we ready?"

"Yep."

I swallowed, and then English pulled the door open. Campbell waited for me when I crossed the threshold. He was dressed in a tuxedo, looking as dapper as I'd ever seen him. His artfully messy hair had been brushed off his face.

His hands were in the pockets of his trousers. And my heart stopped as our eyes met.

"Fuck," he breathed.

I thought he might actually fall onto his knees before me, as English had suggested. His eyes were wide and mouth gaped. We were long past prom, and I certainly hadn't gone in a dress of this quality or this expensive. Nothing could compare to what I was wearing.

The dress was ruby-red silk that flowed around my hips like a waterfall. The straps were paper-thin strips of lace that fell off my shoulders. The neckline was purposely droopy, revealing the top crests of my breasts. I looked somehow taller and curvier and thinner and everything, all at once. It was a fucking miracle dress, and I felt like a queen in it.

"I am the luckiest fucking guy in the world," he told me as he drew me into him and dropped his mouth onto mine.

I almost protested about my lipstick but fuck it. It was supposed to be smudge- and waterproof. If it wasn't, I wanted my money back.

"All right, kids," English joked. "Let's get you into a limo. Have a great time."

"What's your plan for the night?" I asked, pulling away from Campbell.

Court got a look in his eyes that said dirty, dirty things.

English swatted at him. "I'll be available if you need me. But you won't need me."

"Have fun," Campbell said.

Then, Campbell whisked me downstairs and into the limo. The anxiety about the gala I'd been holding off all day suddenly hit me again.

"Are you sure we should be doing this?"

Campbell wrapped his fingers with mine. "I want nothing more than to be seen with you."

"It's just a lot."

"I know," he said. "I know it is. Are you okay with it all?"

"No," I told him truthfully. "I don't really know how to react. People on the internet hate me."

He nodded. "I was worried about that."

"It's weird to say I've mostly had a positive experience on social media, and now, I can see how it would be debilitating. Why you're not on it."

"I wish it weren't that way for you."

I shrugged. "Can't change it now."

"We'll figure it out," he promised.

Even though it felt like a promise he couldn't possibly keep.

The drive to the Beverly Wilshire was a short one by LA standards. But already, Rodeo Drive was packed with fans and reporters, anxious to see the music celebrities in attendance at the gala that supported music education in local schools. If I got past my anxiety, I was excited to go. I'd been to plenty of things like this in Lubbock, but somehow, it wasn't quite the same. Okay, not even close to the same as being in Los Angeles, surrounded by celebs.

Campbell took my hand in his as we got into line with the other limos. "This is going to be fun."

I laughed. "How can you know that?"

"Because I'm here with you. I never thought I'd be here with you."

"Me either."

"So, I'm determined to forget the onslaught of online madness and just enjoy the evening with my girlfriend."

I beamed at that word. I still wasn't used to hearing it from him. Even in high school, the word wasn't something we'd really used. Our relationship had always been so secretive. So, maybe this was what we needed to get past all the errors of our past.

"All right, I'll give it a shot," I said as he drew me in for a kiss. "I want to have a good time, too. Plus, English prepared me for everything."

"She's good like that."

I nodded in agreement.

Then, we were at the front of the line. A man in a tuxedo and white gloves opened the back door. I took a deep breath before taking his proffered hand and stepping out of the limo. When I'd said English had prepared me for everything, I meant, *everything*. She'd walked me through a red carpet step by step so that I wouldn't gape at what I saw in front of me. And still, it was hard not to be awestruck by the beauty of it all.

A long red carpet had been rolled out in front of the famous hotel, leading inside through the arched glass doorways. Either side had been roped off, and reporters waited to speak to the incoming attendees.

Campbell next came out of the limo. He slipped an arm around my waist, giving his best smolder to the cameras that now flashed dramatically. "Ready?" he asked as he pressed a kiss into my hair.

"Ready."

The red carpet welcomed us with open arms. My smile didn't even have to be faked. It was exhilarating, and all my earlier fears disappeared. This wasn't so bad at all. Campbell was charming, and everyone loved every second he gave them. He was still my Campbell, but I could see how he was so much bigger and better in this world. And why he'd prefer to not *have* to be the person they all expected him to be.

The first reporter pushed a microphone toward us. I recognized him as one of the reporters that English had slipped the questions to. "Campbell, it's so good to see you out in public with your new girlfriend. So many of our followers have been asking about this mystery woman. We've heard the rumor that she's the 'I See the Real You' girl we've always wondered about. Can you confirm?"

Campbell laughed, self-effacing. "The mystery woman you speak of is my girlfriend, Blaire." He squeezed my waist. "We dated in high school, and yes, I wrote 'I See the Real You' around the time when we were last together."

"And with this relationship rekindling, will we get new songs about the lovely Blaire?"

I met Campbell's gaze, and he winked. "Guess you'll have to wait and see when the new album releases."

We continued along to the next reporter I recognized. "Campbell, it's good to see you out in LA."

They clapped hands like old friends. English had said that Campbell already had a good relationship with this guy. I could see the camaraderie as they talked.

"Blaire," he said, turning to me, "we're glad to see you in LA. About time someone settled down *the* Campbell Abbey." Campbell laughed and shook his head, but the guy continued, "We noticed on your social accounts that you were close with the internet sensation Nate King."

"Yes," I agreed. "Nate and I have been friends for a while."

"Just friends?" He winked at Campbell. "Sorry, Campbell."

Campbell arched an eyebrow. "Do you think she'd be here with me now if she was dating someone else?"

"We're just friends. Nate and Campbell met when he

was in town. And as you can see on Nate's accounts, he's already congratulated us on our relationship."

"And how are you handling the talk of Campbell and Nini Verona's relationship?"

I stumbled on that one. A furrow forming between my brows. We hadn't discussed this one. That was a name that had come up a couple times while I was around Campbell, but he'd always adamantly denied that they'd ever dated... kind of like I was doing right now with Nate.

Campbell interceded. "Nini and I have never had a relationship. That's an old rumor after I performed at a fashion show she was in. We won't be taking any more questions about that."

We moved away from that reporter, and I leaned over to whisper, "Are you and Nini just friends?"

He shot me a look, and my stomach dropped.

"Oh," I whispered.

"It was a few weeks right before the tour started."

I had no room to talk since I'd been dating Nate more recently than that, but I had purposely not thought about how many other girls he'd dated before me. He was a rockstar. The number was likely staggering. And it didn't matter, did it? He was here with me.

We stopped in front of the next reporter. She wasn't a person that English had prepped us for. She had the same magazine credentials, but we'd been expecting someone else.

"Do you have a minute, Campbell?" she asked politely.

He glanced at me, and I shrugged. Last one, and then we'd be finished.

The reporter asked a few of the same questions we'd already heard from others. She was on the same script as what English had sent out.

Then, she looked over at me. "Blaire, what do you make of the reports that you were pregnant with Campbell's baby in high school and had an abortion?"

Ringing.

There was ringing in my ears.

My vision dimmed to nothing.

My stomach plummeted to the concrete.

Suddenly, I was shrinking in on myself and lying on a bed with blood between my legs and tears on my lashes and pain in my abdomen. There was nothing but heartache and a deep aching sadness that I could never recover from. Just pain and pain and pain.

I choked as I remembered my mother driving me to the hospital for my ten-week OB/GYN visit. Ten weeks. Soon, I'd find out if I was having a boy or a girl. A tiny thing was growing inside of me. No one could quite see it yet, but I could. I could feel it. My breasts ached all the time, and I couldn't stop peeing. I was exhausted and threw up more than I'd ever in my entire life. Even worse than the terrible stomach bug I'd had sophomore year.

I was eighteen and pregnant, against my mother's expressed wishes. And I wanted this baby. This beautiful baby boy or girl would be mine. The only thing I had left of me and Campbell. He was gone. He was in LA, living his dream. I was here in Lubbock, living a nightmare. But at least I had the baby.

Then, I was in the hospital, getting a standard ultrasound. The doctor paused. Her face fell. She said, "Oh."

I sat up straighter at the word. Then, I heard the words in a daze. Something about no heartbeat and unviable and miscarriage. Horrible, terrible, disturbing words. I started to cry. My mom stared, frozen, unsure how to comfort me. I wanted Campbell more than anything, but he wasn't here.

The doctor gave me pills to induce the miscarriage and explained what was coming next. I barely heard them through my sobbing. I was making a scene, but no one faulted me, except my mother, who seemed to be giddy with happiness. She was hardly hiding it either.

The doctor informed me it was common. That fifteen to twenty percent of all pregnancies ended in miscarriage and possibly even more than that if you considered miscarriages before people knew they were pregnant. She tried to make it all sound rational in her soft, careful voice.

I took the medicine and left with my mom. Her words still rang in my ears as I stared forward with red-rimmed eyes and no baby.

"I don't know why you're so upset, Marie. This is the best thing that could have happened to you. You have your whole life ahead of you. This is going to make everything so much easier."

I wanted to vomit, just hearing her say that. As if miscarrying Campbell's baby was exactly what I should have wanted for myself. When it was the last thing I had ever wanted.

Pamela asked if I needed any help. I gave her the list of things to buy to make the next month more bearable physically. Though nothing could fix it mentally. She dropped me off at the house and then went to the store.

My first instinct was to crawl into bed and cry for another decade. Instead, I called Campbell. I hadn't spoken to him since the night I'd told him I was pregnant. I never expected him to answer.

"Blaire?" he asked in confusion.

Wherever he was, it was loud. It was a two-hour time difference to LA. He shouldn't have been anywhere that sounded like a nightclub.

"Hey," I said weakly.

"What's up? I'm at work right now, and it's not a great time."

"I..." I said, stumbling at the dismissive tone of his voice. "I need to talk to you."

"Okay. Can it wait until I get off work? I'll call you back."

"Sure," I lied. I was going to be bleeding for the next four hours. Passing his baby from my body. What else did I have to do? "Sure. Yeah. Call me back."

Maybe things would have been different or at least better if he'd called, but he hadn't. Not that night or the night after that or the night after that. He didn't call again at all.

The miscarriage was the absolute worst thing that had ever happened to me.

But the one word that I'd never used to describe it, that the doctor hadn't even used, was *abortion*.

I'd *wanted* that baby with every fiber of my being.

I *still* wanted that baby.

And now, I stood before some asshole reporter, spitting that word in my face for a headline, and all I could do was return to that eighteen-year-old girl who had felt like she was dying. All I could do was retreat.

36

CAMPBELL

*R*age filled my chest.

All week, it had been creeping closer and closer to the surface. I'd almost lost it on Michael at the studio. I'd almost come apart at the seams when Blaire was mobbed on Hollywood Boulevard. But now—*now*—it was here. A fire-breathing dragon like I hadn't seen in years. Not since I had been in high school and taken it out on my dad for how everything had happened with my mom.

I slapped the camera away from Blaire even though that was breaking rule number one of dealing with the press. "Get the fuck out of her face!"

The reporter took a step back. I'd never made a scene with the press in all my years in the public eye. I'd kept it all carefully put together. The look of shock on her face said she hadn't expected this to elicit that sort of reaction from me.

It would be the talk of the evening. Fuck if I cared. She was out of line, and she had to fucking know it.

"How dare you," she began.

"No, how fucking dare *you*," I snarled at her.

I turned my back on the rest of the interaction. There were cameras everywhere. And half of them faced the commotion I'd just made. Blaire stood frozen, as if she'd turned to stone at the very question. She'd lost all color in her cheeks, and fear crossed her face.

"Blaire?" I said tentatively, reaching for her.

She jerked backward out of my grasp. Sheer panic hit my stomach. She couldn't look at me. She didn't want me to touch her. What had that goddamn question triggered?

I needed to get her out of here. Even if we stayed at the event, I couldn't have her here, in front of the cameras, a second longer.

"Hey, it's okay," I told her soothingly. "Do you want to stay?"

She shook her head. Yeah, I'd expected that.

"Okay. Okay. We'll go. Let me text the driver to come back around."

I gently touched her elbow. She flinched but let me direct her away from the rest of the cameras and inside the hotel. Security was tighter inside, and there were no cameras. I could already see everything spiraling out before us. This was going to be on TMZ in minutes.

The driver confirmed a new pickup location, and I shot off a message to English as well as my publicist, Barbara. No one was going to like this. I certainly fucking didn't.

"The driver is coming around. There's a side entrance we can take," I assured her.

There was no response. She just stared off, as if she were caught in some nightmare. Her hands were around her stomach. Honestly, she looked sick.

"Blaire, are you okay?"

Her cerulean gaze met mine, and she swallowed before glancing away and muttering, "No."

I gritted my teeth. I hated this. I couldn't do anything to fix this. Everything was a mess. Here we'd thought we were going to control the narrative, and then, fucking *somehow*, the world had found out that she'd been pregnant. I hadn't even thought about mentioning that to English. Fuck, we were so stupid.

A few minutes later, the limo pulled up to a side entrance, and I hustled a catatonic Blaire into the backseat. Luckily, no press had gotten wind of our retreat. So, we were in the clear as we drove through Beverly Hills.

English called once we were in the car. "Blaire isn't answering."

I glanced at my girlfriend. She'd scooted away from me in the car. Fuck, fuck, fuck.

"She isn't speaking."

"Oh Christ. Is she okay?"

"No. No, she's not."

"Fuck. Okay, I'm heading to the hotel now. We're about a half hour out. Just stay away from the press and the internet until then."

"English, what the fuck happened?"

She sighed heavily. "Neither of you thought to tell me she'd been pregnant?"

"It was eight years ago. Only her mom knew. How could I have anticipated that the entire world would find out?" I huffed. "How *did* they find out?"

"Apparently, a Campbell Soup girl snooped through her medical records. There's even an actual picture of her file that says she had an abortion roughly eight years ago. Which would have been when you were together or had just broken up."

"A Campbell Soup girl?" I asked, low and furious.

"Yeah, you have some rabid, boundary-defying fans."

"I'll murder them."

"Let's not let that get on record."

"I smacked a camera and cussed out a reporter. I'm already in shit."

English was silent for a minute. "They must have really pissed you off. You always keep your cool."

"I know," I ground out. "Everyone crossed the line with this one."

"Just take care of our girl, okay? I'll be there soon to pick up the pieces."

I said good-bye and then just kept an eye on Blaire as we veered through traffic to a back entrance of The Beverly Hills Hotel. She was still silent and looked like she was holding on by a thread.

We took the private elevator up to our suite, and she immediately swept to the window and stared out with her arms crossed.

"Blaire?"

Her shoulders heaved at the sound of my voice.

"Can we talk about this?"

A small, derisive laugh left her. "Now you want to talk about this?"

I bit my cheek to keep from saying anything stupid. Adrenaline still coursed through my veins. I would not take this out on Blaire. It was the rest of the stupid fucking world that deserved my wrath.

"Yes, I think we should talk about it."

"Which part, Campbell? The pregnancy you didn't want or the phone call you never returned?"

I froze at those words. The harsh reality of them. I hadn't wanted a baby at eighteen. I didn't know anyone who wanted a baby at eighteen. I'd been wrong to treat her the way I had to follow my dream, but the rest...

"What phone call?"

She choked. Her body tensed. "*What* phone call?"

The room was quicksand, and I felt myself sinking. I had missed something vital here. And I had no clue what it was.

"I don't know what you're talking about."

"You left Lubbock, and I called you. You were at work. You promised to call me back."

I shook my head, trying to remember this. It had been eight years ago, and the details of my first few months in LA were fuzzy. I'd worked in a bar, and they'd had me up at all hours of the day. Not to mention the fact that I'd been drunk *a lot*. I had no recollection of Blaire ever calling me. I'd thought she had completely cut me off after I left. I'd deserved it.

"I don't remember that."

She turned to face me, and tears tracked down her perfectly done makeup. "You don't remember?"

"No."

"Great. Just great."

"I'm sorry. I wish I remembered. Those first few months in LA are a blur. I don't remember much, except exhaustion and alcohol."

I was the dick who hadn't called her when she'd been pregnant. I'd been young and so fucking stupid. I wished that I could take it back. When I checked in on her again and saw that she'd never had the baby, I'd known she'd gone through with an abortion after all. I'd been...relieved...and disappointed. I hadn't known how to reconcile those reactions and figured reaching out would only make things worse.

"But this isn't about a phone call, Blaire. You're upset about the abortion. I didn't know the reporter would bring that up."

She took a step backward at the word. "That's what you think I'm upset about?"

I held my hands out to her. "I know it's upsetting, but it's not like what the reporter said wasn't true."

Her jaw dropped at my words. Then, a split second later, she snapped her jaw shut and looked ready to erupt. Before she even opened her mouth, I realized that I'd said the wrong thing. The absolute wrong thing.

"I did *not* have an abortion," she snarled. "I went in for my ten-week checkup, and the doctor said the baby had no heartbeat. I'd had a miscarriage, and the baby hadn't left naturally yet. The doctor sent me home with pills to speed up the process."

"Fuck," I said.

"And I *called* you that day to tell you what happened. You answered and then promised to call me back. Then, you never did."

"Blaire, I—"

She held up her hand. "You have absolutely no fucking clue what I went through. You *weren't* there, Campbell. You weren't there when I told my mom about the baby. When she tried to convince me to get an abortion and I yelled at her that I wanted to keep it. She thought I was insane. I only had her. My mom was the only person who knew and who was there for me. And you know she's the worst person alive with these sorts of things. So, the day when it all happened, she was *happy*. It was the worst day of my life, and she was happy for me. She told me I could have my life back now.

"But all I knew was that you were gone." Tears streaked down her cheeks, and she could barely breathe as she told me all about her hurt. "You were gone, and the baby—the only piece I had left of you—was gone, too. I wanted that baby, Campbell. I wanted to have that piece of you. And on the worst day of my life, you couldn't even call me back."

I felt sick. She'd had to go through all of that alone. All of that without me. And even when she'd reached out, I'd fucked it all up.

"Blaire, I'm sorry. I know I can't make up for it."

She whirled away from me. "No, you can't."

"I wish I could change it."

Her shoulders shook. "I was prepared for everything with you. I was ready to talk about our past. To be the 'I See the Real You' girl after years of avoiding it. I was ready for people looking into my business and past relationships. I was ready for all of that. I would have been okay with it all. But...not this."

I swallowed hard, my throat closing at her words.

"This was too far. This was...over the line. I don't know if I want this level of fame if people can dredge up an eight-year-old miscarriage and then feel okay, bringing it up as a talking point on the red carpet. I don't think I can have that life."

And how could I blame her? I'd wanted to shield her from the worst of it. It was why I had never told anyone who she really was. I'd respected her privacy. And then this had all gone down, and I didn't know how to make the spotlight any easier for her.

"Blaire..."

"I want to go home," she said softly with a sniffle.

"Okay. We can change and head into the Hills."

"No," she said abruptly. "No. I want to go back to Lubbock."

"Okay. We'll get a flight back together."

"I want to go...alone." She met my eyes as she said it and swiped at her tears.

This wasn't what I wanted. I wanted her here. I wanted us to work it out. Had I been living in a dream the last couple weeks? Had everyone been right when they warned me about our relationship? Was it too much to hope that we could make this work when my life was in LA and it was this hellscape for her?

"We can fix this…"

"Please," she said. Her shoulders slumped forward in on herself. "I just want to go home. I can't do this."

"This?"

Her eyes finally met mine. "Us."

My body went hollow. "Us."

I was an echo, but there was nothing else for me to say. My life was not all glitz and glamour. And she'd seen the dark side of it. Could I blame her for wanting to bail? Because I didn't.

"Don't do this," I pleaded.

"Don't, Campbell. Please. It's too much. You don't know what it was like."

"I don't want to let you go," I said, reaching out for her.

She took a step backward and shook her head. "I need time. Just…just give me some time."

And her face was so crushing that I couldn't do anything else. If she needed time, how could I deny it to her? She deserved it after everything I'd done in the past to fuck us up. I was the asshole here. Even if I'd do anything to fix it.

"Okay," I said hollowly. "If that's what you want."

PART VI

THE ONE THAT GOT AWAY

37

BLAIRE

*T*he door burst open after my pronouncement. English read the room and ushered me out. She spoke with Campbell for a few minutes. I didn't even bother listening in. I was sure that she was going to keep him updated on me. When I reminded her that she was my publicist, she nodded and told me that Campbell was her friend.

Which was all I needed to know. I was her priority, but she wanted us to work. I could see it in her sad blue eyes.

She made a sharp and swift apology for what had happened at the event. But we both knew that we couldn't change it. And it was probably better to get me out of the public spotlight until everything died down.

English retrieved my luggage from Campbell's house, and I was on the first flight home. She promised to handle it. I believed her. Because I certainly wasn't fucking handling anything.

When I landed in Lubbock, a barrage of text messages awaited me. One was from Piper, letting me know she was waiting in the cell phone lot. The rest were from Honey. I scrolled through them all, hoping that I'd have something from Campbell. But no, nothing. I'd told him not to contact me, and he hadn't.

But the messages from Honey were never-ending. I finally gave up and called her, thankful for the privacy in first class.

"Blaire! Did you land safe?" Honey asked.

"Hey. Yeah, I just got in."

"Are you sure you don't need me to pick you up?"

"I'm sure. Piper is already waiting out front. I just saw all your messages. What did I miss?"

I'd asked Honey to hold down the fort for the business, which shouldn't have been difficult since I'd also requested that we go entirely radio silent. No more posts. No more comments. No more emails. I wanted everything to come to a screeching halt. The only things we needed to do was pay bills and keep the lights on. Metaphorically speaking. Since I didn't have my own office.

"Just sending you follow-ups from the business email. There have been a lot of media requests."

"No," I said flatly.

"I figured as much but wanted to run it by you. Maybe this would be better in person. I could come over, and we could discuss—"

"No," I repeated.

As nice as it was to have Honey, she was maybe too happy to have me home. She seemed to have actually been concerned that I'd never leave LA.

"Okay," Honey said quietly. "I hope you're okay."

"I'll be fine," I lied. "I want you to hold all of this together. I don't want to think about business for a few days. Can you do that?"

"Oh yeah, sure. No problem. I misunderstood what you

said. I thought you wanted me to still inform you of everything coming in. I didn't know you wanted me to go quiet, too."

I closed my eyes on a sigh. "That's not what I meant. I just need to deal with what happened in LA. Why don't we plan to meet up later in the week? Once I start feeling better."

"Definitely. But if you need anything in the meantime, do not hesitate to ask. Dinner, a movie, a shoulder to cry on. I'm your girl."

"I know, Honey. Thank you." I stood up as we reached the gate. "I have to go. I'll talk to you later."

I hung up and grabbed my boho bag before disembarking. My bag was the first one off at baggage claim, and Piper's blue Jeep waited outside of the exit.

She hopped down and pulled me into a hug. "Aww, Blaire, I'm so glad you're home."

I started crying on the spot and held my best friend as tight as I could. "Piper, I hate this."

"I know." She brushed my hair back. "It's going to be okay."

"I hope so." I swiped at my eyes. "And now, I'm worried someone is going to take a picture of me crying. I can't shake the feeling of being followed."

"Well, let's get you out of here then. You'll be better at home."

I nodded. Though I couldn't help but doubt it. That *being followed* feeling felt inevitable. It had been stronger in LA, where the paparazzi could be anywhere, but knowing that Campbell's fans were stalking me online sure didn't help anything. I felt helpless, and it triggered fight-or-flight in me.

Piper grabbed my bag as I got into the passenger seat.

"Have you heard from Campbell?" she asked as we pulled out.

I shook my head. "No. I told him I didn't want to talk to him and I needed space."

Piper sighed. "Yeah. That makes sense. I was rooting for y'all."

I crossed my arms and stared out the window. "Me too."

We arrived back at the house twenty minutes later. Eve greeted us at the door. But I just shot her a half-smile before retreating to my room. I crashed into the comforter, and tears hit me fresh all over again. Piper was worried. She wanted answers to what had gone down in LA, but I wasn't ready for the conversation. I wasn't ready for anything but crying and sleeping.

Which was what I did on and off for the next couple days. Nothing from Campbell. Only intermittent messages from Honey. A few from English. But even she went silent a few days into my heartbreak.

It felt like the first time all over again. Campbell was in LA. I was here. I had made that happen. I was the heart-broken one. But I couldn't see how it could have happened any other way. I couldn't suppress the pain from eight years ago. I couldn't pretend that none of it had happened.

And worse, all this time, I'd thought he'd abandoned me in the middle of my miscarriage, but he had no memory that I'd even called him. Should I have called him again? I hadn't been rational at that time. I was eighteen years old and had just lost *everything*. There wasn't a moment where it felt logical to call Campbell after he never returned my call. I was alone. That was how it had been.

Again, I was alone. And I missed him.

Everything hurt. And I ached for him.

I hated every bit of it.

"Knock, knock," a voice called from the hallway before someone pushed the door open.

Annie stood in the doorway. "Hey, Blaire."

I was still under the covers. My hair up in a messy bun at the top of my head. My eyes red-rimmed. Four days into this depression, and I didn't feel any better. Maybe only worse.

"Hey, Annie. Are you off work?"

"I am. Residency is crazy but worth it." She stepped inside and sank into the foot of my bed. Jennifer, Piper, and Eve peeked their heads in as well. "We want you to know that we love you and are worried about you."

I sat up on the bed and rubbed my eyes. "I'm sorry. I don't want to worry you."

"You don't have to apologize. I can't imagine what you're going through," she said gently. Annie, who was always brash and loud, was being gentle with me. I must have looked even worse than I felt.

"You know you can tell us anything, right?"

I nodded. "I don't know how to begin to talk about it."

"And that's okay. We were actually thinking...it just might be good to get you out of this bed."

I groaned and flopped back. "I'm not ready to be a person."

"You've barely eaten, and you haven't left this room in four days."

Piper stepped in. "We can all crash in here with ice cream if you'd rather."

Jennifer took a seat opposite Annie. "We're here for you, whatever you want."

"I don't want to be seen in public right now. I'm a mess. And I have this uncontrollable fear that someone is going to photograph me, and everything will be fucked up again."

Piper rested her hands on my footboard. "You can't let

them control you like that. You are bright and vibrant and wonderful. A few paparazzi can't scare you off. What happened was in the past. They shouldn't have dug it up or however it came out, but it doesn't define who you are now."

"That's right," Annie agreed. "And I think Hollin would beat the shit out of any paparazzo who got within a dozen feet of the winery. So, you'd be safe there. He said he'd bring in more security tonight for you in case you wanted to get out of the house and just be a human being for a night with no expectations."

"That's...nice of him," I whispered.

None of them said that it was because Campbell was his brother and he'd do anything for him. But I could feel it.

"I don't know if I can pretend I'm okay though."

"Maybe the best step would be the couch," Jennifer suggested. "Forget going out. Just get out of this bed."

I laughed at her enthusiasm and agreed, "All right. Couch it is."

"Plan B activated," Annie said. "Eve, ice cream."

I shook my head. "You planned for this?"

"Of course. We love you," Piper said.

"But first, shower," Annie said.

A half hour later, after a shower and my long, dark hair was piled back into its messy bun, I was seated on the couch with my girls. Annie had chosen *How to Lose a Guy in 10 Days* for us to watch, and we were binge-eating the ice cream. Eve looked positively excited. I wondered if she had ever done something like this before. She kept looking around at us like we were some rare breed.

"Thanks for the ambush," I finally said after I gave up on my ice cream and snuggled into the blankets.

"Anytime," Piper said.

"Can we talk about what happened?" Annie asked.

I sighed. "I didn't have an abortion."

"It's okay if you did," Eve said softly.

Jennifer nodded. "We'd be here for you regardless."

And so I told them all what had really happened. How everything had been leaked, the mobbing, the red carpet fiasco, and the reality of my miscarriage. They all looked back at me with various pitying looks, but I knew it was more than that from them. They loved me. I could see that.

"I hate that you went through that alone," Piper said, pulling me in for a hug.

"Yeah," I whispered. "I should have called Campbell again. I should have made him be there for me."

Annie reached for my hand. "That is not your fault. None of this is. You were just kids."

"I know. I know, but maybe this all would have been different if we'd been...I don't know—rational."

Eve laughed. "Yeah, all eighteen-year-olds are rational."

"Pregnant eighteen-years-olds at that," Jennifer said.

"You're right. Okay. I know." I held up my hands. "Just lots of fucked up."

"It is," Piper agreed.

Eve bit her lip and leaned forward. "Who knew about you and Campbell in high school to begin with? You said some Campbell Soup girl dug up your medical records, but before that. How did they even find out you'd been together?"

"Yeah, who would have snitched about you being the 'I See the Real You' girl?" Jennifer asked.

"Well, at the time, just my mom and stepdad. But they didn't know he'd written that song about me. They could have guessed, but I don't know why they would. They don't seem to care about my life."

"I just figured someone snooped in your past to find out," Piper said.

"I don't know how they could have. No one knew about us. All the pictures from that time are in a photo album in my room. It wasn't common knowledge. It had to be someone who knew."

"But none of us told," Piper said.

And then a dawning realization hit me at the same time a pit formed in my stomach.

"Someone else had to know, right?" Eve asked.

"No," I siad quickly. Then I paused. "Wait," I whispered. "Oh no."

"What?" Annie asked.

I'd been so terrified by what had happened to me with the press in LA that I hadn't really considered how they'd found out about our relationship. The Campbell Soup girls had dug into my past after they found out we'd had a relationship as teens. They hadn't done that before because no one else had known.

But one other person *did* know. Because I'd told him.

"Nate King."

38

CAMPBELL

*B*laire left.
　　　The city.
The state.
Me.
And all I wanted was to get her back.

She'd told me to stay in LA. I had to be in the studio anyway for the rest of the week. I had obligations. But how the hell did they expect me to play the love songs I'd been working on the last couple months? The ones that were about her beautiful face and kissing her perfect lips and wanting nothing but to bind my life to her?

So, I said *fuck it* to the love songs.

I refused to work on them in the studio. And I wrote as if in a fever dream, of all my pain and heartbreak over her leaving. I wrote five songs in a matter of days. Delirious and desperate, I handed the lyrics off to the band, and we did nothing but burn through the pain. All day, every day, rehearsing the songs that I could already feel would shape the second half of the album.

I had no idea how I'd ever record those love songs again. But it was a problem for another day. Another Campbell.

"Hey, man," Santi said, clapping me on the back. "Get your shit. We're going out."

"I'm not going out anywhere. I have a few more songs in me."

"No," Viv said with a shake of her head. "We're going to go get drunk."

Yorke nodded. "You need it."

Even West agreed. "Come on. Getting out of here will help."

Before I could protest, Viv and Santi looped their arms with mine and tugged me out of the studio and into an awaiting limo. They'd planned this ahead of time. Maybe they were tired of working on my heartbreak songs.

When we arrived at the club, Viv secured a booth for the lot of us, and we sank down into the plush leather seats. She dropped a shot of Patrón in front of my face.

"Drink up, love," she said.

I didn't argue. I tossed the shot back and called for another from our bartender. The scantily clad girl hurried over and poured me a second shot. Her eyes were wide as she watched me down it. I called for another. She hadn't even left.

"Should I leave you the whole bottle, sugar?" she asked with a laugh.

"Whoa," Viv said with alarm. "Slow down. Have a beer or something." She snatched my third shot and passed it to Santi. "We want you to be drunk. Not obliterated."

I glanced up at the bartender. Now that I was here, I didn't want to think or feel anything. "I want to get obliterated."

She giggled and poured me another shot. I drank it before Viv could steal it.

Weston leaned back in his seat and observed the scene. "Are you sure this is a good idea?"

"It's not a bad idea," I assured him. I gestured to West. "Pour one for my friend here."

He held his hand up. "No thanks. I'll just have a beer."

"Good for you," Yorke said with a nod of approval.

Santi crashed into the seat next to him. "No shots, *hombre*?"

West shrugged. "I try not to overdo it. When addictive personalities run in your family, it's for the best. Trust me on that."

"Well, forget it then," I said. "More for me."

But just because West wasn't taking shots didn't mean I wasn't. He'd come for moral support. I'd come to forget that the girl of my dreams had walked away.

I'd been so fucking stupid. I'd followed her on social media. I'd known she never had the baby. All this time, I'd thought that she'd had an abortion. It had made sense in my mind. No baby equaled only one thing. But to hear it from her, it was clear that I'd been wrong. So fucking wrong. And she'd had to relive that on a red carpet with a microphone in her face after a week of other anxiety-inducing shit.

Worse yet, she'd called to talk to me about it. And I'd been so deep in my new LA life, working around the clock and drinking when I wasn't, that I didn't even *remember* her phone call. What a worthless piece of shit I'd been.

I was waist deep in alcohol when I heard a voice call, "Is that Campbell Abbey?"

Cosmere was in a private booth in a VIP section of the nightclub. No one could get over here unless they were also of celebrity status. And even to my addled brain, I knew that voice.

I caught sight of the long, dark hair and her signature pout. "Nini Verona."

"It is you!"

Viv coughed loudly. Yorke put his hand on my shoulder. Santi said, "Uh, man..."

I laughed at them, shrugging off Yorke's hand. "It's fine."

They all looked at me like it was *not* fine. But they didn't realize that I had no interest in the likes of Nini. Yes, we'd had a brief fling before the tour at the end of last year, but it hadn't been anything. And it wasn't anything now.

She crossed into our booth and pulled me into a quick hug. "I heard you were back in LA."

"Yeah? Who hasn't with all my fucking press?" I grumbled.

She laughed. I'd almost forgotten that her laugh tinkled like a chime. She leaned her hip into a column next to the booth, accentuating her curves in her plastered-on black dress. "Well, good thing I'm here now."

"Nini," Santi said with a sigh.

"I'd say it's good to see you," Viv said with an arched eyebrow, "but you have shit timing."

She blew Viv a kiss. "I've missed you, too."

"We are in crisis mode."

"I'm not in a crisis," I slurred.

"I've heard the rumors," Nini admitted. "I just got in from New York for an Cunningham Couture event. Didn't guess I'd see you."

"Take a seat."

Viv's eyes widened. "If you're photographed together, Campbell..."

"I know. I know." I waved her off.

Nini took the seat and asked for a vodka water with a splash of lime. "So, does this mean you're single?"

I cringed at the words. My brain was fuzzy, but I wasn't stupid. "God, I fucking hope not."

Nini pouted slightly. "Too bad."

"As if we would have ever worked. You were too obsessed with your New York boarding school friends."

Nini was old, *old* upper-crust money on her mother's side and super fucking rich from rumored Mafia money on her dad's side. She was the perfect mix of Upper East Side princess and Italian heiress. I'd found out quick that her real life was sort of terrifying in its intensity.

"True," she admitted. "And this Blaire? She makes you happy?"

I nodded. "I'm in love with her."

Nini took her drink from the bartender and sipped it absentmindedly. Or seemingly at least. I'd never seen her do anything absentminded. She had a quick mind and a ruthless edge. People thought she was just a pretty face, but she was sharp as a razor's edge.

"Then, what are you doing here?"

"She doesn't want to see me."

"What girl wouldn't want to see you?"

"Blaire. I fucked it up."

Nini shot me a look. "Did you fuck it up, or is this just your life?"

I shrugged. I didn't want to think about that right now. I wanted to get shit-faced and *not* think. Because, yes, obviously, this was my life. It was always going to be difficult for someone who was outside of the circle to integrate into it. Much harder when I had a troop of people who snooped for clues. Which was how they'd discovered the abortion in

Blaire's medical history. Someone should probably be fired for that shit.

But just because it was hard didn't make it impossible. I didn't want Blaire to have to deal with this shit. I wanted it to be easy and uncomplicated, like it had been these past months in Lubbock.

Except my life was in both Lubbock and LA. I couldn't change that. And Michael had proven how hard it was to have it all to begin with. What would it be like if she was always back in Lubbock? As she was now.

"More drinks," I said, deciding to ignore Nini's question.

"Fine, fine," Nini said. "It's not my place. And the reporter was wrong to bring up her past. But we've all dealt with that shit before."

"She's not one of us though," I argued.

"No. She's not."

"And she doesn't deserve this shit."

"And the rest of us do?"

"It doesn't matter. Blaire is gone. I don't know what our relationship is. But I do know that I'm madly in love with her, and nothing is going to change that. If you're staying, Nini, then let's stop talking and get back to drinking."

She held her hands up. "I see where your heart is, Campbell Abbey. And I am here for it. I just think if she means that much to you, you should go after her."

If only that were an option.

There was no rulebook for this. No easy way out.

She needed space. She needed time.

I could give her that if she needed it. But all I would do in the meantime was pine, drink, and write. Sometimes, all at the same time.

I held my hand up for the bartender. "More Patrón shots here."

Nini shot a look at Viv that said they both had my interest at heart. She may not have known Nini was going to be here, but it was a kick in the ass to see her. I certainly wasn't listening to the rest of them. But Nini didn't sugarcoat, and seeing her only made me want Blaire even more.

Too bad all I had was tequila.

I downed another shot and another until I forgot the entire thing had happened.

My head felt like a bomb had detonated inside it.

I clutched it as I opened my bleary eyes and looked around the room. This was not my bed. It was distinctly feminine. Crisp white and soft blush everywhere. My heart pounded as I jerked upward and then immediately regretted it.

"Fuck," I spat.

Where the fuck was I? It wasn't a hotel room, but I had no recollection of this space either. Which was a bad, *bad* thing. I wouldn't have done anything supremely stupid, like go home with someone else.

All I remembered from last night was bemoaning my loss of Blaire, and then Nini had shown up and...

And then Nini had shown up.

Well, shit.

I threw the covers off me and found I was still in my clothes from last night. That was...a good sign. Even if it left me a lot more rumpled and dirtier than the day prior. I staggered to the door and wrenched it open.

Nini stood there in nothing but a white button-up, holding a glass of water. Her eyes narrowed at my state. "Well, it's about fucking time."

I gaped at her. "We didn't..."

She shot me a licentious smile. "We didn't."

I blew out a harsh breath. "Thank God. What am I doing here?"

"I won't take that as an insult." She shoved the water in my hand and a pair of Tylenol. "How much do you remember from last night?"

"I remember you showing up."

"Well, you got obliterated, as you wanted. I brought the band back to my place because it was closest."

"Did I do anything stupid?"

"You spoke of your deep love for your lost woman all night and bored the shit out of all of us," she said, crossing her arms. "It's past noon. You should get up. Your brother keeps calling."

"Fuck." I downed the water and took the medicine before following her out into the living room. The rest of the band was lounging in her apartment. I picked up the phone as it rang again and answered the video chat. "Hollin, fuck, sorry."

Hollin's face was stone. "I've been calling all morning."

"I just woke up."

Nini waved her fingers at him. "Hello, Abbey brother."

Hollin gaped at her and then narrowed his eyes at me. "Tell me you are not as fucking stupid as you look."

"I am not," I told him, heading back into the bedroom.

"That was Nini Verona."

"Yeah. We met up last night, but nothing happened."

"Jesus, Campbell, I was going to ask what the fuck you were still doing there. Blaire is a wreck. You need to get your ass here and figure it out."

I sighed and ran a hand through my hair. "I want to do that, bro, but she said she wanted to go home alone."

"You are fucking stupid." Hollin shook his head. "She said that, but she doesn't mean it, idiot. She misses you. Piper hasn't said much, but I know that Blaire still loves you. God knows why."

I laughed and leaned back against the bedroom door. "You think I still have a shot? The situation is so fucked up."

"You left her once before. If you don't chase her now, then you'll never get her back."

I nodded. "Yeah, yeah. You're right. I'm coming home. Pick me up?"

"Good," Hollin said with a nod. "I'll meet you at the airport."

39

BLAIRE

*N*ate King had known that I was the "I See the Real You" girl.

I'd told him that day that he met Campbell. I'd trusted him.

"Oh God," I whispered.

"What?" Piper gasped. "Why does he know?"

"I told him," I said as horror dawned.

"Shit."

"He's so into you, Blaire," Annie said with a sigh.

"No, we were well past over. He was looking out for me, and I told him the truth about me and Campbell."

Eve looked skeptical. "He's a guy who is used to getting what he wants. Trust me, they'll do whatever they can."

Jennifer nodded sadly. "I think he was more into you than you were into him."

I looked between them as panic set in. I'd done this. All this time, I'd been freaking out about how it had gotten out. I'd thought it was some kind of fluke where someone had just discovered it even though we'd been so careful. But all along, *I* was the one who had done it.

If the girls were right, Nate was still into me. And he'd done this to, what? Punish me for choosing Campbell? It was inconceivable. I'd never thought Nate was that kind of person. Had I missed all the red flags?

"I have to ask him," I said abruptly. I jumped off the couch and dashed into my room.

Piper followed. "Are you going to call him?"

"No," I said as I threw off my sweats and pulled on jean shorts and a top. "I'm going to Midland."

"What? Why? Just video-chat him or something."

"I have to see him in person. He can't lie to my face. Also, I can strangle him if it was really him."

"Are you sure?"

"Yes," I said vehemently. "I need to find out why he'd do this."

"Do you want me to go with you?"

I paused, the denial on my tongue, but finally nodded. "That would be good."

Piper disappeared to change, and ten minutes later, we were in her Jeep, heading south toward Midland, where the entire King family lived and the Dorset & King oil company headquarters were located. Nate's place was about an hour and a half from mine. He lived in a house surrounded by oil fields. I'd only been there a handful of times. Normally, he drove into Lubbock.

"This is his place?" Piper asked with wide eyes as we drove up to the giant house.

Nate came from *money*. He had a large family, all who were involved in the oil business, except for him. The rest of his family thought he was crazy for being a TikTok sensation when he could work for the family company. But his trust was large enough that it clearly didn't even matter.

Piper parked at the front of the property, next to a huge white truck. "Want me to go with you?"

I shook my head, steeling my nerves. Now that I was here, I was a bundle of them. It had made sense an hour and a half ago. But despite my resolve, I didn't want to face him. I didn't want to find out that he had done this to me.

Before I could back out, I jumped out of the Jeep and headed to the front door. White roses bloomed stark and bright against the white of the two-story house. The white roses of the King family.

I knocked on the front door. My stomach twisted, and I swallowed down the lump in my throat. Nate would tell me the truth. That was my only lifeline.

Hard boots stomped on the hardwood inside, and the door swung open. But it wasn't Nate who answered. It was his older brother, Malcolm. My mouth went dry. I'd only met him once before, but he was the heartthrob of the entire King clan. How he was not married was *beyond me.*

"Hi," I squeaked, unprepared to be met with his hard gaze. Let alone the cowboy hat and boots.

"Blaire," he said, flashing a dimple. "Is Nate expecting you?"

"Uh, no."

He nodded, as if he understood. Though how could he? He turned away from me. "Nate, you have company."

"I'm busy," he called back.

Malcolm's jaw twitched. "I said, you have company."

It was more a growl than anything. Commanding. I shivered. Well then.

Nate must have heard the change in his voice, too, because he appeared a second later at the door. "Who..." He trailed off as his mouth hung open. "Blaire?"

"Hey, Nate. Can we talk?"

"Uh, sure." He ran a hand back through his mussed dark hair and glanced at his brother and then back. "I didn't know you were going to be here."

Was he fidgeting? Did he know that I knew?

"I'll leave y'all to it," Malcolm said. He tipped his head at me and then disappeared through the door. He walked toward the giant pickup. God, he was attractive. What in the hell did these oil fields feed these men?

"Do you want to come in?" Nate asked.

"Sure."

"I thought you were in LA," he said, closing the door behind him.

We stepped through the foyer and into the living room, complete with a vaulted ceiling and a recording setup for his videos. It was beautiful, all hardwood and surprisingly rustic for someone who appeared so modern. Couldn't take the Texas out of the boy.

"I was. I came back early."

"I saw what happened at that music gala." He leaned back against the white marble kitchen island and crossed his arms. "That was shitty."

"It was." I took a deep breath. "Did you leak that I was the 'I See the Real You' girl?"

"What? No," he said automatically.

There was no hesitation, but still, I didn't know if he was lying to me. He was slick. He always had been. It was the reason that I'd driven all the way out here. He couldn't lie to me in person. Not for long at least.

"Nate, tell me the truth."

"I am telling you the truth. Why the fuck would I tell someone something that you'd told me in confidence?"

"I don't know. Because you still like me?"

His eyes rounded, and then he laughed softly. "Don't

flatter yourself, Blaire. I'm not some besotted ex-lover. We had a good time. You ended it, and it was mutual. I'm not suddenly heartbroken and going to ruin your life. If that were the case, why would I work with your publicist?"

"I don't know, Nate. But someone told the press. Someone who knew. You met Campbell and didn't like him. Maybe you were looking for a quick payday."

He gestured around him. "Does it look like I need a quick payday?"

I bit my lip as I looked around at the house I'd just been admiring. It did in fact not look like he needed money. That was for sure.

"No," I admitted.

"And I liked Campbell just fine. But I can be jealous of what y'all have." His eyes darted away from mine. "Not that I wanted it for us, but just in general."

"Oh."

I hadn't considered any of this. I'd been so set on it being Nate. He was the only other person who knew about us from back then besides my friends, and they certainly hadn't told.

"Well, someone leaked it. And no one else knew," I finally said on a frustrated sigh.

"How did they find out about the abortion?"

I flinched at that word. "Miscarriage."

His face dropped. "Fuck, Blaire."

"Yeah, that's why I crumpled on the red carpet. I didn't even know the hospital had listed the miscarriage as an abortion in my file. It brought back a slew of terrible memories."

"I'm so sorry. Fuck the press."

I shot him a sad smile. "Yeah. Well, we need them, but the shit they do to celebrities is not cool. And it was a

Campbell Soup girl who found out about the miscarriage."

"Isn't that illegal? Accessing and sharing someone's medical files?"

"Definitely," I agreed. "But it still happened."

"So, maybe they just snooped."

"It's possible, but if they didn't find it throughout the years that Campbell has been in the spotlight and everyone was looking for who the song is about, I don't think that they'd just find it on their own. I think someone told them."

Nate shrugged. "What about your assistant?"

"Honey doesn't know either."

Nate's silence was louder than anything he could have said.

I stilled. "What? She didn't know. I never told her."

"She was there the day that you told me."

"She was?" I racked my brain to go back to that day.

Had Honey been in earshot of that? The picture that had been leaked *was* from that day. It showed Campbell and me standing close together. I'd assumed someone had seen us and not that it was someone from my team. Someone likely following Campbell. Not *this*.

"She definitely was."

"No way," I said, my voice shaky.

Nate shot me a look. "Maybe she's in love with Campbell."

I gaped at him. "What?"

"I thought she was kind of normal until he showed up."

"Yeah, but..." I trailed off as the past few months came back to me.

Her being a die-hard Cosmere fan, the way she'd overstepped my bounds to get Campbell to do the video, the fringe bangs and dye job, her borrowing my clothes, and all the messages from her when I'd been in LA asking if I was with Campbell. Had she been doing all of that to try to get Campbell to notice her? Had she been *turning into me* to try to get him?

Had she done something to make sure we broke up?

I suddenly felt sick. "Oh my God."

"I would never do that to you, Blaire. I don't need the money, and I want to see you happy and successful."

"God, Nate, I'm sorry that I accused you. I just...couldn't think of who else would do something like this."

"I understand. I probably would have accused me, too," he said with a laugh. "But I'm here, looking out for you, Blaire. Are you sure that Honey is, too?"

Ten minutes ago, I would have said yes.

And now, I didn't know.

40

BLAIRE

"Wait, Nate thinks *Honey* outed you to the press?" Piper asked when we were back on the highway, heading home.

"It was the only other answer we could think of."

"And you're sure it's not him?"

"Pretty sure," I said. "He wasn't acting like someone who was guilty. I came all the way out here, so I could look him in the eye when I asked him. I know when he's trying to be charming to get away with shit. I've seen it on him before. He wasn't doing any of that with this."

Piper blew out heavily. "Okay. Wow. But why would she do it?"

I bit my lip. "He thinks it's about Campbell. Like...she started to borrow my clothes and dye her hair to look like me. She changed when he showed up. Like she was trying to get his attention."

"Whoa," Piper said with wide eyes. "I hadn't considered any of that, but she has been twice as clingy as normal. You think she did it to break you two up?"

"I have no idea. But if Nate didn't do it and Honey has

been acting increasingly strange...it makes sense. She's in love with Cosmere. It's not a stretch for her to be in love with Campbell, too."

"Jesus," Piper said. "Well...what are you going to do?"

"I have no idea."

"Say Honey leaked the info and she's in love with Campbell. What's the first thing you'd do if that was all true?"

"Fire her," I said automatically.

"No, before that. You'd have to protect yourself first. Change all your passwords and freeze your accounts. What does she have access to?"

"Fuck, I hadn't gotten that far," I spat. "Everything. She has access to everything. She even has a key to our place."

I grabbed my phone out of my purse and pulled up my emails. I never checked them anymore, except when Honey highlighted specific things for me. It was how she had gotten that email from Campbell and responded as if she were me. She had been doing that for so long that she hadn't even stopped to think if it was right. Or she hadn't cared because she wanted to get closer to Campbell.

I needed a shred of proof before I imploded the best working relationship I'd had in a long time. Yes, she was overly enthusiastic and sometimes crossed boundaries, but she got the job done. Fuck, it was hard to find a good assistant.

"I don't even know what I'm looking for," I admitted.

I frowned at the endless scroll of bullshit in my inbox. It reminded me why I never got in here. She hadn't been lying when she said that I had a bunch of media requests. I should forward all of these to English to deal with, but I couldn't focus on that right now.

"Do you have access to her email?"

"Yeah. It's through *Blaire Blush* as my assistant. But she

could have reached out on her personal email, too. I might never find anything."

"Can you ask your publicist to ask around?"

I shook my head. "I already did. She's looking into it. She said her contact wouldn't tell her at first, and we all assumed it was someone snooping."

"Hmm," Piper said.

I searched relevant keywords to see if there were any emails to TMZ or something. There were a surprising number of those emails in my inbox, but none of them were what I was looking for. Just junk.

I sleuthed through my inbox for nearly the entire hour-and-a-half drive home and found nothing. Not a single thing out of place. I never would have suspected that Honey had done anything if there wasn't a lot of circumstantial evidence.

My phone started ringing as we pulled into Lubbock. I answered, "Hey, English."

"Hey, how are you doing?"

"Uh, well, I've been better."

"Are you sitting down?"

I glanced at Piper and put English on speaker. "Yeah, I'm here."

"It looks like...*you* outed yourself as the 'I See the Real You' girl."

I swallowed. "What? No, I didn't."

"My contact said it came from your own email, including the photograph. That you just sent it over. Didn't even ask for money. Does anyone else have access to your email? Otherwise, it looks like you've been hacked."

"My assistant has access to my email. I...I think she did it. Do you have more info about when it was sent and to who?"

English rattled off some info, and then I searched the email address. My blood chilled as I found the deleted email still sitting in the Trash. She'd been so confident that I wouldn't look at my email that she hadn't even dumped the Trash. Wow.

"It's here," I said, feeling sick. "I found it."

"Fuck," English spat. "Why would she do that? Wouldn't she have realized you'd fire her for this?"

"Yeah, I don't think she expected to be caught. Plus, we think she was gunning for Campbell."

English blew out a harsh breath. "I'm sorry, girl. Seriously. That's twisted."

"I'm going to secure all my stuff and then go see her."

"Good luck. Let me know if you need anything."

I hung up and sighed.

"Well, that's all the proof we needed." My hands shook as I stared down at the email that had snowballed into the destruction of my life.

I spent the next couple hours locking down my accounts. By the time I finished, I felt drained of all energy. I hadn't realized how much access Honey had to my information. I'd trusted her and left myself vulnerable. Now, I needed to get this over with.

Piper had gone into work but told me to text her if I needed anything. Eve had gotten a job as a realtor for a different real estate agency and was gone at all hours of the day.

So, I was alone when the doorbell rang.

I jogged over to answer it, and Honey barreled inside.

"Sorry, I know that you're not feeling well, Blaire, but something is really wrong," Honey said without preamble.

I jerked backward as she tugged her laptop out of her bag and plopped it down on the dining room table.

"Come on in," I muttered.

It was shocking to look at her with all this new information in my head. Her hair looked *just* like mine, and she was even in a coral athletic kit that I also owned. She had been turning into me, and I hadn't even noticed. All because I'd agreed to introduce her to Campbell that one night? If I didn't have the truth in my pocket, I would still have trouble believing it.

"Something is wrong with the *Blaire Blush* system," Honey continued as if she hadn't heard me. "I was logging in to make some website updates, and it won't accept my password. So, I went to contact the web developer, but my email is also down. It's so bizarre. Must be a server outage or something."

"Honey, we need to talk."

"Okay, sure. But we need to figure out this server problem. I don't know what else to do. Should we contact the server host?"

"Honey," I repeated.

My tone of voice must have rattled her because she finally turned to face me. "God, it's just so good to see you. I really thought you'd never come back from LA."

"But you made sure that I did."

She blinked. "What do you mean?"

"You outed me to the press. You found out that I was the girl from Campbell's song, knowing that I never intended for that information to get out."

Honey opened and closed her mouth. "I...I, uh..."

"And then when I got bombarded by the press, you acted

scared for me. You kept telling me to come home. You wanted my relationship to fail."

Honey straightened, as if realizing this was spiraling. "Blaire, I...it's not what you think."

"There is no server problem, Honey. I stripped your access from all of my accounts."

"Blaire, oh my God, no, please. Don't do this."

"I want my key back." I held my hand out. I was proud of myself for not shaking.

"What?" she gasped. "No, please."

"Key," I ground out.

She must have seen my resolve because she dug into her purse and pulled my key off her keychain. She held it in her hand as tears came to her eyes. Then, she dropped it into my hand.

"Second, you're fired."

Honey looked positively distraught. Like I'd kicked her puppy. Or broken up with her. She looked ready to collapse entirely.

"Blaire, no. This is the best job I've ever had."

"You should have thought about that before you over-stepped my boundaries. I told you if you ever did some-thing like that again, I would fire you. And here we are. You did way worse. You sent my relationship with Camp-bell to the press. Did you locate and send the pregnancy too?"

"No," she said, tears streaming down her face. "I didn't know about that, Blaire. I swear. I'm so sorry."

At least I believed her about that. I hadn't found any evidence that that had been here. Just another psychopath out there digging for dirt to try to break me and Campbell up.

"I don't even understand why you did it. I know that you

love Cosmere, but did you really think changing yourself to look like me would get you closer to Campbell?"

My words were cutting and harsh. Her jaw dropped, and her lip quivered.

"Closer to Campbell?" she repeated in confusion. "I don't like Campbell."

"Then, *why*?" I gasped. "Why would you do this to me? Do you just hate me?"

"No! No, no, no," she said fiercely. "I was trying to *protect* you!"

"Protect me?" I said dubiously.

"Yes, of course. Everything I do is for you, Blaire. You deserve so much better than the likes of Campbell Abbey. Have you not seen the pictures that came out from yesterday?"

I blinked at her in confusion. "What pictures?"

"He was seen out, drinking with Nini Verona. Do you think someone who loves and deserves you would be out, drinking with a supermodel a few days after you left? Do you think he really cares?"

My mind whirled with that new information. I hadn't known that he'd been with Nini. Especially since he had just confirmed that they'd been together for a few weeks before he last toured.

But that wasn't the matter at hand. It wasn't like Campbell had done anything like that when we were together. In fact, he had seemed entirely besotted. I couldn't even see what Honey thought she'd needed to protect me from.

"That's beside the point. You sent that information out, and it's unacceptable. That isn't protecting me. That's invading my privacy."

"It's exactly the point. Campbell is a rockstar. You think he's going to be faithful to you when he's gone on tour? You think it's easier to find out now or later that he's exactly who you think he is?"

"I believe that he would be faithful, but even if he wasn't, it wouldn't be acceptable for you to interfere."

"No one is good enough for you, Blaire," she said. "It was why I vetted Nate when you were dating and why I'll always look out for you."

"Wait, you vetted Nate?"

"He's a player. And I knew that he wasn't as into you as he appeared. I made a fake account and tried to get him to agree to go out with me."

My jaw clenched at those words. She seemed utterly sincere. As if she didn't even realize how insane that sounded. And then I remembered Nate telling me about the crazy person who had hounded him to get more information about me. Had that been Honey all along?

I took a step backward. This had just gotten to be...too much. I'd thought it would be an easy firing. She was in love with my boyfriend. She'd overstepped. It was worse than that.

"And Campbell was going to take you away from me. I couldn't have that," Honey said frantically.

"Take me away from you? What does that even mean, Honey? You were my assistant. I wasn't ever planning to leave Lubbock."

"You say that now. But Campbell was planning it. I just know. And I couldn't live without you."

I took a step backward in fear at those words. I'd thought this had been about Campbell, but really it had been about me all along? She'd changed her appearance to look more like me. She'd borrowed my clothes because she wanted to be like me. She'd been trying to ruin my relationships so that she could have me all to herself.

Was she...in love with *me*?

"Honey, you should go," I said, my voice shaking. "Whatever you did was wrong. With Nate and Campbell and how you've started to look like me, it's too far. You need help."

Honey's face fell, and something dark entered her eyes. "I can't...I can't do this, Blaire. I had to get you back home. I needed you here. Not in LA. Please!"

She stumbled into the kitchen and grabbed the butcher knife from the block.

"You can't do this, Blaire," Honey said as tears ran down her cheeks. She held the knife and then brought it to her wrist.

My eyes widened. "Honey, what are you doing?"

"I can't live without you."

41

CAMPBELL

*H*ollin dropped me off at my Range Rover with a half-smile. "Good luck."

I tipped my head at him. "Hope I don't need it. But thanks. For everything."

It took me ten minutes to get to Blaire's house. Nerves had eaten at me the whole drive. I tucked them safely away, where they belonged, and lifted my hand to knock on the door.

That was when I heard the first shout.

"Don't do this! Honey, stop!"

I didn't think; I just barged into Blaire's house.

What I saw stopped me dead.

Blaire stood with a hand outstretched toward Honey. Her other hand was on her cell phone on the dining room table. Honey stood in the kitchen. A knife was poised on her wrist. Red blood dripped from the self-inflicted wound.

"Campbell," Blaire said with relief.

"Stay back!" Honey shouted at me. Her eyes found Blaire's. "You called him? You told him to come?"

"No," Blaire said. "I had no idea he was going to be here."

"It's true," I said quickly. "It was supposed to be a surprise. What is going on here?"

"What's going on is that you're trying to steal her from me!" Honey shouted. "You show up, and suddenly, she's too busy for anyone else and she's going to LA and she wants to move there."

"I'm not *moving* to LA," Blaire said. Her eyes flickered to mine briefly. "Honey leaked the photo and info about us from high school. She thinks she's protecting me."

I reeled from that information. That her own assistant was the one who had done that. I wanted to lunge for her. She hadn't been there when Blaire was mobbed. When I'd gotten the phone call and thought she was in actual trouble. I never wanted to hear that from her again. I'd thought Honey was off before. That her drastic change in appearance had been suspicious, but I'd never thought it would come to this.

I mouthed, *911*, to Blaire.

She nodded and gestured to her phone. Good. I just needed to keep Honey talking until someone showed up.

"Honey, look, I never intended to take Blaire away from her home. You can hate me all you want, but I love her and want what is best for her." I took another step forward. "I want what is best for you, too. Maybe you should put that knife down and let me look at your arm."

"Stay back," she said, brandishing the knife again.

"Okay, okay." I stopped in my tracks. I didn't want her to turn on me either. "Tell me the problem. Maybe we can fix this."

"*We* can't fix anything. You are a worthless piece of scum compared to Blaire."

"That's true. I agree with that," I said easily.

She narrowed her eyes at me. The one thing that she

couldn't change to look like Blaire. She didn't have Blaire's bright blue eyes. "You're not good enough for her."

"True. I'm not. I've never been good enough for her. No one is."

"Right. That's what I told her," she said. "That you can't possibly deserve her."

"Not even a little."

"You're going to hurt her."

"Now, that's where we disagree." I peeked a glance at Blaire. Tears were welling in her eyes at my words. "I already hurt her. I did it, and I regret it with every fiber of my being. I would never do that to her again if I could help it."

Honey scoffed. "You were photographed with Nini Verona yesterday!"

I nodded. "That's right. I was out, drinking with the band, and Nini showed up. We're not together. In fact, she hooked up with Yorke last night. Not me. I got drunk and *bored* everyone all night, talking about how much I was in love with Blaire."

"That doesn't make what you did okay."

"No, nothing can change the past." I was saying these words to Honey, but they were meant for Blaire. Her hand had gone to her heart. "If I were the same man I was eight years ago, I never would have come back. But I'm not, and I want to deserve Blaire again. I want to make her mine."

"You'll never be good enough," Honey said.

But then the front door cracked open again, and a pair of cops shouldered inside. "Police!"

Honey broke down at the word. The butcher knife slipped from her grip and embedded into the floor in front of her. She dropped to her knees and began to sob, clutching her bleeding arm.

"I just wanted her to love me," Honey said as a mantra

the entire time. She said it as paramedics came in and bandaged her arm. As she was herded out of the house and promised proper medical care. And as she was taken outside and into an ambulance.

"What is going to happen to her?" Blaire asked with a shaky voice to one of the cops.

The cop gave her a sympathetic look. "She'll be evaluated at the hospital and kept on a suicide watch for seventy-two hours. After that, it's up to her and the doctor to determine whether or not she needs to go into psychiatric care or if she's well enough to be out on her own."

Blaire nodded. "Good. She needs help."

The cop nodded gravely. Blaire and I gave him a statement, and then they were gone. As if none of it had happened. And yet all of it had happened.

I pulled her into my arms and pressed kiss after kiss into her dark hair. I held her as she cried, promising her the world and more. I wished that I could make it all go away, but that wasn't possible.

Finally, the tears ran their course. She pulled back to wipe them from her cheeks. I wanted to reach for her. To explain why I was here, but she took my hand and drew me in for another kiss.

"Did you mean everything you said?"

I nodded. "Every word of it."

"Stay," she breathed.

"I'm here," I told her. "I'm not going anywhere."

"Good," she said. "I can't believe that you traveled all the way here."

"Well, I didn't think that I'd be saving you from your assistant, if I'm being honest."

She laughed softly and dragged me in for another hug. "Thank God you were here."

"Blaire," I said, suddenly serious. I drew her back, so I could look down at her. "I am so sorry about everything. I never wanted things to go down the way they did in LA. I can't believe that Honey did that, but just as bad was what I did. I wasn't here for you. I wasn't the person you deserved."

"That's in the past," she told me. "I've been a mess the last couple days. But the reason I fled isn't because of who you are right now. The old Campbell was the one who left me. That isn't who you are anymore. It was wrong of me to hold on to that when you proved you were different time and time again."

"No, I deserved it. I did. I was out of line with the miscarriage. I should have called. I should have been there for you."

She nodded. "It was a hard time in my life. I held it against you for long enough. Maybe now that it's all finally out in the open, we can heal. Together."

"I'd like that. I want to be with you. I only want you, Blaire. I'm so madly in love with you."

"So in love that you bore all your friends with it?"

I laughed. "Yeah. I can't stop talking about you. I can't stop thinking about you. Blaire, you're the only one I've ever wanted."

"I love you, too." She reached on her tiptoes and kissed me.

"I lived eight years without you, and after the last four days, I've realized I can't do it again. I just can't do it."

"I know. I know," she said, her hands coming to my face. "I feel the same way. I thought I needed space, but I don't need space, Campbell. I want us to be together."

I swallowed hard. The nerves that had rattled around inside of me all day came back fresh. But they were new ones. I was doing the right thing—the best thing—and still, somehow, it was the hardest thing I'd done in my life as I sank onto one knee and withdrew a black box from my pocket.

Tears came into her eyes again as she gasped and threw her hands over her mouth. "Oh my God, Campbell."

"You're my one true love. I never want to spend another day without you. Marry me, Marie Blaire Barker. Make me the happiest man alive."

"Yes," she gasped. "Yes, yes, yes."

I pulled the ring from the box and slid it onto her finger. She stared down at it in awe and then launched herself at me. We kissed like the world would never end. This was our moment, our love eternal. And I accepted that kiss as a promise for forever.

Because this was my girl.

I saw the real her.

The one that got away.

Now, she was all mine.

42

BLAIRE

"Thank you all for coming," I said, my eyes drifting around the room.

Campbell twined his fingers with mine. We'd debated just announcing to everyone we knew that we were engaged, but we'd had a better idea. Well, mostly, I'd had a better idea. And now all our family was together in one place.

Campbell's dad, Gregg, his aunts, and brother and sister. Then on the other side of the room, my mom and Hal. We'd left off on such a horrible place that I wasn't sure Pamela would even agree to come today. That she'd snub me for being the insolent daughter she never deserved. But when I told her it was important, she'd agreed.

"This means so much to us," Campbell said.

"What's this all about?" Nora asked. She looked down at her watch. "I have to be at the vineyard in exactly twenty-seven minutes for Morgan's wedding prep."

"It won't take long," Campbell assured her.

"I mean, I want to know, but it's a big day. Our biggest wedding ever."

Campbell laughed. "It's fine, Shrimp."

I swallowed and Campbell squeezed my hand. "We wanted to bring everyone together for this unexpected moment." Then, I held my left hand up and revealed the glittering ring on my finger. "We're engaged!"

Campbell's side of the room erupted. His dad was the first person to spring forward and give his son a hug. "Congratulations! This is the best news."

Campbell grinned up at him. He'd told me he was wary of his father's reaction. Gregg hadn't exactly been pleased that we were dating. He'd been worried that he'd leave me behind and go off and be an idiot. But apparently this had proved to him just how serious Campbell really was about me.

"Thanks, Dad," Campbell said.

Hollin and Nora crowded in.

"Ah, nice, bro! Locking it down," Hollin said.

Gregg shook his head at his oldest.

"This is amazing!" Nora squealed. "Please tell me I can plan the wedding."

Campbell laughed. "Well, can you do it in a week?"

Nora blinked at us. "What?"

"We decided to elope," I told her.

"Oh my God! How romantic." Nora nodded her head. "And I can do it in a week. I have prepared my entire life for this."

"Elope?" Gregg asked. "That's pretty big."

"Morgan and Patrick's day is today. Or else we would be heading to Vegas already," Campbell told him. "And I'd love for you to all be there when we get hitched. I can fly everyone out if you want to attend."

Everyone clambered forward, excited and asking questions about our upcoming nuptials.

And there was Pamela and Hal.

Neither of them had said a word. A knot fit into my stomach. I'd worried about this. She wasn't going to be happy. She was going to ruin our moment. But I wanted her to know. I wanted to tell the entire world. When really the only person I'd confessed to was Piper.

"Go on," Campbell said, pushing me toward my family.

I shuffled forward until I stopped in front of Pamela and Hal. "Surprise."

My mom opened and closed her mouth. Fear spiked through me. She was going to tell me it was a terrible idea. She was going to tell me not to do it. Oh God, this was a mistake. I didn't want her to steal my happiness. This was the best decision of my life. It was what I wanted.

Then, to my shock, my mom smiled. A *real* smile. "Oh Blaire," she said, actually using my preferred name.

I was stunned silent as she wrapped her arms around me and pulled me into a hug.

My mom was hugging me.

She was *hugging* me.

She didn't like any form of contact. We never touched. We definitely weren't hugging people. And here she was breaking all her own rules.

I hesitantly wrapped my arms around her and felt her closeness. The fragility of a matriarch that I had always considered unshakable.

"Mom?" I whispered.

"Oh baby," she said, pulling back and putting her hands to my cheeks. "I am so happy for you."

"You are?"

"I may not have known how to show it, but I did want the best for you."

"I thought...I thought you wouldn't want me with Campbell."

"I didn't want you to get hurt again. I was worried for you. I didn't know how to show that. And clearly I did it all wrong."

She had done it wrong. We'd both been wrong. Time and time again we'd fought against our own stubbornness. She could have been more maternal. But when I'd needed her most, she'd been there for me. She'd been the one to take care of me during the miscarriage. No matter her own feelings on the subject. She'd had to be there for me. And she didn't have to be here now. Actually *happy* for me.

"I'm glad you're here, Mom."

"Me too." She brought her hand to her own cheek and swiped at the one lone tear that tracked down her face. "Look, I'm leaking."

I laughed at the joke. She'd always said that about me as a kid. It had made me giggle and stop crying instead. "You leak beautifully."

She joined me in soft laughter. "You love him?"

"With all my heart."

"Even with everything that's happened with the press?"

"You followed that?"

She shot me a look that was purely Pamela. "You're my daughter. I've followed everything about you. I've watched all of your accomplishments."

Now tears came to my eyes. "I thought you weren't happy about my blog."

"It's so much more than that now, isn't it?"

I nodded. "So much more. And yes, I'm happy with Campbell despite everyone knowing about the miscarriage."

"I wrote to that magazine about their incorrect information, I'll have you know."

God, that was so my mom. "You did what?"

"They reported incorrect information. I sent in a correction as a firsthand witness to the events."

"Oh Mom, you didn't have to do that."

"I know, but I'm glad I did. I know that things with us are...not like other people. I can't help who I am. But I can take my own advice and try to be better."

"I love you. Will you come to Vegas for our elopement?" I looked to Hal too. "Both of you?"

"Yes," she said at once.

Hal nodded too. "We'll be there."

"I'm going to invite Dad too."

"As you should," Mom said. "Now, can I properly meet my soon-to-be new son-in-law?"

I laughed and brought her over to Campbell and his family. He charmed my mom as I always knew he would if he got the opportunity. His eyes were bright and happy for me. I'd been worried and now all the pieces were finally falling into place, exactly how I'd always wanted them to.

Hours later, Campbell was in a black suit, and I'd donned a dress to match the blue of my eyes as we watched Morgan Wright tie herself forever to Patrick Young. Wrights lined either side of the aisle to celebrate their sister and CEO.

Only Patrick's best friend and Morgan's older brother, Austin Wright spoke out of turn in the middle. "It's about damn time."

Everyone laughed and the happy couple just shook their head. Then they were kissing in front of what felt like the entire town. We got to our feet and cheered for their happy union. It was good to see so much love. To see love prevail above all else. Despite the adversity they had gone through.

Morgan and Patrick headed back down the aisle to a ringing round of applause.

Campbell leaned down and whispered in my ear. "That's going to be us in a week."

I glanced up at him. "I can't wait."

"I actually don't want to wait."

I laughed at him. "What? You want to run away without telling anyone?"

"There's a courthouse."

"Campbell Abbey," I said, nudging him. "I've waited all my life for you. I think I can wait another week."

He slid an arm around my waist and kissed me deeply. "I'd wait for you forever."

It was our turn, and we walked down the aisle together. I couldn't wait for it to be our turn to do this in a week. To tie my life to him forever. We'd had our ups and downs. Our trials and hardships. I wasn't naive enough to think that everything would be smooth sailing from here. The album release and tour and long distance was going to be hard.

But it would all be worth it because I was doing it with him.

Just the two of us forever.

EPILOGUE

ONE YEAR LATER

"*A*re you ready?" Piper asked as we stepped through the front doors of Wright Vineyard.

"So ready!"

"Even though the whole album is about you?"

I laughed. She wasn't wrong. The new Cosmere album would officially be out tomorrow, and the release party was being held at Wright Vineyard. It was becoming a tradition to have their big events in the barn. A small thing before the bigger events in LA. But this one was special because it was the album that he'd written and rehearsed in that tumultuous few months when we first started dating again. Half of the songs were the happy *falling in love* songs, and the other half were heartbreak songs, written in that terrible week we'd been apart. It was a masterpiece, and already, the critics were giving it rave reviews. Everyone said the Grammys were knocking on Cosmere's door for this one.

I couldn't be prouder. Especially since I had all the footage from that time and had cinched a deal with Netflix for an exclusive release of the documentary around the new album, *The One That Got Away*.

Already, "Rooftop Nights" was the hottest song of the summer. I still couldn't listen to it without blushing, thinking about the kiss that had ignited it. The whole album made me blush. But, hey, it was true to my namesake.

"I love that it's about me," I admitted.

Nora appeared at my side. "Hey, sis," she said with a wink. She'd taken to calling me that since my wild Vegas wedding with Campbell. "I'm so glad we had the event here. Since, you know, I didn't get to plan a real wedding."

I snorted. I would never live this down. "You got to plan *the* wedding. But considering we did it all in a week, you can't really blame us."

"I don't blame you." She sighed dramatically. "But do you know what I could have done even with a few months?"

"I do know, and you would have made it a dream, but I'm glad we did it spontaneously. It was better that way. Perfect that way."

"It was," Piper agreed.

Nora giggled. "You're right. But you, missy, will not be eloping when my brother finally proposes, okay?"

Piper went a little green at the edges. "Um, I think we have a while before that."

We laughed at her and then headed backstage. All our friends were hanging out with the band. It was good to see everyone together like this. Jennifer sitting in Julian's lap and Jordan arguing with him. West sitting between Viv and Santi while Yorke had his arms crossed and said nothing.

Annie traipsed across the room to hug all three of us.

"I can't wait to hear the new songs live," Annie said with wide eyes.

She and Jen had gotten an early copy of the new album and played the songs on repeat until they knew all the lyrics by heart. They were officially obsessed with every single song. Though we were all partial to "The One That Got Away." I certainly was.

"Me either!" Nora said. "I like this album the best."

Everyone was excited. We were only missing one person. One person who would have been ecstatic for this release.

Honey.

After she'd been arrested, I'd gotten in contact with her family. They'd thanked me for calling the police. They'd apparently been trying to get her help for years, but they couldn't admit her into a facility unless she was a danger to herself or someone else.

It was unfortunate that it had ever gotten that far. I hadn't had contact with Honey personally because we all feared that it would make her relapse. But I kept up with her recovery and her family. What had happened wasn't my fault, but it didn't mean it wasn't my responsibility to see that she got better.

I wished that she were here. The old, vibrant Honey who had loved life. Not the one who had hurt herself in my kitchen.

But she wasn't here. She was with people who were taking care of her.

I even had a new assistant. Though I'd never trust anyone like I had Honey. I'd learned that lesson the hard way.

At least Campbell and I had worked it all out. Life wasn't perfect. We split our time between LA and Lubbock. We both got frustrated with the distance and the timing, but I wouldn't trade it for anything.

Speaking of Campbell...

"Have you seen Campbell?" I asked, peering around the back.

"Still in the dressing room," Annie said.

"Thanks." I said good-bye to my friends and headed to the dressing room.

I rapped on the door twice. This was where it had all started again. The inspiration for "Invisible Girl" was right at this door. And now, that man was my husband.

"Campbell?"

"Blaire, come in."

I stepped into the room and quickly closed the door behind me. Campbell made me stop in my tracks. He was in low-slung black jeans and was just pulling on a T-shirt over his rock-hard abs.

"Uh," I muttered incoherently.

He smirked at me. "Come here, you."

I grinned and rushed toward him. We crashed together. "I missed you."

"I was gone for a few hours," he said as he laughed.

"Still missed you."

"Missed you too, babe," he said as he claimed my lips.

"Everyone is excited to hear the songs live."

"So am I."

"Mmm, me too." I kissed him again.

He bit into my bottom lip, and then he wrapped his arms around my thighs and lifted me up around his waist. "Maybe the crowd can wait a little longer."

"You're filthy," I joked.

"You like me filthy."

He sank into the couch, bringing me down with him. I wrapped my arms around him and gave him a good, long kiss.

"I sure do."

"So, do you think we have time?"

A gleam of excitement was in his eyes. He still couldn't get enough of me. And I loved him every single day for it.

"Actually, I wanted to tell you something."

"More important than a quickie before my set?" he joked.

"You tell me."

I pulled out a pregnancy test from my pocket and held it out to him. His jaw dropped, and he looked up at me with hopeful eyes.

We'd been trying to get pregnant almost since the moment we'd gotten married that wild weekend in Vegas. But it hadn't been as easy as it had been that fateful night when we were eighteen and stupid. That had all changed today.

"Babe," he whispered, "is this..."

He looked down at the two pink lines that confirmed what he thought.

"I'm pregnant," I told him.

He jumped back up and slung me around in an excited circle. "Oh my God, finally. God, I love you." He kissed me and kissed me and kissed me. He was near to tears when he finally put me back on my feet. "I can't wait to start our family."

I took his hand. "We've already had a family for the last year. We're just adding one more."

He dropped to his knees and kissed my stomach. "I am the luckiest man in the world. And I can't wait to meet you in there."

I laughed and pulled him in for another kiss. We were expanding our family in the best way possible. And I just couldn't wait.

I might have been the one that got away.

But now, I was just *the one*.

THE END

ACKNOWLEDGMENTS

Getting to write Campbell & Blaire was like a dream come true. It's no secret that I love second chance romances. I love the newness of that young high school love. I love the heart break of being torn apart when all you want is to be together. And I love finding your way back to the person you were always meant to be with. It was a joy writing their book, and I was so deep in their love that I felt like I could have just kept writing more and more of them. I hope you felt that way too.

Thank you to everyone who made this book what it is: Rebecca Kimmerling, Danielle Sanchez, Staci Hart, Nana Malone, Bethany Hagen, Devin McCain, Rebecca Gibson, Anjee Sapp, Sarah Hansen, Wander, Jovana Shirley, and you lovely reader!

Special thanks to my husband Joel, who has to listen to all my ideas every day, and the puppies!

The soundtrack to this book was: Falling by Harry Styles, Red (Taylor's Version) by Taylor Swift, Traitor by Olivia Rodrigo, The One That Got Away by The Civil Wars, Honey by Halsey, and justified by Kacey Musgraves

ABOUT THE AUTHOR

 K.A. Linde is the *USA Today* bestselling author of more than thirty novels. She has a Masters degree in political science from the University of Georgia, was the head campaign worker for the 2012 presidential campaign at the University of North Carolina at Chapel Hill, and served as the head coach of the Duke University dance team.

She loves reading fantasy novels, binge-watching Supernatural, traveling to far off destinations, baking insane desserts, and dancing in her spare time.

She currently lives in Lubbock, Texas, with her husband and two super-adorable puppies.

Visit her online:
www.kalinde.com

Or Facebook, Instagram & Tiktok:
@authorkalinde

For exclusive content, free books,
and giveaways every month.
www.kalinde.com/subscribe